FALLING FOR THE PLAYBOY

S.L. SCOTT

Published in the United States of America

ISBN: 978-1-940071-84-8

Cover design by Kari March Designs

You're the sky.

1

MALLORY

"Flight attendants, please prepare the cabin for landing. And to our passengers, the crew would like to take this opportunity to thank you for choosing our airline to start your Hawaiian adventure. Aloha!"

Taking a deep breath, I close my eyes just as the tires touch the ground. We land with a hard bump and a strong pull back. Palm trees and floral bushes surround the Oahu airport. The plastic plane window has yellowed and is scratched, but the expanse of blue in the sky and green flora on the ground is a marked difference from the mountainous landscape of Colorado that I'm used to. After months of planning, I'm finally here. The realization that I get to spend the next two and a half months, my summer break from university, in this tropical paradise makes me smile.

Walking through the crowded terminal toward baggage claim, I squeeze through the gathered sea of Hawaiian shirts, flip-flops, and leis. I pass through the secured area and encounter kissing families, couples hugging, and hear endless 'alohas.' None of it holds my attention. What does is a young couple, around my age—early twenties—kissing with abandon. The tall, wild-locked boy with sun-lightened brown hair could easily be mistaken for an earthbound Hawaiian God. My stomach tightens with envy of the girl who is lucky enough to receive untamed passion from such a hot looking guy.

Jealousy can be the killer of confidence and often is for me. Unreasonable irritation settles in as I become frustrated with my lack of self-esteem, and huff. '*Stupid, pretty, blonde girl.*' I allow my opinion of her to be voiced freely inside my head. It doesn't bring relief to reality, but it does make me feel a bit better.

The perfect looking couple is entrancing and my eyes stay locked on them as my pace slows. While observing their amorous interaction, my gaze is drawn to his physical perfection. That's when I see that she is clearly more into the kiss than he is. My eyes trail from long lashes down a few days of unshaven stubble to his lips which part as I stare. He speaks and the second I hear his voice, my world shifts on its axis. "I'll call you," he says, rubbing her shoulders with reassurance.

"You promised to write too." She's pouting as a tear slips down her cheek.

Do guys really find sulking girls sexy?

He wipes the tear away from her cheek and gives her a small, inauspicious smile. Just as she wraps her arms around his neck, his eyes lift up and meet mine. I continue to stare when he tells her, "I'll write every day." He embraces her, but at the same time, with an air of arrogance, he flirts with me—a smug smile aimed directly at me.

Over her shoulder, his eyes stay bound to mine as he feeds her another line and my axis shifts right back onto its normal rotation. *What a jerk!*

When I pass them, he tells the pouty girl, "I'll miss you.

Don't forget to text to let me know you landed safely." After a quick peck on her lips, he turns and leaves her standing there alone with her tears.

I look down at my feet and shake my head, disgusted that he just flirted with me while kissing his girlfriend good-bye. *Guess guys aren't any different in Hawaii than they are back home.* I may be in paradise, but I can't escape the fact that guys are the same everywhere. This realization causes my anxiety and disappointment to spike.

Removing my large suitcase from the carousel is a struggle for my five-four frame. An older man in a colorful floral design shirt grabs it, setting it upright on the wheels for me. "Thanks," I say, but he's already down the line chasing his Samsonite spinner that mine had trapped on the belt.

I can handle the hard case once it's on the wheels and pull it to the curb to wait for my ride. After laying it down on its side, I sit on top of it and begin searching through my carry-on bag for a cigarette. I feel the need to alleviate the stress that has built up in the last ten minutes, defeating the calm I experienced on the long, uneventful flight. Smoking is a bad habit I picked up in the last six months. I don't smoke all the time, but when I'm stressed, I crave the nicotine. It's another thing to add to my growing list of things I want to change. That's what this summer is all about. It's the summer I break free from the protective barriers I've built and live my life without boundaries or judgments.

My hair has grown out. I probably should have gotten a haircut while I was on the mainland, but my flight here was a day after finals ended. I grab my long brown hair out of my face and spin it into a sloppy knot at the nape of my neck. It won't hold long, but hopefully long enough for me to dig through the bag with an unobstructed view.

While waiting for that adventure to begin, I become frustrated because I still can't find a damn cigarette. Anxious, I glance at my watch, realizing I didn't change the time to make up for the four hour time zone difference. I quickly unhook my watch and turn the dial. From behind, a familiar male voice sweeps over me. "Do you need the local time?"

Looking up, I see Mr. I-might-have-a-girlfriend-but-I-can-still-flirt standing just a mere two feet from me. Now I really need a cigarette. Ignoring him, I turn back to my bag again, feeling desperate to find that sinful pleasure that will make me feel better.

"Are you here on vacation?" He's persistent. I'll give him that, but he's still not worth my time after that gross and disrespectful display inside.

I finally find my much needed cancer stick and ease it into my mouth, savoring the feel of it while anticipating the relief it will bring.

A lighter appears in front of me. Without bothering to look up, I move forward into the fire. I try to ignore the ridiculously handsome guy as he tries to pick me up after sending his girlfriend away.

He's unsettling and ... confusing, and apparently doesn't take a hint, so I make myself crystal clear. "Just so you know, your bullshit lines won't work on me. Anyway, I'm sure there's a fresh batch of girls about to land who are looking for that fling they will always remember and reflect upon fondly for the rest of their lives."

The Hawaiian God's heat emanates from beside me.

He's too good looking.

He's too close.

"Speaking of bullshit, a thank you would be nice," he says, moving to stand in front of me.

"For what?" I ask.

"For the light."

"Thank you," I mumble, rolling my eyes and wishing my ride was here to save me from this situation.

"That didn't sound sincere."

"That's because it wasn't." I tilt my head, take a long drag, and look up into his blue eyes. Yep, it's official. He's too good looking with bad intentions mixed in. That combination does all kinds of tingly things to me—good and bad.

"Bitter much?"

I stand, stubbing the remains of my cigarette out in a nearby ashtray. Without a word, I lift my suitcase and drag it about twenty feet away from the pretty boy who seems to get what he wants too often in life. Not only do I not have time to waste on guys like him, but I'm also way too selfish to even want to compete with their egos. My ex was too much work. I'm not looking for a repeat of that relationship.

He remains standing where I left him on the curb, and I look down at my phone as it beeps with a text: *Sorry! At the ER with a broken hand. Catch a cab. I'll pay you back. x Sunny.*

Worried about my best friend, but irritated about being stuck at the airport, I toss my phone into my bag and look for the cab line, which doesn't seem to exist in Hawaii. I sigh aloud, frustrated.

"Looks like you've been stood up, sweetie. How about I give you a *ride*?" He draws out the last word for me to catch his double meaning.

I look at this smug, narcissistic jack-off and reply in my own smartass way. "Giving me a *ride* will probably put you out."

"Only if it's good, and I've got all day to find out."

There's something about him. Yes, he's arrogant. Yes, he's hot, but all that aside, his confidence is also sort of attractive.

Sunny convinced me to spend my summer on the islands, encouraging me to come here and live a little. Well, here I am. Might as well start living it up now, and really, he is just too delectable to refuse. He might be exactly what I need—a carefree goodtime. Ridding myself of all logic and good reasoning, I say, "My day just opened up. I think I'll take you up on that ride."

He swings his arm in front of him, directing me to the parking lot. "Right this way." As we walk next to each other in silence, once again I feel like I'm moving into the fire. Somehow though, I know that the burn will be well worth the ride.

Flipping the seat forward after opening the car door, he loads my suitcase into the back. He adjusts the seat back into position and backs up to allow me to get in.

I restrain my smile, trying to play it cool while sliding down into the car as he holds the door open for me. The car is a brand new silver Maserati GranCabrio. I might be impressed, but I would never give him the satisfaction of knowing that little tidbit. It's ridiculous that I even know what type of car this is considering I never cared when my ex-boyfriend used to drag me from car show to car show when we dated. So here I am sitting in one of the most coveted cars in the world with a guy too pretty to be any good for my insecurities, going to God only knows where. I make a split second decision. After shutting the door, I text Sunny: *I'm here and heading to the hospital to see you.*

As he slithers like the snake I know he is into the driver's seat, he turns and smirks. "Didn't your mom ever tell you not to accept rides from strangers?"

Though I wish I could say panic squeezed my chest, it didn't. He may be working girls from all angles, but for some reason, I can tell he won't hurt me. But just in case he tries, I tuck my hand into my bag and prepare my keychain pepper spray ... *just in case*. Looking at him, I study his strong jaw and straight nose until the side of his lips quirk up. I roll my eyes because he so caught me checking him out. Attempting to distract him from my embarrassment, I ask, "What's your name?"

With a chuckle, he starts the car then casually responds. "Evan."

"Well, Evan, I'm Mallory." My head drops back on the seat, and I close my eyes, feeling the exhaustion from travel settle into my bones. "I guess we're not strangers anymore."

He revs the engine then peels out. I'm definitely not surprised, but remain a little horrified that he would treat such a fine piece of machinery like a souped-up Honda Civic from *The Fast and the Furious*. "So, where to, *Mallory*?"

"The ER on the north side."

His turns quickly, worry covering his expression. "You need a hospital? Are you all right?"

"Yes, I'm fine. Thank you for your concern," I say, hinting of sarcasm, though I'm actually touched to see a true emotion from him. That may be the first one I've witnessed since we met all of twenty-five minutes ago. "My friend is at the ER with a hurt hand. Hence, no ride."

"Well, I was heading up north anyway, so this works out perfect."

I look at him surprised by his word choice that seems almost deliberate. "Perfect, huh?" I smile knowing that I don't really need him to confirm anything, but in a small way kind of want him to.

He looks at me, tilts his head and smiles. "You're quite the pot-stirrer, aren't you? Do you always like to put people on the spot?"

Now he's making me feel bad. "No, I mean yes, uh ... I

don't know. I'm sorry. I'm being rude. I'm a little cranky because I'm tired from the flight."

"Sarcasm is a defense mechanism. Do I make you feel defensive?"

He's watching the road and I'm unabashedly watching him. I lower my eyes to his arms, admiring the definition of his biceps and triceps working together with ease. My gaze travels further down past his elbow to his forearms where the muscles alternate in the tiniest of ways to manipulate his movements on the steering wheel. Then I notice his hands. They're very masculine, strong hands with long fingers that seem like they could play every note to perfection—every one of *my* notes. I sigh aloud, feeling squirmy in the concept.

"Mallory?"

"Huh?" *I didn't just sigh out loud, did I?* "Yeah?"

"I was just asking you if I make you feel defensive, unsafe." He smiles again as if he knows exactly what I'm thinking, which is annoying.

Pausing to think about what he's asking me, I shake my head before I answer. He makes me feel safe, maybe too comfortable for just having made his acquaintance. "No, I feel … this feels *okay*."

"Wow, thanks for the ringing endorsement. Well, would you still feel *okay* if I asked for your number?"

I don't know why this catches me off guard, but it does. It's amazing how fast a boy with a little stubble, perfectly kissable lips, and deep blue, oceanic-colored eyes can make you forget your name and have you under his devilish spell. But the memory of airport girl rushes back too soon. "I don't think your girlfriend would appreciate that you gave me a ride, much less my number."

He laughs as if what I just said is completely absurd. "Girlfriend?"

"*Uh*, yeah. Remember the blonde you just left at the airport? The I'll – write – you – everyday – and – text – me – when – you – land - girlfriend you just lip locked with before you walked away leaving her tears to dry themselves? Does that girlfriend ring a bell?"

"Whoa! Voyeur much?" He accuses, conveniently turning the topic back to me.

"*Voyeur?* You were making out in a crowded airport. Wait, don't sidetrack me."

"You're a cynic, Mallory."

"That's very psychoanalytical of you to assume. But I guess I'm not sure how my cynicism has anything to do with you having a girlfriend."

"I don't have a girlfriend," he states, pulling that little smug smirk he seems to sport a lot.

My mouth drops open at the nerve of this guy. My arms arrange themselves into a defensive position across my chest, and I huff out of frustration. "Seriously, you are so disrespectful."

"I don't have a girlfriend!" His tone is firm, but he struggles to sound lighthearted.

"Fine, whatever." Turning my attention to the amazing scenery passing outside the car window, I decide pursuing this level of ludicrousness is not worth my efforts. I don't even know why it bothers me that he won't admit it, but it does. "If you don't want to tell me, fine! But I think you're being disrespectful to the girl you were just tongue fucking at the airport." My anger flares because he's pushed every one of my buttons and now I'm sitting here aggravated like an idiot over a guy who clearly doesn't understand that women are not on this earth just for his amusement.

"We hooked up a few times, but she's not my girlfriend. I don't do the relationship thing." He says the last part like he's not allowed to have a relationship.

I look over at him, take a deep breath to calm my irrational behavior toward him and ask, "Why not? What's wrong with being in a relationship?"

"There's nothing wrong with it, but I can't do them. I gave up trying a couple of years ago. It wasn't worth the headache or the heartache."

"Yours or theirs?"

He laughs, and I take note of the great sound he makes. It's genuine, as if it's reserved for something that strikes him just the right way and then he releases it out with honesty. But deep down, I have a feeling honesty and Evan *are not* friends. "You've got me there. Probably theirs. It sucks being the bad guy."

"Then don't be." It's hard to stay mad at him for some unknown reason. I'm thinking it's because even though what he says should anger me, he's authentic in his words. There are no pretenses.

"Easier said than done, my dear. Years of hard work went into cultivating this bad boy image. It's not going to come crumbling down over a girl anytime soon. So, I spare the chicks some tears and grief and try to play as truthful as possible."

The man sitting next to me is a paradigm, confusing in the most interesting ways. His words don't match his mannerisms or the sensibility he so strongly projects, and yet his words are his truth. He's being honest—at least more honest than he should be with someone he apparently is trying to pick up. Then another thought occurs to me, inspiring me to speak before I lose my nerve. "You're telling me this so I know not to expect anything from you, aren't you?"

There's the smirk, but watching him this time, it wavers before he speaks. He doesn't rush to answer. His quick tongue waits for the thoughts to back him up. "I'm giving you a ride, Mallory, that's all. Did you expect more?"

"You're good at turning the tables on people."

"And you're very clever. More clever than most, I suspect. So I'm not going to fool you into anything. That's not my style. Contrary to what you might believe, I don't usually encounter much resistance."

"Oh, I believe it all right!" *Wait!* I might have just admitted something to him that I'm definitely not ready to admit to myself.

He doesn't say anything, but the knowing, self-satisfied grin beaming across his face says he understood perfectly. *Damn it!* He gets me all flustered. My phone beeping brings my attention back to the present, and I pray he doesn't respond to that last comment. The text from Sunny reads: *Stuck here a few more hours. Don't waste your time here. Go to the apartment. The spare key is under the potted plant on the porch. Sorry.*

I text back: *Call me as soon as you can. I'm worried.*

She's quick to respond: *I'll call you later.*

"How's your friend?" Evan asks.

"Fine, but she's stuck awhile longer. Do you mind dropping me off at her place? I have the address."

He looks over at me then back to the road. His tone is kind. "Why don't I take you out for a bite to eat? I'm sure you're hungry after traveling and then I'll deliver you to your friend's place in time to greet her."

"I'd like that." My brain is not functioning properly because I know if it was then all of my instincts to protect my heart would be telling me to end this now. But since it's not, I find myself being driven on a date. *Is this a date?* No, it can't be because he has a girlfriend even if he's not admitting it yet.

He pulls into the parking lot of a palm frond themed diner. I reach down to the floorboard and grab my purse when suddenly my door is opened and he's standing there offering me a hand. He may be trying to charm the pants off me, but I won't fight against a polite gesture. Maybe it's time for me to look past his surface suave moves and have some fun. "Thank you," I say, taking hold of his warm hand.

He follows me into the restaurant, also holding that door open. "After you," he says, smiling. It's a more kind, relaxed smile than before.

After a few minutes perusing the menu, he places his hands on the table and intertwines his fingers. His eyes focus on mine, penetrating me more than I'm accustomed to. "So, in the short time I've known you ..." He looks at his watch jokingly, "... I think I've got you all figured out."

"*Really?* Let me hear it. This should be entertaining, if nothing else."

The waitress interrupts his ridiculous assumptions and we place our orders.

He smiles then proceeds with an in-depth description that hits too close to home to admit to him. "You're an only child who's originally from a state with heavy winters on the Mainland. You've had boyfriends, but you're currently single. You've probably never had a guy do his due diligence in bed thus making sex for you almost a chore instead of pleasure—"

"No! What? I don't ... *what?*" My words stumble out of my mouth in disbelief of the gall of him to talk about my sex life. "That's way too personal for you to be talking about."

"I'm just telling the truth and that's what you like the most in someone—*the truth*."

"No one likes to be lied to," I justify, shrugging.

"No, but not everyone wants to hear the truth either."

I roll my eyes. Quite riveted by his summary of me, I close my mouth and act like this doesn't bother me at all. Sitting back, I cross my arms over my chest and try to gain some control back from him. Without warning, he continues. "You can handle the truth even if it's not pretty. But, let me get back to the good stuff. You like to make-out, but you make guys wait a pre-determined amount of days before hopping into the sack with them. That has nothing to do with the guy, but just to make *you* feel better about letting them into your panties in the first place."

"Please keep my panties out of this conversation," I scold with disdain.

"Yes, ma'am." His arms slide off the table to his sides. "You're a good student and ambitious. You don't work because your parents saved all their pennies to send you to college and want you to 'concentrate' on your studies?"

"Grants and scholarships," I interject, correcting him as our food is delivered and set down in front of us.

"I'll allow the adjustment, but I find it funny that you choose to correct only that part of my analysis, meaning I'm not wrong when it comes to your sex life." The smirk reappears and broadens in delight, but at my expense.

My cheeks heat as humiliation creeps across my face. I don't know if I should say anything so I sit there looking out the window and stew, but this time annoyed at myself. I shovel a big bite into my mouth to stop the smart-ass remark threatening to come out.

"C'mon, Mallory, I didn't mean to embarrass you. I'm just giving you a hard time."

I finish chewing and say, "We don't know each other well enough to give each other *that* hard of a time."

"Okay then. How can I get to know you better because I really want to?"

My mouth drops open as I witness earnestness wash across his face coloring him in a whole new light. "Tell me who the girl at the airport was?"

"Her name is Kelly. She was vacationing here and we kind of ... hooked-up." He shrugs, dismissing any importance of the situation.

"How long was she here on vacation?"

He hesitates and for some reason that makes me nervous for his reply. "She was here for a week—"

"A week! By the way you two were attacking each other's mouths, I would've thought you were a couple for a lot longer than a week." I'm shocked. This guy might be even smoother than I originally thought.

"I never said I was a knight in shining armor. I'm not and I never will be. I'm way too selfish to try that hard."

His confession makes me sad for him. Leaning forward, I lower my voice and ask, "Not even for the right girl?"

"*The right girl?* I'm one of those guys who believes in the right *now* kind of girl. I'll openly admit I'm a relationship-phobe. These girls—"

"*These girls?*" The way he refers to them is insulting. They've become of mish-mash of females to him, losing their identity once they leave the island.

"Yes, *these* girls. I don't lie. I tell them the truth." He looks down at his food, shifting in the booth, suddenly uncomfortable in his stance. "I think I just lied to you." He clears his throat. "I don't lie to them about what to expect from me when it comes to a real relationship, but I do tend to send them off on a little lie. In my mind, it makes their long journey home more bearable."

"Because otherwise, they would be crying themselves to sleep on the plane? What if they didn't? What if they used you just like you used them? What if they lied *to you*?"

"The difference is I don't care if they lie to me. It's all inconsequential in the end. Obviously, in the time we spent together, it didn't rock my world enough to change my course or theirs."

He's sitting across from me and his shoulders ease, like a burden has been lifted. For some reason this conversation is cathartic for him. His eyes settle on mine, and as we look at each other, both unable to eat, I feel a tugging at my own burdens.

"I'd like to take you somewhere," he whispers.

"Is this the same somewhere you take all the ladies to impress them before sexing them up?"

"Sexing them up?" He tilts his head and looks at me like I'm crazy.

"You know what I mean."

I can tell he's already over the comment. After an awkward few minutes, I ask him about Hawaii and he tells me about some hotspots to check out. By the time we're finished eating, he shifts, obviously preparing to close the dating deal. Staring into my eyes, he says, "Mallory, I'd like to take you to one of my favorite places on the island." Here it comes, his out. "I've been honest with you and already said too much, but I can tell you that even though I won't be a knight, I am a good person. I also promise to be honest with you, *always*. I've got your lunch." He pays the bill as I mull over what he just said.

His words hit me harder than expected. He's telling me not to rely on him, but to trust him. It's an interesting situation because I want to spend more time with him, but I really don't want to set myself up for heartache. With the unfamiliar feel of the aloha spirit taking over, I find myself open to his proposal even at the risk of a little heart damage.

My phone buzzes as we walk to the car. Deciding to ignore these typical girly feelings swirling inside of me at the sight of this too cocky boy actually getting his way with me, I answer the call. "Hi," I say thrilled to hear from Sunny while sliding into the leather seat.

"Mallory, I love *youuuuuu*."

Shaking my head, I close my eyes knowing she has to be on some strong meds for her to sound this out of it. "How's your hand?"

"My hand?" Silence takes over until she blurts into the phone. "Yes, my hand! It's good. I'm feeling no pain at all. Now I'm going to sleep with Johnny."

"What?"

"Mallory?" A strange male voice comes over the phone.

"Um, yeeesss?"

"Hi, this is Johnny. I'm a friend of Sunny's. We work together." He releases a shaky breath then explains, "She's on pain meds and a little out of it. I know she feels terrible about this happening on the same day as your arrival. Are you settled in? Do you need anything?"

So this Johnny guy is with Sunny and it makes me wonder if she's safe. He seems friendly and she trusted him enough to have him at the hospital, so I guess I have to as well. "I'm fine. I'm, uh ... out with a friend right now. I don't think I need anything, but if I do, I'll manage and I'll take care of it. What can I do for Sunny?"

"She's good. Falling asleep right now. I'll have her at my place for the night. Don't worry, the doc told me she'll pass out before the car ride ends."

"Don't touch her—"

"I would never take advantage of her. She couldn't drive, and the doctor wanted her to be supervised because of the medicine, so she asked if she could stay with me before he dosed her. She's told me a lot about you. Guess I'll finally get to meet you tomorrow."

The name Johnny finally connects in my head when I recall her mentioning him to me and saying they were close. "Yes, she mentioned you, too. Okay, so you're sure about taking care of her tonight because I can do that?"

"She's no trouble. A little mouthy sometimes," he says, laughing. "But harmless."

"That sounds like Sunny all right."

"Welcome to Hawaii. Oh, and call this number if you need to reach either of us."

"Thanks. I will."

After I hang up, I realize that my plans just dramatically changed. Perhaps it's fate that has made me available for the remainder of the day. I turn and look at Evan, trying not to get caught, which is difficult when he's already staring at me. He smiles softly, with kindness, no trace of smugness in it at all. I smile then announce, "Is your offer still good?"

The smirk quickly returns and he floors the gas pedal. I guess I got my answer.

2

MALLORY

Evan pulls up a long drive that leads to a mansion. Considering his cocky attitude, he would probably only call it a house. After parking to the left, near a paved walkway, he gets out and opens my door. With a nod over his shoulder, he says, "C'mon. It's this way."

The path is shadowed by the house, giving way to an expansive view of the ocean. My breath catches and I'm in awe of the beauty of this vista. Wanting to take a closer look, I stop next to the large pool. Between where I stand and the ocean is a guesthouse with huge windows. And here I thought they only had those on trendy teen dramas.

"I live back here," he says, leading me to the guesthouse.

I roll my eyes. *Of course, he does.*

He slides the glass door open, and I walk inside. My mouth drops open in awe of the view through the two large windows overlooking the ocean. The sun is setting, which creates a glow that surrounds us making the view even more spectacular. "I can see why this is your favorite place."

He takes me by the hand, causing my heart to skip a beat ... or three. His hand is warm and strong, his confidence felt as his pulse beats against my stuttering one. Pausing, he does a minute shake of his head then continues toward the back door with my hand still tucked neatly in his. When the door is opened wide, the breeze flowing through the large room, combined with the view, and the company of a bewildering boy, sets my head spinning.

"I'll be right back," he says, leaving me alone with this natural beauty.

I sit down on the step that leads to the grass, unable to imagine any place better than this. The word paradise could easily be overused if I spent a regular amount of time here. This place is perfection come to life. Until he sits down next to me, and hands me a glass of white wine. That's when my perfect world gets even better. The wine choice surprises me. "I didn't take you for a wine guy." I sip.

"I like to enjoy a good glass now and again. But, shhh, don't tell anyone." He laughs at his joke.

I laugh at the whole set-up. "Wine with this view, Evan? I'm sure there are not many girls who haven't had this move played on them. I think your secret might already be out."

He shakes his head, disappointment coloring the defined features of his face and his tone. "Can we drop the games and just enjoy each other's company? I'm not going to lie to you, remember? I think it's fairly obvious that I find you attractive. You're pretty and smart. I like that. Sometimes that combo is not easily found." He chuckles to himself while swirling his wine in the glass. "Or ever." The last part is just a whisper, but I hear him.

Before I can respond, he looks at me and says, "I'm gonna overlook that biting charm you use to feel secure because I can tell it's not the real you." He stands up and walks a few feet ahead of me, staring at the ocean.

I stand, but I don't join him. Leaning against the house

for support, I debate whether I should be insulted or not—
no matter how true his assessment of me is. Even if I'm
slightly offended, I can't take my eyes off him. He's athletic,
his shoulder muscles highlighted by the thin cotton of his t-
shirt.

I down two gulps of wine, needing the respite it
provides.

He turns around and looks me in the eyes, puzzled, as if
he doesn't know what to do about me. Then he's in motion,
rushing forward, his mouth crashing into mine. There's no
asking and definitely nothing polite about this kiss. It's
needy—he's needy—and I inwardly smile that I've made
Mr. Smooth desperate for me. My body reacts and I become
just as needy in return. I wrap my arms around his neck
without warning, struggling to hold the wine glass in the
other. When our tongues meet, he backs me through the
open doorway, taking my glass from my hand. I'm dazed,
lost in desire for his sexy, heated body against mine. His
hands glide over my ribs and down my hips then back up to
the sides of my breasts where they linger.

My breathing picks up, the anticipation for what's to
come, building deep within me.

His palms squeeze lightly, pushing my breasts closer
together as his hands grip me tighter, grounding me to the
spot and to him. His tongue is gentle, unlike when his lips
first took possession of mine.

I let my hands roam up his shoulders and toward the
back of his neck and push my fingers into his incredibly
sexy hair. Just from the little kissing we've done, I don't want
to leave him either, now sympathizing with the girl at the
airport. I open my eyes to sneak a peek at the Sex God I'm
making out with and am once again beaten to the punch.
His eyes, though hooded with desire, are already watching

me. Clamping them shut again, I moan. "Oh, Evan." *Wait, what? Where'd that come from?*

He takes that as a sign to continue, which makes me realize how much I want this to happen—how much I *need* this to happen. It's been too long and ... well damn, look at him. His face alone turns me on, so I start to appreciate it with my mouth. I hear him groan internally and I can't help smiling again at the carnal pleasure I derive from that sound.

Kissing down my neck, he stops and asks, "What? What are you smiling about?"

I sigh, answering him despite the sex drunk state I'm currently in. "This feels so good."

A smile flashes across his face before exploring my jaw with his mouth, leaving a wet trail across my skin. "This?"

"*Um*, yeah, that."

He reaches the base of my neck, and his warm tongue traces the curve of my collar bone. "How about this?" he asks.

I nod enough to encourage him to slide his hands down my body as he continues his kissing journey. Even though I'm taking all he's giving, I still want more.

"And this?" he asks, teasing with the tip of his tongue flexed flat on my skin.

I don't even bother with an answer because my body's response is answer enough. His hand slides between my legs and rubs roughly up and down, twice, before leaving me well bothered and craving more.

His words are just a whisper, his breath hot against my ear. "What about—"

"*Yes! Jesus!* Evan, right there, *especially there!*" My voice is screechy, not even recognizable to me. The word wanton comes to mind.

"*Okay*, settle down. I was just asking," he says, but I can hear the playfulness in his tone.

My hands work their way down his backside, his muscles flexing under my touch. I take the open invitation and squeeze his ass. *Oh good lord, why'd I do that?* It's fantastic, hard and rounded. Images of seeing it move up and down as we have sex fuels a surge of ultimate boldness.

My words sound more like a demand than a request. "Take off your shirt." Maybe they are.

His lips stop on my cheek, his hands pause on my waist just under my shirt, and he leans back away from me. With a furrowed brow, he asks, "What kind of guy do you take me for, Mallory?"

"I'm hoping a guy who can back up that bad boy reputation you've worked so hard to create."

His hand graces my face and he places a sweet kiss on my forehead. "Oh, baby, I can back it up. Don't you worry your little cotton panties about that. But, I'm a firm believer in *ladies first*."

His cockiness is growing on me and I'm starting to think he probably *can* back it up. His hands reach the bottom hem of my shirt and he starts slowly pulling it up, never losing eye contact.

It's too slow for how much I'm revved up. Feeling confident, I take the shirt into my own hands, lift it over my head, and toss it onto a nearby chair. In these situations, which hasn't been many times, I usually hide a little, but I don't want to here. He allows me to feel good about my body. I'm fit, not an athlete and there's a softness to my curves.

He quickly follows, lifting his shirt off and tossing it to the floor. His abs are not bulky like bodybuilders. His are defined and strong, more natural in form, probably from sports and a healthy lifestyle. I run my fingers over his stomach again as he kisses me with passion. If I allow myself, I might venture to say it's laced with deeper developing emotions.

We continue with our lips freely occupying the others and our hands deceptively close to operating on their own accord. I can sense that I'm already in too deep. All I can do is pray that I'm as strong tomorrow as I am right now, here in this moment.

He unbuttons my jeans and slides them down my pale legs. Kneeling, he remains eye level with my center, leaning gracefully forward, his nose and mouth land on the apex of my thighs. My mouth drops open in shock as my middle heats up. My right eyebrow shoots up when I hear him inhale and then feel his hot breath released back onto me, my knees weakening at the sensation. He slides his nose against my wet panties and upwards not stopping until he lands between my breasts.

"This won't do at all," he says, unfastening the bra as if he's done it a million times, which he probably has.

My back is arching my exposed chest toward him, an offering he'll hopefully accept. The playfulness has disappeared, only to be replaced with a lustful burden. A crease forms across his forehead, backing my intuition. He kisses me quickly to cover then says, "Let's move to the bed."

Taking me by the hand, he leads me to his platform bed that sits as the dominant feature in the open space. We stop at the edge and he strips his own jeans off before we slowly lay down together. Looking at each other, we study, learning the other's features. His leg slides between mine. His are long and muscular, and I wonder if he plays soccer or tennis.

He looks me over, taking one of my breasts in his hands and kneads. "You're incredibly sexy," he says.

I have a decent sized chest, average, I suppose, but he seems satisfied and his words make me feel beautiful. Eyeing each other without a word, we give one last out of this unexpected turn of events. Neither of us takes it and we move closer, our bodies tangling.

He rolls on top of me, taking the lead and suddenly we're moving together, intense pleasure I'd long forgotten building quickly. Our kisses are fevered and we moan in unison pushing the other towards our mutually desired goal.

Evan's tongue enters my mouth, and unlike the frenzy we felt moments earlier, this time it caresses mine. His hands glide along the side of my body then stop and gently play with the back of my knee. He pulls it up, wrapping his arm around my thigh and holding it against his side. This new position makes me squirm with desire, needing more.

My mind focuses on his fingers tucking under the sides of my panties as he continues trailing wet kisses down my body, over my hips, as he removes my panties.

Lifting up abruptly, he stands at the base of the bed, his eyes locked on mine while he removes his black boxer briefs. Black equals bad boy. *Will wore white.*

I prefer the black.

My breathing deepens as anticipation starts to peak. He lowers himself back down, hovering over me. A small smile reveals his appreciation of my body beneath his. I've never felt more confident or comfortable being naked in my life, and I briefly consider leaving on this high. But knowing his history with women, I'm curious as to what makes them cry when they have to leave him. I have a strong suspicion it's related to his skills in bed. As a matter of fact, *I'm counting on it.*

On his hands and knees above me, he lowers himself

down, resting his body lightly on top of mine as he kisses me again. Our lips part and we look at each other. I can't hide the fire I feel for him as his erection presses against my center, adding the fuel that makes me heat and lust for more —more contact, more sensations, just more of all of him.

"Are you sure about this?" he asks although we both are well aware that no woman ever says no to him.

I try for casual. "Never more." I don't know how I sounded, but he definitely gets the message. His lips find mine with more pressure, but yet still gentle in their quest.

He pulls back and stretches toward the nightstand, pulling the drawer open to retrieve a condom. Sliding down my body, he kneels between my legs, taking the packet between his teeth, and ripping it open. As I watch him put the condom on, I realize I hadn't taken in the full view properly. His cock is larger than I've had inside me before and I'm daring enough to think it's handsome. *Wow!* I can't believe I just called *it* handsome.

When it's covered from tip to base, he leans over me in a push-up position, his gaze roving from my middle to my stomach and stopping on my breasts to admire. His eyes flicker up to meet mine and a small smile forms on his lips. "You ready for me?"

I nod, feeling a bit breathless at the moment.

With that, he drops himself back down and slowly pushes into me. My head lulls back and my eyes automatically close. I feel his breath and lips against my neck as a low rumble escapes him. "Mallory." His voice is low and raw, bordering on wild.

My eyes flutter open to take in the sight of Evan on top of me. His head is buried into my neck and hair as he moves gracefully. The act itself surprises me. It's not that it doesn't feel amazing, but it's more like he's making love to me rather than fucking. I thought we had an understanding that we were going to fuck—maybe not a verbal one, but an understanding of what this was when we started.

My body responds to his and I join him in the action. I moan and my voice is breathy and uncontrolled as I wrap my arms around him, pulling my body closer to his. I spread my knees further apart and he lifts above me, going even deeper as our connection intensifies.

Pulling my thigh up, he anchors it with his arm while thrusting faster and harder, our breathing becoming jagged when his fingers find my most sensitive center. Playful, deliberate moves make me jolt reflexively under his touch.

As his mouth moves steadily along my jaw, I can tell he's nearing his release. That knowledge, along with these overwhelming sensations twisting inside, sends me into an abyss of sexual vertigo, something I haven't had in well over five months and nothing as glorious as this before. While I'm lost in my own orgasmic heaven, Evan reaches his peak. My mind lands safely back on earth as he soars in his release while his breathing and moaning into my neck makes my skin react and tingle.

He relaxes on top of me for too short of a time before he rolls off, tossing the condom in the trash can near the nightstand. The action reminds me that this is his everyday, nothing special to him. I try to remain happy in the here and now, and by the smile on Evan's face when he flops down next to me, he is too.

A leisurely kiss is placed on my lips before he says, "You're a really beautiful girl." He pauses. "Did you enjoy yourself?"

"Immensely," I answer without hesitation because it's true. I actually did enjoy myself, which is more than I can say about my previous sexual encounters back home. As much as I hate it, he was right in what he said earlier at the diner. He does have me all figured out. This annoys me, but doesn't seem important anymore after what we just did.

"Would you like something to drink?" he asks, sitting up.

"Yes." I glance at the clock. "I'll take my wine and a glass of water please."

He laughs as he saunters across the room into the kitchen area completely naked. After grabbing two bottles out of the fridge and our wine, he returns to my side and hands me my glass. I sip the wine as he opens the bottle of water for me. Alternating between the two, thirsty yet needing something stronger than water to keep my mental state in check, I crave both.

Watching him go into the bathroom, I hear the shower start seconds later. He pokes his head out. His smile is huge as he suggests I join him. "Come in here with me."

Now I hesitate, but I don't know why. He senses my reluctance and comes back to the bed and sits down next to me. Taking my hand in his, he tries to comfort me. "There's nothing to be embarrassed about. We just made love, Mallory. I want you to shower with me." He tugs at my hand and I give in, following him into the steamy room. The warm water relaxes my body as I think about his words '*made love*' when he steps into the shower stall behind me. He's right. We did just make love. This stall is very close quarters, and he amusingly prods me out of my thoughts when he asks, "Can you share?"

I tilt my head surprised by his lightheartedness. "Yeah, of course, Evan. Sorry about that." I'm embarrassed for hogging the water.

Stepping aside, I let him under the water. He runs his fingers through his hair, soaking it under the spray. Looking back down at me, he says, "I like the way you say my name."

"Really? How do I say it?"

He shrugs. "Um, I'm not sure. It's your accent, I guess. Where are you from?"

"Colorado."

"Ah, that must be it." He taps me on the nose while reaching for the shampoo. Squirting a capful of shampoo into his hands, he massages it into my hair, dragging his fingers carefully through to the ends of my long hair. I've never had a guy do this before and it's erotic on a physical and an emotional level. I hum my pleasure aloud which makes him chuckle. As he rinses my hair, he asks, "Repeat?"

"Absolutely, magic fingers."

That makes him laugh even louder, enjoying the ease and fun of the moment. I return the favor, adding a few fun flair techniques I developed myself, causing him to groan in pleasure. Minutes later, we dry off, and he says, "You're different now."

It's just an observation, but it shows how perceptive he is. "I feel more comfortable after what we did."

"Any regrets?"

"Not yet. I can't promise I won't have any tomorrow though."

"What you're saying is that I have tonight to make sure regret never crosses that pretty face of yours?"

He's attentive and caring which makes me question that maybe this whole bad boy thing really is just an act. My changing feelings don't matter though because he's been more than clear how this is going down. We've only got tonight and I need to enjoy it.

When I walk back into the main room, he's already dressed, but hands me a t-shirt, a pair of briefs, and ibupro-fen. "I'll get your suitcase out of the car, but you can wear these if you want." He hands the pills to me, and adds, "You might need these before morning."

I'm not sure why I would, but figure it will help with the soreness of sitting on that airplane for more than five hours.

I take the clothes, dropping the towel. Evan watches me dress with interest as a darkness clouds over his eyes. He comes closer as I pull the shirt over my head and then he's on me. His hands are on me, his lips are on mine, and his legs are tangling with mine.

All of Evan, all on me.

I kiss him back before he abruptly turns and leaves the room, walking outside and up the path towards the car. This gives me a minute that I desperately need for clarity. I sit on a barstool, swiveling and taking in my surroundings. I have so many questions, but with the short amount time we have together, I don't want to waste words on topics that don't really matter in the end. I feel giddy inside that he just assumes I'll stay with him. He's already accepted that as fact which leads me to believe he wants me to be here as much as I want to spend more time in his arms.

He returns with my heavy suitcase in his hand and walks to the corner of the room, moving about like it weighs nothing. He sets it down on its side in the corner, and while scratching the back of his head, asks, "Are you hungry or tired? Do you want to watch a movie or go to bed?"

He's quite a caring host, and I appreciate that in him. "I'm still full from the earlier meal, but I am tired."

I watch his reaction and as he stands in the middle of the room, he seems befuddled. For some reason, though I know it can't be true since we're on his turf, he seems out of sorts. I walk over to him taking his hand in mine, and say, "I'm really tired. Can we just lie together until we fall asleep?" I know that cuddling is probably pushing his personal limits, but I want that closeness with him. Anyways, he can always say no.

"Yes."

My lips part, but I catch myself before it drops open all the way, and smile. He's a riddle that isn't easily solved. Unpredictable.

"I know you have your suitcase here, but if you don't want to dig out your toothbrush you can use mine." He looks at me as if he's waiting for more than just a yes or no answer.

"It's no problem. I carry mine in my purse," I reply, walking to my bag. He doesn't say anything and retreats into the bathroom. By the time I walk in there, he's already done. He leaves the bathroom in silence, giving me privacy.

When I walk back into the main room, it's dark and he's already in bed. The curtains are drawn along the wall of windows that face the mansion on the other side of the pool which makes me realize that they were open earlier when we did ... *the deed*. I try not to wonder if anyone lives there and saw us. That would embarrass me too much, so I block that thought from my mind. I slide under the covers just as his arm goes out to hold me. He tucks me into his side. My eyes feel heavy as my breath slowly steadies in sync with his, a calmness washing over me.

I dream of Hibiscus flowers and trade winds, tropical storms and white sheets, bronzed skin and crying girls at airports.

3

MALLORY

I attempt to roll over, but can't. My eyes flash open and I gasp. *Where am I?*

The weight of an arm draped over me is heavy and hot breath hits the back of my neck. *Will?* No way! I don't care how drunk I get, I could never be drunk enough to hook up with him again after what he did. And I don't feel drunk, a little sore, but not drunk. I look at the hand holding mine against my chest and don't recognize it. It's nice looking though. Freeing my hand, I drag my fingertips lightly along the muscular arm and up until the warm body stirs and tightens around me.

My eyes adjust to my surroundings which give me a sense of where I am—Evan, Hawaii, traveling. Another mystery solved and my dignity is still intact even though I broke my rule of no one night stands. It's nice being here for the summer where no one will judge me like they do at home. More importantly, I feel good about my choice, what we did, and that's what he gave me, a choice.

Without moving, he whispers, "Mallory?"

I snuggle back, pressing against him even more. "Yes?"

"Are you having trouble sleeping, baby?"

Why do I like that sound of 'Baby' so much? "When I woke up, I was wondering where I was?"

"I'm that forgettable, huh?"

I giggle softly. "Unfamiliar surroundings, that's all." I'm starting to feel more awake.

He props himself up on his elbow behind me, and I roll onto my back and under what appears to be an adoring gaze. "Do you want to go for a swim in the pool?" he asks.

I don't want any of this to end and not wanting it to end means still going along with it while I can. "Okay."

He rolls out of bed and reaches his hand down for mine. Graciously accepting, he helps me to my feet. I want to kiss him and am about to but his smile lessens as he looks at me, his other hand rubbing the back of his neck. His gaze drops away for the briefest of seconds and when his eyes return, they are confused, mystified. My hand is released, and he walks away. I don't know what just happened, but he looked at me like I'm an enigma of sorts.

The door opens, letting in a faint light from the outside, and I follow now unsure in my decision to stay. He was happy, endearing in bed and now ... now he's back to the guy in the Maserati.

I walk outside and see him strip his briefs off just before diving in. Walking to the edge of the pool, I sit down with my feet dangling in the warm water. Swimming the length of the pool, he touches the other side then comes up for air. Gripping the edge of the pool behind his head, he asks, "You're not coming in?"

I shake my head, confused by him. In the silence of the night, I hear the rustling palm fronds high above my head, the tide crashing on the beach, and Evan's every stroke through the clear water as he swims closer. He stops, takes my legs in his hands, and floats in front of me. Staring into the blue of his eyes, his beauty has depth and yet his heart is so closed off. Regret was imminent. I had just hoped that it wouldn't come until morning.

"I'm sorry, Mallory."

I tilt my head down to look at him. He's all wet and glorious in the water. "Why'd you act like that?"

Releasing me, he sinks under water avoiding my question or maybe he needs time to come up with the right answer. When he surfaces, he tugs my legs forward dragging me down into the pool. He pins my back against the side of the pool, pressing his chest against mine. One of his hands finds my waist, and he says, "I don't know, but I'm sorry. I could see I hurt your feelings and I didn't mean to." His face is inches from mine, his breath chilling my wet skin.

I pull an *'Evan move'* and drop from the confines of his arms straight down into the water. When I'm fully submersed, my languid body frees the tension, and my mind clears. I feel him against me. Opening my eyes, he's glaring at me under water. He embraces me and carries me upwards for air. The air feels harsh against my throat as I gasp and then cough.

He shakes his head, angry when he speaks. "Are you trying to do yourself in?" Swimming to the side of the pool, he stares out into the blackness from where the sounds of the ocean drift toward us. "Don't pull that shit again."

I'm taken aback by his reaction and words fumble from my mouth to fill the awkwardness between us. "I wasn't doing anything. I was only under for a few seconds. I'm sorry. I'm sorry if I scared you."

"You were under for at least a minute, and I don't know your water skills."

"*My water skills?*"

"Do you even know how to swim?" His tone is harsh and it makes me defensive.

"Yes. Why are you so mad?"

He dives under, pushing off the wall, and swims to me. Feeling his way up my body, he reaches my mouth and kisses me. I don't return the kiss ... at first, but give in knowing this is obviously how he copes with his anger *and* because he's so sexy when he's angry.

The rage dissipates from his face as we part. His hand moves to the base of my neck and he pulls me closer. I glide gracefully through the water to him wrapping my arms and legs around his body. He holds the edge of the pool, supporting us then pushes forward, pinning me against the wall. His kisses become more aggressive as his tongue sweeps into my mouth like it owns the place, and he presses his erection against my already tingling sex.

He lifts his body up a few inches to appreciate the sensation that it brings to both of us which makes me moan into his mouth. I don't know why he makes me do that. I never used to do that with Will. I'm not a moaner—usually. This makes me realize that A: We were either doing it wrong, or B: The sex just wasn't moan worthy. I'm guessing B since it's kind of hard to mess up the basic concept of intercourse.

My mind flashes back to the present as Evan's mouth covers my neck with passionate kisses and his hand finds its way into my undies—technically, his undies, but I'm wearing them and staking claim because possession is nine-tenths of the law. *Nine-tenths? Who cares about that right now?* I berate myself because Evan is in my underpants, and I'm not paying attention.

His mouth is mesmerizing. I lean my head back to enjoy the magic he's working on my neck. He nips, sucks, licks, and kisses all together in the perfect arrangement. His fingers rub across my wanting sex. When he parts me, they slide inside, and I sigh.

Forehead to forehead, we both try to catch our breath. Dipping down, his nose nuzzles mine in the sweetest of gestures. Evan leans back and looks at me through lust-filled eyes. His lids look as if he doesn't have the strength to hold them open any longer, but he does, just to watch my reaction as his fingers begin their sexual dance.

My breathing is uneven and affected, and when I look at him, he appears the same. His hand moves effortlessly, causing a whimper to escape me before I can process the thought to stop it. Before embarrassment reaches my cheeks, he leans in, taking my bottom lip between his and gently sucks on it.

His mouth releases me, and I lean my head against his arm that's stretched next to me, supporting us against the wall, and I close my eyes. Rhythmic fingers pump, edging me closer to bliss. At some point, I stop caring what sounds I make, or that I'm in a pool, or that I might drown in this sensation. As I strive for another slice of orgasmic heaven, my insides implode, leaving me calling his name and begging for more. "Evan! Fuck ... I need you in me now."

Without delay, he jumps out of the water, spins me around to face him, and hastily hauls me out of the pool like a ragdoll. He kisses me quickly then pulls me by the arm inside. Taking my soaked shirt by the hem, he pulls it over my head and tosses it out the open door and then strips off my underwear, throwing them outside without care.

Naked, dripping wet, and standing next to the bed, I shiver. The tension in the room is thick, heated, engulfing until he takes my face in both his hands and brings me to him. We kiss like we're in love and for the time being I pretend we are. I lower myself to the bed, not waiting for an invite. He follows, mimicking a sexual version of a cat and mouse game. I move on my bottom to the top of the bed as he stalks me, hovering over me the entire time. My head bumps the headboard and he seems to delight in my entrapment. Evan tilts his head, taunting me, and asks, "Mallory, do you want me inside of you?"

I quirk an eyebrow. He's egging me on, teasing me. "You know I want you inside of me," I reply coolly. Two can play this ego game.

He leans down to kiss me, and I close my eyes anticipating his lips on mine again, but they don't come. My eyes pop open when I feel his breath enter my mouth because he's so close. "I want to be inside of you too, baby."

Baby. I inwardly sigh at the joy of hearing that nickname again.

After grabbing another condom from the nightstand, he rolls it down his large and very ready length. Leaning forward on one hand, he strokes himself once then swipes up my entrance with his fingertips. It's kind of crude and kind of hot at the same time. I move down a bit to a more comfortable position and prepare. He lowers himself, his lips meeting mine tentatively then he forges forth.

"*Ahhhh.*" The only sound I manage when he fills me, making me whole once again.

Then he hums. "*Mmmmm.*" The sound fills my mouth and heightens my pleasure and it tells me he feels the same way I do. I relax into the bed, dropping my weight even further. His body descends and I wrap my legs around his waist, still holding my mouth to his. I don't want to complain because he feels amazing, but I need him faster, harder, and rougher. I just need him so much.

"More," I beg. My orgasm gathers in strength as he

relieves my mind of worries and thoughts. I can tell by his body's movements that he's getting close too.

"Mallory, *beautiful*, Mallory." His words inspire my body into submission and as I tighten around him, he speeds up and peaks.

Evan weakens on top of me, lightly digging his fingertips into my wet, matted hair and he covers me with kisses. Our bodies become one as we lay there together all panting breaths and tired sighs. He whispers in my ear, "You're incredible."

Once again, I challenge his words against everything he said and did earlier in the day. He still leaves me beyond bewildered and yet utterly blissful. "Evan?"

"Yeah," he mumbles, sounding half asleep.

"You're too heavy."

His head pops up and looks concerned as he apologizes. "I'm sorry. I'm so tired." He rolls off of me and smiles while adjusting onto his side.

"Evan?"

"Yeah?"

"That *was* incredible." I lean forward and give him a nice chaste kiss then crawl out of bed.

I walk into the bathroom shutting the door behind me to freshen up. Standing in front of the mirror, I expect to find tired. I expect to see bags under my eyes from traveling. I expect a rat's nest on my head from all the wet hair sexing. But I don't find tired, bags, or a rat's nest. I find beautiful and eyes that gleam with happiness. My skin is practically glowing from the inside out. I haven't looked this good in a long time *or maybe ever,* and I owe it to Evan. That cocky, obnoxious, egotistical guy in the next room made me look and feel beautiful and sexy. I run my finger over my swollen lower lip when a small knock on the door breaks me from my most self-indulgent moment.

I open the door, still naked, and now proudly working my God given assets. My arm goes to the top of the door-frame and I lean against it tilting my hips in the opposite direction. Evan's lips part, and though I like that as a start, I know I can do better. I drag my finger down his nose and catch his bottom lip with it, hook and release, hook and release, hook then release that pouty lip of his until he breaks his stance, succumbing to my trickery.

"You are so fucking hot, Mallory."

That's more like it.

"I thought you might want dry clothes." He hands me another pair of briefs and another t-shirt.

I walk past him waving off the clothes, and say, "I'll sleep naked." Sitting down in the middle of the bed with one knee bent and the other leg straight, I lean back on my hands and toss my head back. In other words, I strike a pose just for him. "Unless you'd prefer me to get dressed."

His mouth more than drops open, it hits the ground with a crash. His manhood stands erect to get a gander at me and I smile knowing he can't hide his thoughts.

"Yeah, naked. Sure, you should ... naked." He doesn't make much sense, but enough for me to know that I've gotten to him. There are absolutely no signs left of the narcissistic ass from the airport.

He backs into the bathroom, his eyes glued to my body while mumbling, "Naked, hot, nakedness ..." After he shuts the door, I hear a whimper. I have him thoroughly bewildered just like what he does to me. Perfect!

I lay down, pulling the covers up over my still sensitive skin and wait for him to return to me. He stays in there a few minutes longer than I expected and I hear an occasional

'*You can*' from the bathroom. He might be psyching himself up to return. I don't know, but it's the only logical answer I come to before the door bursts open and he saunters back to bed. He lays flat on his back then hurriedly kisses me on the cheek, and says, "Good night, Mallory."

I'm left dazed by the sudden change in his behavior, but too tired to over-think it. "Good night, Evan. Sweet dreams."

I roll onto my side and he sidles up behind me hooking his arm around me and pulling me back, curled against his naked body. I fall asleep and dream of Evan's kissable lips, diving into a pool filled with ecstasy, and hands roaming all over my body. That last part might have actually happened, but I can't be sure.

4

MALLORY

The morning sun awakens me to an empty bed and I sit up to look around. My heart drops into the pit of my stomach feeling the emptiness of the large room—Evan's home.

Glancing at the nightstand for a note, I don't see anything of interest. I walk into the kitchen and find no clue to where he has gone. After dressing, I open the back sliding glass door and take a deep breath of the sweet island air. A surfer far out in the ocean draws my attention.

I don't know where Evan's gone, but it stings waking up alone, left here to deal with my growing humiliation.

I continue watching the lone surfer and get lost in thought, eventually wondering if I should call a cab. I don't. Walking back to bed, I lie down, not ready to leave this small taste of paradise. And being honest with myself, I can admit that I want to see him again and want him to make me feel better, to make this all right.

Another half hour passes and I hear my name called. "Mallory?"

I look up from the bed and glare at him. "Evan."

He points over his shoulder, and says, "I did dawn patrol."

"You were working?" I stand up, crossing my arms over my chest protectively.

He remains standing there, dripping wet and magnificent. "No, dawn patrol is surfing before sunrise. There were some great waves today."

"So great that you couldn't leave a note?" Sarcasm spills into every word.

"I, uh, didn't think it would be necessary—"

"It's not necessary? It's a courtesy to leave a note."

He doesn't respond and stares at me with unsettling eyes. Raising the towel, he rubs it over his head, messing his hair up even more than it usually is, and ignores me.

Finally looking back at me, he says, "I see you're dressed. Let me throw on some shorts and I'll drive you to your friend's place."

My heart drops to my feet. How can he drive me to Sunny's after the time we shared last night? *Oh God!* I think I started falling for him and he was being truthful. My eyes well with tears as regret colors my vision of last night, of Evan, and the memory of beautiful Mallory in the mirror. I fell for it. I fell for him. I let my carefully, crafted guard down and fell like every other girl who's walked through that door.

I grab my purse. "Let's go," I say, pretending I'm not hurt that the old Evan is back and currently looking at me with no emotion whatsoever.

He trails behind me, keeping his distance, and it makes me wonder if he feels that is the safer thing to do. The car alarm chirps as we approach the Maserati parked in the driveway. I don't look back, but I can feel the distance growing both physically and emotionally between us. I don't wait for him to open my door though I remember from the airport and diner that it's something he normally does for girls. Getting in, I shut the door quickly behind me before he can say anything, before my emotions free themselves and I cry. He loads my suitcase back into the car in silence then slides into the driver's seat.

"What's the address?" he asks. Nothing more. His voice steady, unfeeling.

I hand him my phone with the address not wanting to talk for fear of either saying too much or saying the wrong thing, though I'm not sure there is anything I could say to damage us more than we already are.

He starts the engine, turns the car around, and we're up the long driveway in seconds. It's as if we don't even know each other. It's as if last night didn't happen. It's as if he didn't have his dick inside of me less than eight hours ago. "Damn it!" I mutter, frustrated.

He looks at me, but says nothing.

That phrase 'deafening silence' applies to the feeling in this car. The heavy tension from the morning engulfs the vehicle and swallows us with it.

Pulling off the main road into the apartment parking lot, he mumbles to himself, "Building A." He parks the car and comes around to open my door. His actions are too eager to feel polite. The gesture feels like he's ready for me to go, so I take my time sliding out and walk around him. He doesn't make eye contact with me, but turns his entire attention to removing my large suitcase from the backseat. After rolling it to me, he shoves his hands into his pockets. Not able to look or sound more awkward, he says, "I had fun."

I scoff ... loudly. *Fuck him and his fun.* I take the handle on my case and turn on my heel, wheeling the suitcase to the sidewalk.

Just feet from Sunny's front door, he says, "Mallory, c'mon, don't be like that."

I stop and turn around. But my hurt heart and wounded ego keep me from saying what I really want. Instead, I steal the remaining shared seconds to memorize his physical beauty. But he's different to me now, marred like a bad taste that lingers in my mouth. He doesn't deserve to be that handsome. Evan abuses the world with his good looks and so-called truths.

I turn back around not giving him the pleasantry he wants and walk away. He's gone before I have the door unlocked, but I'm not surprised. I'm just glad that I can use my anger to ward off the tears that would have normally been there at his parting. I realize I should've thanked him now. His demeanor this morning has made the hint of regret I was feeling dissipate altogether. I can already look at the situation for what it was, *a fuck*, mentally and physically.

5

MALLORY

I shut the door behind me and look around the one bedroom, first floor apartment. It's cute and very much Sunny. The couch is navy blue with pale pink throw pillows and the small grey entertainment center has a pink metal picture frame. It's the one I gave her last Christmas of the two of us and makes me smile to see it displayed so prominently. Peeking into the kitchen, I see more pink ... a lot more pink.

The bedroom stands in stark opposition to the girly-ness of the other rooms. It's calm, serene in soft green and white. Seeing the bed makes me tired and I yawn already beginning to relax in my new home. I need to check on Sunny though, so I call her, hoping she's awake.

"Mallory! You're up. Are you all settled in?" She sounds cheery.

"Yeah, but more important, how are you?"

"So much better. Did I tell you I didn't break it? It's just a bruised bone. I was really stressing about missing any work. I need the money, you know?"

"That's good news. You sound like you're doing better which is great. When are you coming home?"

"We already sound like an old married couple, don't we? Johnny's gonna drop me at my VW. I can't believe you're finally here!"

"Me either. I'll see you soon."

After hanging up, I spy my suitcase. Making a snap decision to hide all evidence that I was not here last night, I unpack some of my stuff and mess up the blanket and sheets left on the couch for me. Flopping down on the couch, I press my body into the cushions that surround me, denting them and making them less perfect looking.

I open the drapes in the bedroom and head to the bathroom with my toiletries and spread them out on one side of the sink. I kick off my shoes and change my clothes. When I decide the staging is done, I flick on the TV, hoping to take my mind off of my previous night.

That's impossible though. My body can still feel his touch and a vivid image of him moving so gracefully on top of me fills my mind just like he filled my body. All my senses remember the feel of his masculinity, his smell, his body, even his taste, in the pool and out. "Stop!" I shout ... to myself and out loud. He's making me crazy.

That's when a key in the front door lock draws my attention away from Evan and back to the present. I jump up and stare.

The door flies open, and Sunny runs in, arms open. Grabbing me into her arms, she squeezes the air right out of me. I hug her back just as tight. "I missed you," I say, gasping for breath.

She leans back and looks me over. "Damn girl, Colorado is treating you better than I thought. I like your hair all mussed up like that. It's wild and sexy."

Sex hair is more accurate, but I don't feel the need to make that correction, although I'm figuratively sweating bullets. I delve into a different topic to distract her. "Let me see your hand."

She holds up the black brace wrapped around her wrist, and says, "I hope you're a quick learner because I'm gonna need you tonight."

"I'm there. I'm ready."

Hugging me one more time, she whispers, "I've missed you so much, Mal."

After she changes clothes, we make breakfast together and curl up on the couch, sharing a blanket like when we were kids back home. It feels good to be here and to be with my best friend again.

I don't poison our day with talk of Evan or what I got up to yesterday. Fortunately, Sunny doesn't even remember talking to me yesterday, so she hasn't questioned my whereabouts. By mid-afternoon, we head into her work and my new summer job.

Big Kehones, is a bar and restaurant disguised in the form of a large shack on the beach. It's off the main road, but easily accessible by those in the know. We park in the dirt lot out front, and Sunny introduces me to the regulars as we make our way to the bar. The owner, Alana, is working the front. She has me fill out some paperwork and gives me the grand tour which takes about ten minutes inside and out. I already like the place. It's not pretentious, but seems to have a loyal following. It's almost four o'clock when she sets me free to manage the bar, which consists of pouring pitchers of beer and serving sodas and water. I also carry Sunny's orders to help her out.

Johnny clocks in at five, and when I meet him, he's different than what I imagined. He's quite cute and seems like a nice guy. I look at Johnny and Sunny whispering to each other and I can tell by their demeanor that they're close in a platonic kind of way. I didn't think they were dating because Sunny would have told me, but by the way he took care of her yesterday, I thought maybe there was a chance.

Sunny is beautiful, light blue eyes and model pretty with enviable, long sandy blonde hair that frames her face. Her hair is lightened even more from living in paradise. Her name has always fit her disposition, but it fits her lifestyle more here than back home in Colorado. The best thing about her though is that her heart is kind. I've always been surprised that she doesn't have a boyfriend with the next already lined up waiting in the wings.

The three of us work well together. The small dinner crowd seems pleased which reassures me that I can handle the job since I've never worked in a restaurant before today. I get a break just after six and take a burger to the beach, spending my time in reflection of the first twenty-four hours in Hawaii and what a whirlwind it's been.

I've started smoking again, which disappoints me. I'm not a heavy smoker, more of a nervous one. I picked up the bad habit after Will broke up with me. I quit a few months later, but something about Evan and seeing him at the airport drove me back to the habit. While walking to the designated smoking spot out front, I kick up some rocks with my toe. I lean against the wall and light up.

Four rowdy guys in a black Jeep pull into the lot and park after performing a donut, which sends dirt flying everywhere, including on me. I hack from the dust that fills the air. Right, hacking from the dirt not the cigarette, I sarcastically think. I dust myself off wanting to call them my favorite swear word, but I resist knowing they are customers of Big Kehones and I need this job.

The driver rushes over. "Hey, I'm sorry about that." He swats at my jean clad legs to get the dirt off. "I didn't see you there or I wouldn't have pulled that stunt."

I hack one more time just for effect before taking another long drag of my cigarette. His warm brown eyes watch my mouth the entire time. Dropping the cigarette into the dirt, I shrug. "That's cool. No harm done."

He smiles. I can tell he's relieved. His friends walk toward the large garage door style opening into the restaurant, but one stops and says, "Come on, Kalei. I'm hungry. Get your ass in here or you're buying."

"I think your friends want you." I point out the obvious since he's still standing here looking at me.

He glances over his shoulder, and yells, "Fuck off. I'll be in, in a minute."

"I see you're close?" I add, my smart-ass side kicking in.

He laughs. "Yeah, too close, we're cousins."

"Ah."

"You're new around here."

"You're very observant." I leave the opening for him to tell me his name.

"Nohea Kalei."

"Nohea Kalei." I stick my hand out to formally introduce myself, "Mallory Wray."

"You can call me Noah. It's easier for a haole, though I'm impressed you got it right the first time."

There's something about his eyes that intrigue me. A depth and kindness that draws me in. "Today's my first day."

"This place needed some new blood. Don't get me wrong. Sunny is hot as fu ... sorry about the language. I have a problem with swearing too much. She's hot, but she's waiting for Mr. Right."

"The swearing doesn't bother me. So, you use this as more of a pick-up joint than a place to eat and drink?"

"No, that's not what I meant. I mean Sunny is sweet, but unavailable and that only leaves Alana and her sister who sometimes works a shift."

"That doesn't really answer my question."

"Um, no ... it's not why we come here."

I look at my watch and as much as I enjoy eyeing up this tall hottie, I need to get back to work. It is my first day and all. "Well, Noah Kalei, it was nice to meet you." I walk around him and then backwards towards the door. "Will I see you inside?"

He nods and I get back to work.

When I return to the bar, I watch Noah enter, the small crowd greeting him. The old men are waving, Alana says 'hi', and his friends are laughing at him, most likely because of me.

Sunny comes out from the kitchen and stands next to me. "That's Noah—"

"Yeah, we just met."

She responds with, "Mmm, I see." I can tell by her tone what she's insinuating, making me see him as a prospect for the first time. He's at least six-two, but I'm guessing closer to six-three or four. He has short, almost black hair, gelled, and each lock appears to be carefully arranged. His body is killer. He's handsome in a *Men's Health* magazine, rugged kind of way which is the only way to be handsome if you ask me. Who says you need pretty, GQ boys like Evan!

Sunny stays and chats with him when she delivers his food. She turns around and looks at me at the same time Noah does. Since they are busted they both quickly look back down to the table she's been perched against for a few minutes. They both laugh and then she hits him playfully on the arm before pushing off the table and coming back to the bar. "So, Noah, huh?" she asks with raised eyebrows.

"So, Noah, huh, *what?*"

"Oh, Mallory, you have an admirer over there who just said the nicest things about you."

"He obviously doesn't know me then."

"I'd say he knows you quite well actually."

I roll my eyes as I walk over to check on some older men playing cards.

Good to know hottie is interested in me, but with Evan recently ripping my heart, I can't bring myself to appreciate the 'catch' that Noah seems to be. Looking up as I wipe down the bar, he's smiling at me. I return one because he's cute, but notice that when he smiles, he's really hot, too. The few days I've been in Hawaii are already better than my entire last year in Colorado.

I hear Sunny laugh from across the restaurant. It's annoying because I know why she's laughing. Walking back to the bar, I toss the towel down. "What?"

"Just go for it. Noah's a good guy and look at him. He's damn good looking." She moves closer, leaning her back against the bar.

"Noah Kalei, huh?" Johnny pipes in while sitting down on a barstool next to us.

"Why does everyone keep saying that?" I laugh at the ridiculousness of the gossip going on, but my body starts to crave a cigarette. "And I thought Boulder was small."

"This island is smaller than you think, Mallory. Get ready for everyone to be in your business." Sunny says, sitting on a stool next to Johnny.

Johnny looks over his shoulder at Noah then turns back

to me, and says, "That's his gang, his posse, whatever. Some people don't care for them, but I've known them since I was little. They don't cause any real harm. Noah is kind of like their leader. Ironically, he's the nicest of the bunch. I'd hate to think what kind of trouble they'd cause if he wasn't there keeping them in line."

"A girl can't resist a bad boy. Can she, Mal?" Sunny adds.

Johnny laughs. While looking at Sunny, he raises an in-the-know eyebrow and says, "At least, it's not Ashford."

"I think he gets a bad rap," Sunny says.

"Who's Ashford?" I ask curious to who makes such an interesting impression on them.

Johnny leans forward and lowers his voice. "He's a guy that comes in here every now and then." He glances over to Noah. "Kalei and Ashford don't get along. Their groups don't mesh."

"Is it a territorial turf war or what?" They talk in hushed tones like they're opposing gangs.

Sunny giggles. "Nothing like that. More like locals versus the haoles."

"What's a haole?" I ask, recognizing it from when Noah said it earlier.

"Haole is basically someone not of Hawaiian ancestry. It's kind of divided here still."

"So this Ashford guy is not from here, but he lives here now?"

Sunny hops off the bar stool. "Listen, as fascinating as this conversation is on the biases of the island, we need to clean up or we're going to be here later than I want. My hand hurts and I just want to go home and relax."

She checks on the tables and we start the clean-up process. I look up and see Noah bringing his empty pitcher to me. Leaning against the bar, his voice is low, obviously not wanting to be overheard by any of his friends. "Will you be working here?"

"For the summer. Do you come in a lot?"

He shakes his head. "Not much lately, but I will now." He reaches his hand over for mine and when I take it, he smiles. "It's very nice to meet you, Mallory Wray."

"Likewise, Nohea Kalei."

"Noah."

"All right, Noah."

He winks at me, but it's not creepy or cocky. His expression is friendly and kind. He walks towards the door joining his friends, and says, "Goodnight, Mallory."

"Goodnight."

6

MALLORY

As soon as Sunny and I walk into the apartment, she goes into the kitchen to take her pain medication. "I'm exhausted and going to bed. You bunking with me or taking the couch?"

"I'll take the couch."

"Remember, the place is your home too, so help yourself to whatever. Goodnight."

"Goodnight," I say, straightening the sheet and blanket on the couch. Crawling under the covers, I adjust the pillow under my head and stare out the sliding glass door in front of me. I didn't bother closing the blinds since I enjoy the view of the darkness outside. My eyes get heavy and I drift off to sleep.

Dreams of Noah wrapping his strong arms around me, and me lifting up on my tiptoes to meet his supple lips while his big hands handle me the way I like, dance around my head. But, when I stop kissing him and open my eyes, it's Evan. Blue eyes looking into my green eyes, hands gently caressing me how he already *knows* I like to be touched, and our bodies aroused by the chemistry we share.

I sit up startled from sleep and see the start of a sunrise in the distance through the glass. My heart races as I calm myself back into reality. I lay back down hoping for sleep to take me again, but it doesn't. Five- fifteen in the morning and I'm wide awake. I sit up again and rub my eyes and decide to walk the two blocks down to the beach. Dressing in my my cut-offs and tank top, I slip on my sneakers and leave, hoping I don't wake Sunny.

The walk is easy, breezy, and before six in the morning, very quiet. Birds are tweeting in the distance and the seagulls flying above signal I'm near the water. When I land at the edge of the beach, I pull off my shoes and carry them with me down to the water. The sand is surprisingly fine and soft under my feet.

I sit a few feet from the water's edge watching the tide roll in and marvel at the sight before me. I still can't believe I took Sunny up on her offer to visit for the summer. This has to be the most daring and adventurous thing I've ever done, and as I look out at this beautiful turquoise ocean, I definitely don't regret it. Another thought challenges my happy moment. Evan might now be the most daring and adventurous thing I've ever done. Chuckling at the comparison, I realize I don't regret him either. Even though he treated me poorly the next morning, it's hard to regret the best sex you've ever had.

I take a walk down the beach and watch as the sun rises higher over the horizon. Looking ahead, I see surfers on the beach preparing for their own adventures. Some are paddling out and some are waxing their boards. They're tan and fit. I don't get too close, but take a seat in the sand and watch them.

After awhile, I get hot and decide to head back to the apartment. I dust my feet and slip my sneakers back on, knowing that I'll probably always have sand in my shoes while I'm on the island.

When I arrive, Sunny is sipping coffee on her little patio that faces the parking lot. "Good morning. Did you walk down to the beach?" she asks with a small smile.

I nod. "It's beautiful. How's the hand?"

"Better than yesterday." She stops to yawn then says, "I made coffee."

"Good because I need some caffeine." I walk inside and pour myself a cup before rejoining her on the patio. Sitting in a plastic chair, I tuck my feet under my bottom.

"I think Noah might come by this week again," I say, trying for casual.

"Did he tell you that?" She sits up giving me her full attention.

I smile. She never changes which I love. "He said, now that I'm working there, he might come by more often."

"So, what'd you say?"

"Nothing really. I'd just met him." But I can't hide my smile.

"You like him. Mallory Wray likes a boy!" She jumps up and hugs my head.

I swat her off. "All right, all right. Get your jugs out of my face, lady!" I tease. "I think he's kind of cute and nice."

She sits back down. "He's very cute and he's always been super sweet to me."

"Yeah, he said you were waiting for Mr. Right."

"You know I'm not dating anyone. This year hasn't been my best as far as men go."

"You have your pick of any guy out there, Sunny. You always have. So why aren't you seeing anyone?"

Leaning back in contemplation, she looks at me before

she gives me an obviously rehearsed answer. "Just haven't been asked out by Mr. Right, I guess."

I sense her hesitation, which is strange because we've always been so open with each other about everything. Until now that is. She seems to be keeping a secret and I have no right to push since the guilt I carry from keeping my rendezvous with Evan a secret weighs on me. But like her, I'm not ready to share. So I don't push.

We sit a few minutes longer before heading in and getting dressed for the day. Our shifts are scheduled together since we share Sunny's rusted VW bus that she bought for fifteen hundred dollars when she started school here two years ago.

We're at work by eleven and raise the large open-air doors on both sides of the place, which allow the breezes to flow through the building.

When the lunch crowd leaves and the restaurant dies down, I grab a barstool and watch the two older men argue, accusing each other of cheating.

"Hi, Mallory."

I jump, startled from behind. When I turn, it's Noah standing there. "You scared me."

He smiles, it's shy. "Sorry about that. I'll try to announce myself next time." His smile turns playful. "How are you?"

"Good, how about yourself?"

"Really good except the service in here is slow."

"You're full of jokes today," I say, sarcastically. "What are you having?"

"Cola, straight up."

"Cola no ice coming right up." I fill a glass and set it on the counter between us.

He stays for a while and I talk about my life back home at the University of Colorado and my studies. He talks about his passions—surfing and customizing cars. "I've been dying to get my hands on Sunny's VW."

"Really?"

"Totally. I could get rid of the rust damage and make that car sparkle." He slides off the stool and says, "C'mon. Let's go look at it."

"Sunny?" I call into the kitchen. "Grab your keys and come out front."

She joins us a few minutes later out in the parking lot. Noah raises his hands and she tosses him the keys.

"He's gonna look at it. He might be able to get rid of the rust and paint it."

"I can't afford that, Noah. I appreciate it though."

"Just step back and let me have some space," he says, waving for us to back up.

Noah bends over and looks under the bumper, analyzing something as he picks at the flaking beige paint. I take the opportunity to do a little analyzing myself. He's wearing a fitted black tank top that shows off his muscles quite well. He has a tattoo that wasn't visible yesterday under his shirt.

"The structure of the body looks solid. That's a good sign," he says, rising back to his full height. Sunny and I gaze upon him as he crosses his arms over his chest. He's gorgeous. "I can come over one day while you're working or to your house when you're off and take a closer look. I'd really like to work on your body." My mouth drops open and I feel the heat reach my cheeks as he smiles looking between us. I glance at her and she's blushing too.

He chuckles and the sound breaks the stunned silence we're in and he clarifies what he meant. "The car's body. Do you want to go with the original color?"

Sunny laughs, blushing. "I'm ready for something more

fun."

"We could go vintage red. I'll do some research."

"I love that idea," she says, beaming.

The three of us walk back inside and Noah taps his hand on the bar. "I need to go. I've got some work to do for my family." He turns to me, but hesitates, all confidence gone. "Um, so, you think you'd like to hang out later ... maybe after you get off work tonight?"

His eyes go to the floor while waiting for me to respond, but the words don't come fast enough and an awkward silence fills the air. He looks back up, and suggests, "We can watch a movie or hang out and talk on the beach."

I look to Sunny whose eyes are bugging out telling me to go for it, but I'm still unsure for some reason. Feeling the pressure to respond, I reply, "Sure. That sounds fun. We're closing at nine tonight."

"Great. I'll pick you up out front."

"Okay. Cool."

He walks out with a spring to his step and a smile on his face. I just said yes to someone that seems to be a nice guy, so I should feel happier than I do. Instead I feel weird inside.

"Way to go, girl!" Sunny smiles and I force one on for show.

When she disappears into the back, I rest my head in my hands willing myself to feel good. My head jolts up when a raucous group walks in.

"Get your game face on, Mal. We've got company."

The group heads straight for the large table in the back, taking over like they own the joint. Sunny turns to me, and asks, "You want this table?"

A bunch of college age guys who look hot from here. Yeah, it's a bit intimidating. "No, you can have it."

Johnny strolls in behind them and greets me as he sits at the counter. "I see Ashford's in today. Weird since we were just talking about him. His ears must've been burnin'."

"Which one's Ashford?" I ask, leaning forward to get a better look at the customers. Sunny is at the table and moves around to the other side and that's when I see him.

Evan.

"He's the one in the green shirt."

I'm too stunned to say anything, so I stand there like an idiot. Of course, it couldn't be as simple as leaving that night in the past. Of course, he would walk into the place where I work. *Of course*, the guy in the green shirt is Evan Ashford! That's how my luck works—it doesn't. Whatever I do, karma kicks my ass for doing it.

The people at the table are watching him and his blonde friend, especially the two girls with them. My only saving grace, as I duck down to pretend to be washing glasses, is that he hasn't seen me yet.

A tall guy wraps his large, muscular arm around Sunny's waist and pulls her to him. She laughs, comfortable in the overly friendly gesture. But the guy sitting across from them, the blonde one, seems to be bothered, almost irritated by the move. He gets up and walks away from the table, heading for the beach. Standing just outside the door, he looks back once before taking a deep breath. Evan takes command and rules the roost inside, knocking the big ones arm away. They keep it friendly, but Evan appears protective over her.

Sunny yells in my direction. "Four burgers, all the way with fries. Two draft pitchers."

I nod, entering their order in then taking two pitchers from below the bar and start to fill the first. Laughter covers the space between, closing the gap and drawing my attention back to the group. Evan's standing telling some kind of story and using his arms to demonstrate. The group is entranced by his over the top dramatics.

Me—*not so much*.

When I look back at the pitcher, I curse, "Shit!" The beer has overflowed, so I quickly shut the tap off and move that pitcher to the side. Feeling the heat of a dozen eyes staring at me, slowly, I peek. My eyes land on *his* first. Evan is glaring with his mouth open in shock. Everyone else starts laughing, but they return their attention to their own business. My thoughts are racing as fast as my heart. I feel like I've flown straight into hell. "Damn it!" I swear under my breath and close my eyes for a second trying to regain my sense of dignity I left lounging in his bed that night.

Focusing on my job, I move the second pitcher under the tap and start filling it.

"Can I take that one?"

I look up and the blonde guy who left Evan's table earlier is standing on the other side of the bar from me. His smile is gentle, his eyes sky blue, and his hair sun-bleached. I briefly wonder if every guy on this island is so good looking because everyone I've encountered is. The thought makes me smile. "Sure, it's ready. Six cups?"

"Uh," he shifts uncomfortably while looking back over his shoulder at the table in the back. "Yeah, that's good. I'm Zach. You're new here, right?"

"Hi, I'm Mallory and yep, I'm the new girl."

I don't bother giving more than what was asked of me. Instead I concentrate on my job and place the second pitcher on the bar.

"Thank you." With a nod, he turns and leaves with the cups under his arm and a pitcher in each hand.

When I finally dare to look back at the table, Evan is

now sitting. He's staring at the table as if willing it to be something other than beat-up wood. His glare is intense and then he slowly lifts his eyes up and looks right at me.

My heart begins to race again and I need to leave. I need fresh air. "I'm taking a smoke break, Johnny. Will you cover for me?"

"Yeah, no problem."

I grab my pack and lighter and cross the threshold of the bar. Before I'm out the door though, Johnny asks, "Are you okay?"

With my head down, I don't look up and I don't break my pace. "Yeah, peachy keen."

When I make it out the door and am out of sight from everyone, I run to the corner of the building and try to keep myself from panicking. I won't panic over Evan Ashford. He will not get that satisfaction.

I inhale two cigarettes in the time it normally takes me to finish one, and I have a third tucked between my lips, unlit. His Maserati is parked twenty feet from me, demanding my attention the entire time. It's perfection, like it's owner, makes me want to flick lit cigarettes on it and slash his tires. My thoughts fire off in a fit of rage in my head. How dare he come into my place of business and look at me like I did something wrong. *Screw you, Evan. You're the asshole here, not me.* I smile, delighting in the pleasure of knowing exactly the right thing to say at the right moment. But, it's sad because these are wasted thoughts since I won't be making the effort to talk to him. I won't be the next girl in line crying over him. I refuse to be.

I spend the next two hours in a silent showdown with him. Both of us unwilling to cross the imaginary line that has clearly been drawn, dividing the bar in half, his half and mine.

Evan's group finally seems to be winding down. With a sudden stand in solidarity, they get up from the table and head for the door. Evan takes the tail, letting his friends lead the way. His head is lowered and he's focused on the ground in front of him. The only weakness he shows is one small indulgence. Without raising his head, he sneaks a peek in my direction, making eye contact one last time before he leaves. I give him nothing, but a glare.

Zach stops at the door, and yells, "Thanks, Sunny. Good to meet you, Mallory."

"Zach seems nice," I say, leaning forward against the counter.

"Yeah, he is." Sunny's reply is light, but her mind is elsewhere.

Thankfully, the dinner crowd starts arriving within the hour and we're kept busy which keeps my mind off Evan and his crew. At closing time, the cook locks up after we slip out the back door. When we walk around the corner to the parking lot, Noah is standing by his Jeep, which is parked next to Sunny's VW. He looks tense, his arms crossed and his jaw is tight, but he's not looking at me. He's staring at Evan who is leaning against the front of his car on the other side of the gravel lot. Evan stands upright, his body is rigid and his eyes are locked on me. Sunny and I stop in our tracks, and look between them several times.

My brain tells me to go to Noah, but my still shredded and traitorous heart tells me Evan's the one, encouraging the behavior that got me into this mess.

"Mallory?" Sunny, Noah, and Evan say my name at the same time wanting an answer, wanting me to choose.

I look between the three of them one more time, and start walking.

7

MALLORY

Evan takes a few steps forward, but I walk to Noah. The showdown between them is over and the corner of Noah's mouth lifts up, reveling in his victory as he greets me. He takes me gently by the wrist, and whispers close to my ear, "You look good, Mallory."

Tilting away from him, I feel awkward about the situation, the present company making me uncomfortable. I dare a glance over my shoulder and see Evan getting into his car. Zach is next to Sunny and they're talking. Her eyes flick to mine and then Zach's follow hers, but he looks quickly back to Sunny again. In that instant, I see a look that can only be described as longing between them. It's fleeting, but there.

Noah helps me into his Jeep and shuts the door. He jogs around to the driver's side just as the sound of Evan revving his engine fills the awkwardness of the parking lot confrontation.

"Mallory?" Sunny says, climbing up the side of the Jeep, standing on the step guard which puts her eye level with me. "You didn't tell me," she whispers. *She knows about Evan.*

"Can we talk about this later?" I hate leaving everything

like this, but I'm not going to talk about this with Noah sitting right next to me.

"Yeah, sure. Have fun and I'll see you at home." She hops off and goes to her car.

I peek back to where Evan is parked, just out of curiosity, but he's already gone.

"What'd you decide? The beach or a movie?" Noah asks, tapping my shoulder.

I ponder both options for a moment. If we go to the beach, it will be us talking which I wouldn't have minded ten minutes ago. I'd like to get to know Noah, but after this stand-off of sorts, I don't want Evan to seep into the conversation, especially since they seem to be enemies. I choose the alternative. "A movie."

An hour later, I'm sitting on Noah's couch with a large bowl of popcorn on my lap. He's next to me, eating from the bowl that I'm not. The awful comedy we're watching gives me a chance to think about what I've tried to disregard for days now—Evan. I have trouble enjoying the lame jokes on the large flat screen because I know Sunny is at home waiting for answers. I hear Noah laugh and insert my own forced laughter to be polite.

I can't figure out why Evan was there tonight. It seemed like we had said all we needed through the exchanged looks earlier in the day. My appetite is gone and I hand the bowl to Noah to hold since he's the only one eating the popcorn anyway. He accepts the bowl without question, never losing sight of the movie. His expression is happy when I glance over at him. He's a nice guy and I wish I could enjoy my time with him, but I'm too distracted. Evan tends to do that to me.

8

EVAN

I don't act on impulse—at least not much, but I never know my journey's end until I arrive. Tonight, I wish she didn't live so close to the main road. Mallory is too accessible, and I'm too weak to stay away. I couldn't stop thinking about her after I dropped her off the morning after we hooked up, so seeing her at Big Kehones this afternoon felt like an opportunity. After watching her at the restaurant, I knew my initial thoughts were right. I needed to take that opportunity and explore it further.

It didn't matter that I'd been fighting to rid her from my memory for days. When I laid eyes on her again, every emotion resurfaced. I hate feeling out of control and she makes me feel that way, which pisses me off. I've worked too damn hard to let her in. My mind is at war with my heart because of her.

I'm completely mind-fucked over this girl, and thoroughly disgusted that I let her affect me like this. I need to get control back, some perspective on the situation. I need to put closure to this mess, refusing to let her win me over. I always win, even if I have to cheat to do it. And yet, I drive by her place finding some semblance of peace just by being near her. After she chose Noah tonight, I know she won't let me in, so I don't bother trying. She's probably not home anyway. I stick to the road, setting my cruise control and drive by slowly. When I near, my gaze shifts toward the apartment, hoping to see something—the TV on, her hanging with Noah, or any sign of her.

My car veers into the parking lot, making a deliberate decision ... maybe it's my heart calling the shots, but this feels a lot like something I shouldn't be doing, but can't stop myself. Maybe this is what I do in life, feels like a familiar pattern of going against better judgment.

I park, but don't get out. That's where I draw the line.

My breath is stilled, knowing this is wrong. *When did I become this person*? She's done this to me. I can't tell the guys. I'd never hear the end of it. Driving by seemed innocent enough, but now I'm parked in the shadows of the complex lot, hoping to get a view of her from thirty yards away. The lights are out, and I can only assume she's asleep, so what more do I expect from doing this?

Leaning my head back, I slump down in my seat, and close my eyes. Images of her fill my thoughts—images of being on that couch with her, and holding her. I was once in heaven. Now I'm in hell. I don't know where I went wrong, but an unfamiliar feeling has hijacked my normally careless thoughts. I'm thinking its regret.

Getting out of my car, I stumble forward, escaping that emotion. I pull out a cigarette and light up, inhaling the calming addiction deep into my lungs. I decided a long time ago that if I was going to smoke, I was gonna do it fully. No light cigarettes for me. Only full on tar, nicotine, tobacco, and whatever other shit they put in these to make them taste and feel so fucking fantastic. I smoke the entire cigarette then toss the butt into the air, deciding I'm not going to do this anymore, but not quite ready to leave.

9

MALLORY

"Mallory," Noah whispers from above. "Mallory, wake up."

I open my eyes and gasp when I see him standing over me.

"You fell asleep."

"Oh." I sit up, regaining my bearings. "Oh, sorry."

"I didn't wake you because the movie kind of sucked. You didn't miss anything." He sits next to me and rubs my back.

There's a clock ticking on the mantle, and my eyes flash to the numbers. It's almost midnight. "I should head home," I say.

"I'll drive you back."

We chat on the way, keeping it light considering the late hour. He has lots of good stories and we don't lack for conversation, even joking at one point over the easiness of the relationship. The car idles when he stops in front of the apartment building. He angles his body toward me, and says, "Mallory, I know you were asleep half the time, but I had a good time anyway. I'd like to hang out again."

"I'd like that too. Sorry about that whole falling asleep

thing by the way. Guess I'm more tired than I thought." I lean forward to hug him.

His hands grip my waist and he pulls me closer. I feel trapped and noisily gulp. When he leans back, our eyes meet and the awkwardness worsens. Before I have a chance to say anything, he leans forward with that look—a look that says 'Prepare yourself because I'm going to kiss you.' I turn away as words fly from my mouth. "So, I'll see you around, okay?"

"Yeah, okay, see you around," he says, but disappointment darkens his tone as he sits back.

I jump out and move to the sidewalk, watching him drive off then head inside. Sunny is asleep and all the lights are off inside the apartment. I shut the door quietly behind me, but I have the small place memorized, so I keep the lights off finding comfort in the darkness. After brushing my teeth, I slip into a tank top and shorts. I climb between the covers of my makeshift bed on the couch, and lay there looking out the glass door ahead of me.

The parking lot lamp in the distance is dim and blackness surrounds the building. But a small orange glow and shadowed figure is seen despite the dark. An errant thought flashes in the form of hope filled anticipation as my heart races at the realization, and I bolt upright. The orange glow moves as fast as I do then quicker. I struggle to unlock the sliding glass door, but finally get it open, and run after the spark. "Evan," I call, hoping my hunch is correct.

The orange ember at the end of the cigarette gets flicked, and my eyes follow it as it loops through the air and falls to the ground. When my eyes finally adjust to the night, I can tell it's him as he stops next to the car door. He remains in the safety of the shadows, a shrouded mystery.

"Evan?" This time I say his name gentler, hoping he can

hear. I'm not going to chase him any further and I don't want to chase him away.

I stand there waiting for any response he's willing to give, but none comes.

Under the soft glow of the tall lamp in the distance, he shifts, his body appearing to fight an internal battle.

My heart pounds in my ears waiting for anything. I deserve an explanation. I deserve answers to his behavior. "Fuck." I deserve something more than silence in the middle of the night.

His resigned body comes closer, his face not visible under the cloud covered night. Stopping one short foot in front of me, his features are seen, the emotion on his face clear. He's not angry Evan, or bewildered, or even Mr. Smooth Evan. He's vulnerable and open as his expression pleads with me to make the connection. With caution, he takes my face in his hands, his eyes seeking the permission his lips won't ask.

I feel a lump in my throat as confusion sets in. He can't regret how he acted. He chose that path, not me. Nothing makes sense with him, nothing except his lips on mine, willing my mind to settle and my heart to calm. This is right. This kiss makes sense.

His lips aren't hurried or panicked. He's sharing this moment with me, taking his time to enjoy the rewards of his patient waiting. My hands are drawn to him and ghost up his chest and around his neck, my fingers locking together. His hands find my middle and pull me closer. My body moves, knowing exactly where it wants to be. My mind has no say in this because logic is overruled by need. I need to be with him and he needs to be with me.

When our lips part, he looks, analyzing me. His eyes search my face then land back on mine. I don't know Evan well enough to judge his moods by only his expressions, but I know he's resisting something already set in motion. "You didn't kiss him. Why didn't you kiss him?" he asks. His breath is warm and tinged with cigarettes and peppermint.

"I didn't want to." I don't feel the need to say more. I didn't want to kiss Noah, but can't admit to Evan that it's because he was on my mind at the time.

He slides a hand down my arm gently taking my hand in his and leads me toward the open glass door. I willingly follow him. I would probably follow him anywhere right now. My mind is weak and my body is strong when we're together. We make no sense, but right now we are the only logical conclusion that exists in a world of problems.

Leading me to the couch, we sit, the silence starting to weigh on my heart. Evan strokes my cheek acting as if it is meaningless, but I know his gentle touches give him away. He may be a bastard, but he's not heartless.

He leans toward my exposed neck, tasting just the edge of my earlobe before slowly pushing me back onto the couch. I kiss him, feeling relaxed, knowing this is right as my traitorous heart opens up to the one person who battered it without care just two days ago.

Our kisses become eager, our tongues mingling together and are bodies anxious for more. His hands slide to the hem of his shirt and he pulls it off while giving me a look I would normally view as lust, but it's different somehow. *This is him caring.* Standing up, he takes his jeans off, confident in our silent agreement. He drops something on the coffee table then pulls me to my feet.

I mimic his actions, leaving me equally exposed and vulnerable. After sliding my panties off to up the ante, I lay down on the couch under the covers. Without losing eye contact, he slides his briefs down his legs and joins me under the covers. "I want you, Mallory." His breathing deepens as he hovers over me.

My breath staggers, my heart finding instant relief from hearing his voice again. It's smooth and strong and has an authoritativeness to it. He makes me want to obey though he didn't give any orders. I lie back and get to the point. "Take me then."

His hand moves between my legs and my head pushes back into the pillow, enjoying the way he touches me, the way his touch owns my body. A finger swirls, making me moan then disappears. He reaches to the table, and then I see the condom in his hand, the wrapper being ripped open. Turning to the side, he rolls it on then repositions himself above me. The couch is small and uncomfortable, but perfect for us to reconnect.

As he kisses me, his hand appreciates my breasts. I squirm beneath him, my body responsive to this pleasant torture. He smirks knowing the sexual devastation he's delivering as he eases into me.

Not able to control my reaction, I moan again, louder this time. His hand covers my mouth, and he whispers, "Shhhh." It's a reminder of my best friend who is sleeping in the next room. He tilts my head back and takes the opportunity to kiss my neck, working me with his tongue and caressing lips. I feel his stubble against my skin, scratching me, marking me as his even if only temporarily. Shifting to put his weight onto his arms, he raises his body higher to look at where we're joined as I enjoy the wonderful ease of his movements.

"God, Mallory." His own moan is low and anguished and so breathtakingly beautiful.

My hips move to meet his. I lean up to see where our

bodies are joined, but it's too much. The feelings over-whelming me, so I drop back down.

"I'm sorry. I won't last," he says, the words not matching the plea in his tone.

Why is he apologizing? Aren't we achieving the purpose of the act? Isn't this the reason we're doing this—to orgasm? Oh! Sudden realization strikes. I guess *we* won't be and that's what the apology is for, but for some reason, that just doesn't matter. He feels too good to worry about such details.

His hand lowers to my sex and I can tell he's holding himself back to try to please me. I tug his hand away, causing him to look up then shake my head.

He's not a selfish lover. He's proven that to me before. I'll take that he's so turned on that he'll peak faster than he likes as a compliment and a huge boost for my ego. So I'll trade my orgasm for one ego boost this round knowing, maybe just hoping, that he'll return the favor soon enough.

Kissing me, he starts moving slowly again, over and over in rapid succession. Another moan escapes me, this time in a lowered voice, remembering we might get caught, but somehow the thought turns me on even more. I grab his shoulders and raise my legs up higher with him centered between them. Watching the glory that is his face, his expression shows he's desperately trying to hold on and failing as he succumbs to his desire. He drops his head into the nook of my neck, and groans. "Holy fuck, Mallory! You're so—" He interrupts himself with a deep breath.

His body drops down on top of me. He's sated and heavy, but I love the weight on me and try to pretend it matches a depth of emotions he has for me.

All too soon, my mind flips and I go from contented to confused in the span of a second. Rolling onto my side, he holds me against him. The sex with him is incredible even when I don't orgasm. But it's the *after* that I dread and we are now firmly lying in the *after*. I gulp and it's too loud and embarrassing in the quiet room. He strokes my hair away from my face and gathers me closer against his chest. I have to give him credit. He's trying and as the minutes tick by my heart starts to heal, to trust him again, little by little.

The warmth of his body must have soothed me because I don't remember falling asleep until the sounds of cars starting outside mixed with the light of day awaken me. Smiling, I roll over. What my brain fails to realize, my heart already knows and mourns the loss. *Evan is gone.* I'm not surprised, but I am hurt.

10

MALLORY

Sunny walks out of her room and straight into the kitchen to start the coffee pot. "Good morning," she says, tired sounding.

"Morning," I mumble, sounding about the same.

She comes into the living room and crosses her arms over her chest. "You have a lot of explaining to do."

I freeze, knowing she heard us last night.

"Noah and Evan showing up at Kehones was crazy! I didn't even know you knew Ashford." She walks past me and opens the glass door, but when she turns back around something catches her eye, and she stops. "What's that?" she asks, pointing.

I look to the coffee table and see a note. My heart melts just a little as I read my name written across it.

"Um, nothing. I just remembered something I had to do last night and left myself a note." I hate lying, especially to my best friend, but I'm not ready to share the whole ugly truth with her just yet.

She accepts the lie and returns to the kitchen to pour a cup of coffee.

I grab the note as soon as she's out of sight and smile, holding it to my chest. He remembered to leave a note this time and my heart swells with emotions I don't want to acknowledge quite yet. I snuggle onto my side and flip open the folded paper.

Mallory,
    Sorry for leaving, but I had to go and you need the rest.
    Evan

My hope deflates reading the unfeeling words written before me. He apologizes for sneaking out which I guess is a start, but why'd he have to go so early? And when did he become my parent determining how much rest I need. I would have rather lose a few winks and told him goodbye. I would have rather kissed him goodbye. I close my eyes sinking lower into the couch and tucking the note under my leg. I would have preferred that he stayed with me and we started the day together.

"What are your plans today?" Sunny sits on the other end of the couch near my feet and steals some of the covers.

"I'm not sure. I might hang out with you at work for a while. I want to go to the beach, too."

"You should definitely come by Kehones. You can hang out at the beach up there. We can talk when it's dead and you get free food and drinks. It's a win all around."

"You're bribing me with food, drinks, and beach so you're not bored all day, aren't you?"

"Totally. Now promise you'll come by for a bit."

I laugh because although we've been working together

and have gotten to catch up, it doesn't feel like we've really had the chance to talk since I've arrived.

"How's your hand today?"

She holds it up. "I'm still wearing the brace, but the pain is gone unless I carry something heavy. It's just hard to remember to go easy." Patting my leg, she asks, "Do you want to talk about Noah and Evan?"

Looking down at my lap, I catch sight of the edge of the note still tucked away. "I'm not quite sure how to answer that."

"How about starting with why Evan was waiting for you last night? I didn't even see you guys talk yesterday."

"We haven't talked much." I look at her not wanting to reveal what we've done instead of talking. "Sunny, I should have told you the other day, but I didn't want you to think poorly of me. I, uh … I met Evan at the airport when I arrived." I can see the confusion written across her face. "When I got your text about going to the hospital, he offered to give me a ride."

"You accepted a ride from a total stranger? Oh wait, one of the hottest strangers ever," she says, amusement in her eyes. "Yeah, I would too." She smiles, reassuring me. "Mallory, like I said before, I think he gets a bad rap. I don't know him that well, but he's always been nice to me and his friends are cool. The only thing I would warn you about is the Noah factor."

"Noah's a factor now?"

"Kind of. They don't get along, but Johnny told me they used to be good friends. Something went down and now they hate each other. So be careful. The guys around here tend to get possessive. It's kind of a you're either with us or against us deal."

I bring my knees into my chest, wrapping the blanket tighter around me. "Sunny?"

"Yes."

"Would you date Evan or Noah?" I'm worried about her answer, but want to know what she thinks. She knows these guys better than I do and I trust her opinion.

"Um, that's a hard one. You know I give everyone a chance—sometimes to my own detriment, so I'm inclined to say yes. My logical side thinks I would go on a date with both of them, but I'd keep my guard up. My girly irrational side would totally go out with both those hotties too and keep that guard down." She laughs, flopping dramatically onto the couch cushion. "I'm no use."

I laugh, feeling exactly the same way about them both. "Do you prefer one over the other?"

She chuckles under her breath, and looks me straight in the eyes. "Mallory, Noah has always been a sweetheart to me. He asked me out once—"

"Why didn't you go?"

She sits there hesitant in every way though I can tell she wants to say something. Finally, she takes a deep breath, and says, "I haven't been honest with you. I've been crushing on someone for a while now. Others guys just don't bring out the same feelings that ..." She looks down, twisting a loose thread on the blanket around her finger. "... Zach does."

"Evan's friend?"

She confirms with a shamed nod.

"Sunny, hey, that's so great. He's seems really nice." Remembering how they looked at each other the night before, I add, "I actually think you two could be good together."

"You think so?"

"Yep, I do."

"Thanks." She stands up, all smiles and happy. Walking to the bedroom, she stops in the doorway. "And about Evan. Just be careful with that one. He's not known as a lady killer for nothing."

When she leaves, I stretch my legs out and think of the lady killer himself. Heart killer is more apropos. I pull the note out and read over it one last time before wadding it up and throwing it away in the kitchen trash. The words on it hold no true feelings for me, so discarding it is easy.

That afternoon, I ride with Sunny to work. I eat lunch, sunbathe on the beach out back, and visit with all the regulars I now consider friends. Johnny spends his break with me and fills me in on the locals' histories. I'm too embarrassed to ask about Noah or Evan and feel it's best not to show too much interest anyway.

Since Johnny is closing with Sunny, he offers to drive her home. I take her VW and drive back to the apartment late afternoon. After making a sandwich for dinner, I curl up at the scene of last night's sexual hit and run and watch a movie.

I doze off before the movie ends, but wake up to the sound of rain and a knock on the sliding glass door. The apartment is dark except for the TV and bright enough for me to see Evan standing on the other side of the glass, soaking wet.

I remain still, unsure how I feel about another late night visit. Sighing, I get up and slide the door open, but block him from entering.

Angling his head, he smiles that cocky half smile that usually works for him. "May I come in, Mallory?" He leans against the door, mere inches from me.

He's gorgeous and gleaming in the warm rain. His hair is

flattened enough to make me feel sorry that he had to stand out there, but my heart hurts more just looking at him. I stand upright, straightening my shoulders. "No, you can't come in tonight."

His smile falters then returns as his hand touches my arm and runs the length of it, taking my hand in his. He lowers his voice, and leans closer. "Please."

That plea goes straight to my knees, and they weaken. I lower my eyes from his not feeling as confident this time when I answer. "I don't think that's a good idea. We're not a good idea."

He stands there in silence, but I sense his gaze on me, weighted with our baggage. The heat between us starts to engulf me. I can't stay here or he'll be back inside of me in less than point four seconds. "You should go." I look beyond him to the outside, attempting to be direct. "Sunny will be home any minute."

"Is this about last night? I'm sorry that, I should've ... You should have gotten off, too. I came back to take care of you."

I lift my head up as anger swells inside. "You don't have to take *care* of me, Evan. This is not about me, ugh. This is not about having an orgasm or not." Frustrated, I demand, "I want you to leave!"

After taking a step back inside the apartment, I pull my hand back, our connection broken, breaking us apart. I slide the door closed, locking it as if somehow that will hurt him like he's hurt me. He stays, soaking and magnificent, staring at me through the glass. By the time I get the curtain from the far side of the door, he's gone. The curtain may be somewhat sheer, but I still feel the need to close it. He's shut out and my stomach turns, making me think I might have actually made the wrong decision.

Fortunately, I don't have too much time to reconsider the

situation because Sunny arrives home. She flops onto the couch, exasperated. "You sure do have these boys in a tizzy, Mal."

"What boys?" I'm curious if she saw Evan in the parking lot. I'm hoping she didn't, exhausted from the whole encounter.

"Noah and his crew stopped by. They didn't stay long after I told them you had the day off." She laughed. "He looked disappointed when I told him he missed when you were up there sunbathing."

"You said 'boys,' " I wonder aloud.

"Yeah, Zach was in today, too. I think he was fishing for information for Evan." She purses her lips then asks, "Evan wasn't with them though. How was your day?"

"Uneventful," I reply too fast to sound natural. "I made a sandwich then napped when I got back." I really want to redirect this conversation. "Did you make a lot of tips?"

"Okay, but no shop talk. I have a chick flick that's due back tomorrow. I've popcorn and we can watch the movie together just like old times." She's persuasive with the popcorn offer.

"How can I resist."

She walks toward the kitchen. "I'll make the popcorn. You load the movie."

A romantic comedy was probably the last thing I should have watched. When it ends, the knots that had formed in my stomach slowly untie.

She stands to stretch then yawns. "I have to work the lunch shift tomorrow. Do you mind returning the movie after you drop me off and see if they carry the sequel? I have to see how this relationship plays out."

"Sure. No problem."

"Night, Mallory," she says, flicking the kitchen light off on her way to bed.

I turn the TV off and sit in darkness for a minute before opening the curtain back up. The rain has stopped and the moon is shining and bright. Car lights at the back of the lot flash on and from here it looks like a Maserati. As it drives out of the apartment complex, I look down conflicted between the emotions I feel for him and my logic. I think Evan's just as conflicted.

I dream of expensive Italian cars, handsome men too beautiful to touch, and broken hearts.

My eyes open just before the sun rises because my sleeping habits are completely thrown off here in Hawaii. With no obligations of school and a job that has minimal requirements, I've found myself falling into laziness quite easily.

Pulling on my new Hawaiian uniform of a tank top and shorts, I walk down to the beach. I'm starting to like this new ritual, the calm and peace of the surroundings as the breeze blows my untamed hair while watching the sunrise. I'm at one with this place, but I'm really at one with myself this morning which feels even better. I smile then actually laugh letting it drift into the wind.

When the sun is strong and solid in the sky, I walk down the beach closer to the surfers who are floating on top of the water in a jagged line. One by one they claim their wave and ride it in. I watch for a while, but decide I need to get back, so I stand and dust the sand from my bottom as I start walking.

"Mallory!"

Stopping to look back, I see a tall, well-built body jogging towards me. He drops his board into the sand and calls my name again.

I smile, recognizing Noah. "Hey there."

His smile is effervescent, his tan skin glistening with water. "Yeah, I thought that was you. I traded waves with my cousin so I could ride in to find out." He glances over his shoulder. "What are you doing out here so early?"

"I'm still on Boulder time. I've started coming out here to watch the sunrise when I wake up too early." I look across the ocean and at the palm trees hugging the coastline. "This place is magical. It really is paradise."

"I should show you more of the island. What do you think about me taking you to a few of my favorite places? We can start with a beach bonfire this Monday. I'll be training all weekend. Promised my dad I'd stay home and hang with the fam, so the guys made plans for Monday."

Our friendship is growing and he looks so genuinely optimistic that it's hard to say no. "I'd like that." I try to remember my schedule for the rest of the week. "Monday works."

"Cool. I should get back before the waves die down." His fingers graze across my forearm.

"Okay. Bye, Noah."

WHEN I OPEN THE DOOR, Sunny is dressed and eating cereal in the kitchen. I lean against the counter opposite of her. "Good morning, best friend."

"Whash haz you so chespper?"

"What?"

She chews quickly then asks, "What has you so chipper?"

"I have a date with Noah on Monday."

"It's eight in the morning. How'd you get a date before

eight in the morning?"

"He was down at the beach surfing. We got to talking. There's a bonfire on Monday."

"Please tell me some of your luck is going to rub off on me. I don't think I can go much longer without some lovins."

"Sunny, my dear friend, you have every guy drooling after you—"

"Except the one I want—"

"That's not true. He's available and happens to be coming into Kehones quite often these days. Connect the dots."

"Only to get info on you to relay to his friend."

"Not true. I want you to stand there quietly and listen to my reasoning. This is how I see it. He's just using *'his friend'* as a cover to be able to talk to you. You aren't pursuing him and almost seem shy when you're around him which is un-Sunny like behavior if you ask me. But, maybe, he's also shy around you." I throw my hands into the air. "Where's that gonna get us? I'll tell you where. No where!" I take her by the hands pulling her from her slouchy position against the counter, and say, "Now stand up straight, stick out those boobs, chin up, and work what your mama gave you. Be the Sunny I know you can be and go get that man." I lead her to the living room and slap her ass as she passes.

"Owww!" she says, rubbing her bottom with her hands.

"Understand, girlie?"

"I understand, Sergeant Wray. I understand," she says, marching proudly into the bedroom. "I should change into something cuter just in case Zach stops by again today."

"Smart thinking. That's my girl!"

She peeks her head out of the bedroom, and asks, "So, you and Noah on Monday, huh?"

"Yep, seems that way. Me, Noah, and a date on Monday."

11

EVAN

Five days have passed since I last saw her, and although I thought not seeing her would bring some relief to this messed up obsession, it hasn't. Earlier this evening I hung out with the guys at their house before I needed a Mallory fix, and drove by her place. I'd been better, but a few beers seem to make me want to see her, even if only from a distance. She has a routine, and the lights are usually out when I cruise by. Tonight I'm sticking to the road. I don't like to admit it, but she's moved on just fine from all appearances, probably because I've left her alone ... or was told to leave her alone.

While walking up the path to my house, I notice the corner bedroom light is on in the main house. That only means one thing, my sister's back on the island. Like a ninja, I work my way to my sanctuary, locking the door behind me and leaving the lights off because I don't want her to know I'm home. Tomorrow seems like a much more agreeable day to deal with her.

Stripping down to my briefs—my new favorite briefs—I smile when remembering how Mallory looked when she was wearing them in the pool. Grabbing my last cigarette, I open the back door and stand there trying to find some peace from my troubled thoughts of a girl who refuses to talk to me. The ocean reflects the moon in the distance and my mind begins to calm.

After tossing the butt into a metal bucket full of sand, I go back inside. I brush my teeth and climb into the bed that hasn't felt right since she left nine days earlier. This girl is driving me insane and after telling me to go away last week, it finally occurs to me that maybe she meant it. *She's really not interested in me.* It's an unsettling thought and foreign to me, causing me to shift uncomfortably onto my side and curl up. Eventually I fall asleep to the sounds of the ocean through the open door, but I don't dream.

The next morning, I make coffee and throw on my board shorts and a t-shirt, feeling more like my old self. I can't put my sister off forever, but I'm not quite ready to see her. Spying on the main house from my window, I don't see any movement which is my cue to dash and get the hell out. My escape is swift and clean.

Thirty minutes later, I'm scanning the surf lessons appointments chart left in my cabana on the beach. Giving surf lessons was the only thing I considered when I needed to fill my time. Working for a large hotel on the beach just made it easy for me to show up, do my job, and clock out at the end of the day. The access to honeys is just a perk of the job.

I do my usual inspection of gender, age, and names. Names are the least important to me. I don't need to know them after today and if I score with one of the clients then I can memorize it long enough to get by. I spot two opportunities listed on the roster today: females, both twenty-one, Ginger and Tiffany. Using fake names for their vacation means they want to party and I can bet money those aren't their real names.

I set the clipboard down on the counter, unlock the surf-boards, and set them up neatly on the beach. I may seem like a total fuck-up, but I take my job at this hotel seriously, at least the teaching portion of it. By nine o'clock, my first clients show up. They sign the release waiver then I set each up with a board. Once I have their attention on the sand, I show them the basic strategy to surfing. The thirty minute lesson in the sand flies by and soon I'm in the water pushing them on the board towards the shore and encouraging them to hang ten.

Five hours and eight clients later, the end of my day looks very promising. Two girls bounce through the sand straight for me. "Hi, we're here for our lesson," the bleached blonde says, giggling with her friend.

"You're at the right place, ladies. I'm Evan." I offer my hand.

"I'm Tiffany, *Evan*," she says, drawing out my name and insinuating everything I want to hear.

I direct my attention to her friend, who quite honestly fits more of my standard pick-up from work—strawberry blonde, light eyes, tan, big breasts. "Hi, I'm Ginger."

Our hands linger a beat longer than appropriate, but I can already tell this lesson won't be just about surfing. I need to get Mallory off my mind and the best way to beat a habit is to break it. I flash my brightest and widest smile at them and watch as they become putty in my hands.

Our lesson consists of lots of hands-on assistance. These girls are either extremely dense or, by the way they act, horny as fuck. By the time we're in the water, they've completely lost interest in surfing and are whining it's too hard. But by the end of the lesson, Tiffany says, "I'm hungry." She laughs, giving Ginger a look as if that is code for something other than food.

I'm not sure how I'm feeling towards them anymore. I like hot, but I don't like dumb, and Mallory hasn't left my mind like I hoped. I know these girls will be a poor substitute for her. But I'm also not a quitter, okay, I'm kind of a quitter, but I won't let Mallory win. She made herself clear the other night when she shut the door on me.

Fuck that!

I've got nothing to lose and lots of fun to gain. "You girls want to grab some nosh and a movie? Are you staying here at the hotel?" Please let them be staying somewhere else.

"How about we just go back to our room?" Ginger asks, pointing to the hotel and then adjusting her too-tiny bikini top.

"I can't fraternize with the hotel guests on property. I'll take you to a nearby restaurant and we'll go from there." I don't bring girls back to my place either, so I might have to take them to Zach and Murphs to make this happen.

"I don't want to fraternize, whatever that means. I just want to have fun and mess around." Tiffany turns to her friend, and says, "I want him. He's hot!"

There's a silent debate exchanged between them, but it doesn't take them long to figure out what they want to do. Ginger takes the lead, and says, "Sounds like a plan, but we want to shower and change clothes first."

"I have to close up the shack anyway." I hand them a twenty dollar bill for a cab and say, "Meet me at Kailua's restaurant in an hour. I'll buy you dinner—"

"I'm not hungry for food," Tiffany whines.

"Honey, trust me, you're going to need the energy tonight." I play up the whole lothario act for them, but they're so easy it takes no effort.

They begin to giggle again and the sound starts to grate on my nerves. Ginger steps forward and runs her finger across my chest. "We'll see you there."

I put all the boards in the cabana, lock up, then stride into the employee locker room to take a shower. A quick change into clean clothes, kept in my locker for just these sorts of occasions, and I'm out the door.

I beat the girls to the restaurant just as I suspected I would. I never worry if they're going to show up because they always do. Ten minutes late, they walk in, in full club-bing fashion—wearing sky high heels and skirts that invite every man in the room to stare. Ginger's white shirt gives a sneak peek of what's to come through the sheer material. Tiffany's cropped top is too small and too tight, highlighting her surgically enhanced breasts. I'm not really into the fake ones that much, but have never been known to turn them down either.

Ginger slides into the booth next to me and Tiffany pouts because she has to sit across from us. Dinner with these girls is interesting. They're pretty enough, overtly sexual, and horny; a combination that usually works well for me. "So ladies, you want me to call a friend over ... to *watch the movie* with us?" I throw this out just in case I've been reading their blatant signs all wrong. While waiting for their response, I finish my second beer, needing it to calm the anxiety building inside even though I don't know why I'm anxious.

Ginger, who's hand hasn't left my thigh since she sat down, whispers in my ear, "No, baby, just us three tonight."

I pay the check.

In the parking lot, Ginger and Tiffany's hand tightens on my arm when they see my car. They are like all girls, all girls except Mallory, and get wet at the sight of my expensive automobile because it means I have money. I'm not stupid. Women like these have an extra sense to sniff out men with money.

Ginger slips into the backseat and Tiffany slides into the front. I'm disappointed. She's hot, but the airhead act doesn't turn me on.

Walking into the movie store, I nod to the desk clerk while leading the girls to the back curtained-off section of the store. Mallory remains at the forefront of my mind, so I take action to rid myself of her once and for all. I'm not messing around anymore. I'm gonna bump this party to the extreme if that's what it will take to forget her.

As they run their fingers along the large pornographic boxes lining the shelves, I psyche myself up for tonight's adventure. I don't normally do porn or maybe I should say that porn doesn't normally do it for me. But my feelings have been all over the place with these girls and I'm feeling a bit insecure about my performance since being rejected by Mallory. It's really starting to drag me down. They each pick a movie and take to each side of me, rubbing up and down.

As Tiffany licks and nips at my neck, Ginger nibbles my earlobe while copping a feel of my bulge. Knowing we're bordering on our own porn, I need to get these girls out of the store before we get thrown out. Moving forward with an arm around each of them, we stumble out from behind the curtain and towards the front check-out desk. I'm finally starting to feel like my old self again and breathe easier knowing this where I shine. I've got my mojo back.

Rounding the last aisle, we run straight into Mallory. She drops her movie as the girls drop theirs. Instinctively, I bend down, catching her arm and trying to help her, but she yanks it out of my hand. Her face is pale, paler than her usual Mainland shade of pale.

"Don't touch me," she says, warning me while eyeing the girls.

Still squatting, we both look down at the movies lying on the ground. She's quiet, probably processing the information. The girls behind me giggle, and I see Mallory's eyes look up and over my shoulder. Her cheeks flush with the sweetest shade of pink, reminding me of our first day together. I gulp, too humiliated for words.

Apparently, she's not. "You're disgusting, Evan!" Her voice is low. Her words are for my ears alone.

My heart drops to the pit of my stomach and I want to tell her this is all because of her. *I need to forget you and these girls are going to get me over you.* But I can't, and it's better that I don't. She's too smart to believe that bullshit and too beautiful to have to listen to it.

She stands up with her movie in hand, still pink-cheeked and embarrassed, even though I should be the one embarrassed. While she fumbles for her wallet, the girls reach down to pick up their movies. I stand, silent, unable to say what I really want, and watch Mallory completely shut down in front of me. All the emotions that she so readily wore on her sleeve before are gone. There are no witty, smart-assed comments to accompany this awkward situation.

My heart breaks even more watching her tell the clerk that she can't find her money in her purse. She's frantic as she glances back at us, digging in her bag. Looking at the girls caught up in their own world and oblivious to what's happening right in front of them, Mallory says, "Just forget it. I'll come back."

"Take the movie. I'll pay for it on my account," I offer with a shaky voice.

"No." She starts to walk off holding her head high, but I can tell she's struggling.

I grab the movie and run to her before she exits. "Take the movie, please."

"She owes a late fee to be able to rent that," the clerk shouts at us.

I look back at him, and snap, "I'll cover the damn late fee. Just put it on my account."

When I turn back, Mallory is leaving the store, movie in hand. She doesn't know I'm watching as she runs to the car, gets in, and leans her head against the steering wheel. I stand there stunned to the spot and watch as she cries. I want to go to her, but I know it's better if I don't.

I have royally fucked this up and the only thought that crosses my mind is that I lost her before I even had her.

12

EVAN

I pay the rental fees for all three movies, including Mallory's late fee. The girls and I get back into the car just as my stomach churns at the reckoning of my decisions, the choices I'm making. The girls' high-pitched giggles fill the car making me realize I need a drink, and a very strong one at that.

I drive to the nearest liquor store, this time leaving the girls in the car to wait because they are a spectacle in public. I find the bottle of whiskey I'm looking for and go to the counter to pay.

That's when I hear it. "What's up, baby brother?"

Taking a deep breath, I turn around slowly, taking in the sight before me—Kate. I lean my back against the counter, cross my arms, and smile while shaking my head. "Big sister, you're in town for what, like twelve hours and already stocking up?" I eye the three bottles she's holding.

She looks at me with a smirk so familiar it could be my own, and says, "I like to be prepared." Setting the bottles down, she tells the cashier, "He's buying."

I pull out my wallet and toss two large bills on the counter.

"It's good to see you, Evan," she says, hugging me.

I embrace her because sometimes I really do have the coolest sister on the planet. Yes, and sometimes she's the biggest bitch, but she caught me in a sentimental moment. Strange enough, I'm happy to see her.

We walk out of the liquor store, and she points at my car. Tiffany has joined Ginger in the backseat to fill the time by making out in my absence. "Evan, dump the trash, and let's go get drunk. I just got in, and I'm ready to party."

I laugh knowing everything about these girls is wrong, very wrong. My sister's demand lays out the facts to face what I knew I was doing was wrong. *When did I become such an asshole?* "Where are we drinking?"

"Home," she says, smiling. "I'll see you there."

When I open the door, Tiffany says, "Come back here and join us, sexy."

"Ladies, I'm gonna drop you back at the hotel."

"Why, because of that blonde girl you were talking to? Ah, c'mon, we'll be better than her, I promise," Tiffany whines.

Ginger cuts in. "Or, we can ask her to join us."

I scoff, completely grossed out by the thought. "That's my sister! And, yes, because of her. She just flew in and I need to deal with some family business." I start the car and they pout all the way back to the hotel.

After stopping the car before I reach the hotel carport, I jump out to open the door for them. Ginger runs her finger under my chin. "Maybe a rain check?"

I chuckle, now noticing the bellhops and valet guys up ahead, rolling their eyes at me. It's not the first time I've stood here dropping a girl off before. Looking back at her, I say, "I'm sorry. I've got a crazy schedule right now. Have a good vacation." I leave no opening for another rendezvous.

They turn without so much as a goodbye, and I get back into my car and drive off. I don't feel bad. I actually feel like that might be the best decision I've made in days, at least since meeting Mallory. *Mallory. Mallory ... Mallory.* I still don't know what to make of her. She's invading my thoughts more than anyone ever has and I'm just not comfortable with that.

When I get home, I walk into the main house and straight for the kitchen. "Hi, Ms. Chart," I say, greeting our longtime house manager. She's great, but I usually avoid the main house and any potential witnesses to my behavior. I know she would never rat me out to my parents, but for some reason I don't want to disappoint her. I respect her too much to let her see the person I've become.

"Evan, what a pleasant surprise. How are you?"

"I'm good. You know, just working—"

"Lots of partying I hear, too," she says, teasing with an all-knowing smile.

"Yeah, a little of that, too."

"Katie's upstairs changing clothes. She told me she'll be down in a few minutes. Can I get you something to eat, honey?"

"No, thank you."

"Okay, well, I'm off in thirty, so let me know if you need me before then."

She's a great woman. She's really the mom I never had. I have a mom, just not one like that.

"You going to call your loser posse over?" Kate asks, sauntering into the kitchen.

I lean my hands on the counter between us. "I thought it

could just be you and me tonight." I take the liquor out of the bag and twist off the cap of my bottle.

She ruffles my hair, and says, "You old softie. Now get me a drink, baby brother."

Out back, we plant ourselves on loungers in the grass overlooking the ocean with a drink in hand. We don't talk. Instead, we enjoy the view.

As the sun sets, Kate looks at me, and says, "They're not happy if you were wondering."

"I wasn't," I reply, my tone as cold as the drink in my hand. I swirl the ice around in the crystal glass and listen to the tinkering it makes as it hits the sides.

"The Fourth of July party is still on. Mom will be here in two weeks to finish the planning."

"Of course, how could I forget about the annual party? It doesn't matter what's happening in the world, in their marriage, or with their son, but hell, the party must go on. A toast." I hold my glass in the air, letting my sarcasm drip. "To the best family a kid could ever have."

"You're being overly dramatic. It's not that bad."

"Look around, Katie. This house, our cars, our education, none of this has ever been about family. It's only about how we look to the outside world, how we're perceived. Would you spend time with them if they weren't paying your expenses? If you were broke? Think about it. We only *fit* the mold of what the 'proper' family should look like. That doesn't make us the perfect family. I'm sick of it. I'd rather have a family than possessions. I guess that's where we differ."

"You're not sick of that hundred and twenty-thousand dollar car. You're not sick of your free rent in this house. You're just sick that they don't cater to your every bitch and moan, Evan. Well, it's time to face it, they aren't perfect parents, but they're all we have. So this is it. This is your life. Welcome to it."

I down my drink then toss the glass over my head into the pool.

"Why do you do that? You know that could break in there."

I get up, begrudgingly, and walk to the side of the pool where I dive in. Water is my safe haven. I find solace in the water, whether it's a pool or the ocean. I always feel better when I'm surrounded by it. It's so easy to block out the rest of the world in here. Opening my eyes, I see the sparkle of the crystal on the bottom and force myself deeper to grab it. I emerge, setting it on the side. "There it is, all in one piece."

"Good. Now get me another drink, please."

After tossing my soaked shirt poolside, I make another round of drinks in the kitchen. I hand Kate hers before I jump back in the pool and hang on the edge, resting my chin on the rock border.

She moves to a chair that faces me. "Tell me what else is on your mind. I can tell it's more than just the parents."

I duck under the water debating if I want to share my thoughts, my concerns with her. When I come up, she says, "It must be bad if you're hiding in there."

"I'm not hiding—"

"No one knows you like I do. Just talk to me."

She's right. She may be a pain in the ass, but when the chips are down, she's always there for me. "There's this new girl—"

"Wait, let me get this straight, Baby Bro. You're all worked up over a girl? That's a first in forever." She laughs then sips her drink. I give her a pointed look, so she softens a bit when she says, "Okay, I'll be nice. Tell me about this new girl and what's so special about her that she's got you all twisted inside."

I sink a little lower in the water, embarrassed I've exposed a weakness, but needing to talk about this with someone. "Her name's Mallory. Sunny told Zach she's here for the summer."

"That's better than just for a week like your usuals."

"I'm going to ignore that comment, Kate. She's also working at Kehones—"

"Wait, Sunny from Kehones?"

"Yeah, you remember her?"

"Uh-huh. So, her and Zach finally hooked up?"

I chuckle. "No, he still doesn't have the balls to ask her out. But he finally started saying more than 'I'd like a burger with fries' to her."

"He's sweet, but I might have to get involved in that situation or we'll all be old and gray before he makes a move. Now tell me more about this Mallory or is her name all you know?"

"I know a little more," I say, closing my eyes. Memories of her body moving against mine and the feel of her heated skin flood my mind. I open my eyes. "She's smart, which is a complete fucking turn-on—"

"And to think I thought you were just into tits and ass."

"I am, but when she also has a brain, she's perfect." I jump out of the pool, sit on the edge, and take three gulps from my drink. "She's different. There's something about her. She's frustrating too, so fucking frustrating and strong." I stop to think about if I'm willing to share anymore, but I don't think I can. This conversation is getting way too deep for my comfort level.

Kate has a thoughtful expression as she leans back in her chair absorbing what I've told her. "What was up with the girls in the car if you're this in love with someone else?"

"I'm not in love!" *I'm not in love*, I repeat to myself. It's only been two weeks. *I'm not in love!* That is one thing I do know. "I was trying something ... sort of like an experiment."

"It wouldn't have worked. You know that, right? It could've been the best sex of your life and you wouldn't see it that way because they aren't her. And if you were using them to get her off your mind, it would have only been a temporary fix." She takes a sip of her drink and smiles, like a big sister who actually loves her brother kind of smile. "If you're so hung up on her, why aren't you with her?"

I lean forward, running my hand through the water. "I'm not sure." I pause before adding, "I can't. I can't do a relationship."

Kate sits next to me, dangling her feet in the water, and putting a comforting arm around my shoulders. "You need to let all that stuff go. You deserve to be happy. It's time for you to move on." Standing up, she offers me a hand out, and asks, "Are you sure you want to be with a girl that's leaving in a few months anyway? That might not be the wisest choice."

I take the offered hand, and get out. "She's the wisest choice I could make these days."

After kissing me on the cheek, she walks away. "Go with your heart, baby bro, and fuck expectations. Goodnight."

"Night, Katie."

I thought I had spent the last year flipping the bird at all expectations placed on me by my family, university, and everyone else only to have it pointed out by my sister that I am doing exactly what has been expected of me for years—a self-fulfilled prophecy. I'm screwing my life up just like they said I would.

I grumble into my house, stripping off my shorts, and flop down on the bed—the bed where I can feel her presence suffocating me. I roll over, burying my face into my pillow, as memories of her crash over me like a tidal wave. *Mallory.*

13

EVAN

Chirping birds and sunshine are my alarm clock—a typical morning living in the islands, a far cry from the busy street sounds of Manhattan. Glimpsing the time, it's past noon. *So much for the morning.* When I sit up, Zach is lounging on my couch reading a book.

He looks up, and says, "Morning, pretty boy."

"What are you doing here?" I would've normally thrown a fuck in there, but I actually don't mind Zach hanging out in my digs. He and Murphy are my best friends.

"Did you know that 'the quick brown fox jumps over the lazy dog' uses—"

"Every letter in the alphabet? Yes."

"What about a duck's quack doesn't echo? Freaky, huh?"

"What's up with the weird facts, Z?" I ask, stretching my arms.

"Just making conversation. You want to grab a burger?"

"Yeah, give me ten and I'll meet you out front."

As I ride in his truck, I wonder aloud, "Let me guess where you want to eat." He gives me that guilty expression that says so much. "Why don't you just ask her out?"

He stares forward when he answers. "I don't know. Sunny is different. I don't want to screw it up. If she says no then the fantasy is over. I know that sounds strange, but I would rather have the fantasy then nothing at all."

"What if she says yes?"

"I haven't been able to take the risk and hope for that outcome yet."

I shake my head, and laugh. "Dude, really? You haven't been able to properly formulate a theory that results in that conclusion? It's called life. Ever heard it of it? Life is all about decisions, risks, regrets." I knock him in the arm, and say, "I've kept my distance from that girl for six months now. If you don't do it, I will."

He gives me an evil look that I didn't know he was even capable of giving. "You better not, man. She's a good girl. Don't even look at her."

"What? I don't deserve to date a good girl?" The lack of response kind of says it all. I throw my hands up in surrender. "All right, all right. I won't go near her," I say, knowing that comment would incite him. I would never hit on my bud's dream girl. I'm actually hoping to provoke him into action. How could Sunny turn Zach down? Zach is the best person I know. Everyone loves him. She'd be lucky to have him.

We pull up to Big Kehones and suddenly I'm faced with my own dilemma that I had conveniently buried on the drive over. *Mallory. Is she working today? Do I want her to be?* My stomach turns and suddenly I feel like I might be sick. I press on my stomach without thinking.

"You all right there, E?" Zach asks, concerned.

"Yeah." *Just irritated I have such a physical reaction to that girl.*

We walk into the restaurant, but I don't allow myself to

do the only thing I really want to, which is look over at the bar. I don't have to, I know she's here. I can feel her presence. I give in and angle my head, scanning the bar without reward. Disappointment fills my chest.

I follow Zach to our usual table, but don't even have a chance to sit before Murphy barrels in. "Boys, how the hell are ya?" He fists bumps both of us, sitting across from Zach and next to me.

"What has you in such a good mood?" Zach asks him.

"More like who's got you in such a good mood?" I correct Zach's innocent assumption.

"Who says a girl is involved when it comes to my good moods?" Murphy puts his hand on his chest like he's offended. "Maybe I'm just happy to hang with my braddahs."

"Whatever," I grumble.

"What's with him?" Murphy asks, knowing my mood is not typical.

Zach glances at me then looks at Murphy, and not so subtly signals to the bar with his head. Both Murphy and I follow the signal and there she is—*Mallory*. She quickly turns her back and lowers down as if looking for something.

"See something you like, guys?" Sunny asks, pulling all of our attention to her. She looks over her shoulder, letting us know we're busted.

Zach sits up straight, clasps his hands on the table, and says, "Hi, Sunny. How are you today?"

She smiles and in that smile I see ... hmmm ... maybe *like*. Yep, she likes him. Sunny isn't the type to flirt for tips. I may not know her well, but I know she's genuine in her affections. I chuckle at the scene playing out before me—both of them too nervous to push this surface relationship any further in fear of rejection. They're so sweet it makes my teeth hurt.

Turning back to the bar, my eyes meet Mallory's. My heart tightens like a hand is squeezing the life out of me. Despite my discomfort, I stare at her as pink covers her cheeks and she hurries into the kitchen.

It's time to face reality. I can't stop thinking about her. The girl has gotten to me. I don't know how, but what I do know is if she asked me to give up all the vices I love the most, I would do it. If she asked me to make love to her on this bar right now, I would definitely do it. But what scares me the most is, if she asked me to be in a relationship with her, I would do it *and I don't do relationships*. I don't know why this girl makes me feel this way and I don't like it, but I'm coming to terms that these feelings are too strong to deny anymore.

She returns from the kitchen and the grip on my heart loosens, providing some relief. Stealing a few seconds to stare, I take her in. Her long brown hair draws all the attention to her large and bright green eyes. Her outer beauty might have been what drew me to her, but it's her brain that keeps me fixated. She's too good for me. I drop my head down lost in this self-deprecating thought.

"Evan ... E?"

A punch to my upper arm brings me back to the present. I look at Murphy annoyed he hit my arm. "Why'd you—"

"Would you like to order something?" Sunny asks, smiling and waiting for me to answer.

My eyes flash to Mallory once more. The way she looks at me is unsettling. It's like she sees the real me, sees beneath the image I hide behind. My chest tightens again, and I quickly look back at Sunny. "Cheeseburger, fries, and a soda please."

As soon as Sunny walks away, Murphy leans forward and whispers, "Dude, you really need to get a grip. She's just another girl. Hit it and let's get on with our summer." Though rationally I know he doesn't mean to insult Mallory, everything about his suggestion is all wrong.

I bite back. "She's too good to be treated like a whore, so don't talk about her like she is one. Ever!"

Zach laughs so hard his head goes back. I hit him on the arm pissed because I know he sees right through me. The room is closing in on my little charade, and I don't like it.

"Don't stand up or anything, guys!" Kate says, sitting down next to Murphy. "I guess manners don't matter in Hawaii."

"Sorry, Kate," Murphy says, checking her out, his voice clear of his usual obnoxiousness.

Looking between Kate and Murphy, I sense something different, a shift in their behavior. I know he's smart enough not to mess around with my sister, so I'm going to let that too-friendly of an exchange go … this time.

I'm frustrated and I know it's because I'm losing control of my own reactions to the girl currently cleaning the bar. Feeling the heat from my sister's glare, I look up. "What?" I snap.

"Oh, nothing," she says, shrugging and looking over her shoulder.

When Sunny sets our drinks on the table she starts chatting with Kate. I block their noise out, but then I hear Kate say, "No, thank you. I'll order from the bar." As soon as she gets up from the table, I stand, not liking the looks of this at all.

14

MALLORY

The blonde leaves their table and sashays toward me with a self-righteous smile plastered on her face. Taking a deep breath, anticipating the worst, my defenses go up. This girl is on a mission and heading straight for me. I've never been in a physical altercation before and I really don't want to start now, but she looks kind of mean. I'm just hoping she's not Evan's girlfriend—at least not this week's girlfriend.

Stopping right in front of me, hazel eyes narrowed and hands on her hips, she says, "So, you're the one that's got my brother all in a tizzy."

Sunny races over with a nervous smile on her face as if she's here to rescue me. Although I'm uncomfortable, I smile at the ridiculously beautiful blonde, tilt my head, and lean forward. "Who's your brother?"

"This is Kate, *Evan's* sister," Sunny replies.

When Kate smiles, it reveals her confidence and is more compassionate than I expected. Looking over her shoulder, I lock eyes with Evan who is standing up for a better view and looking quite worried. There's no trace of his usual cocky smirk in sight.

"Yeah, so, it's Mallory, right?"

I turn back to blondie. "Yes."

She leans closer, lowers her voice, and says, "Any girl that can knock my little brother off his high horse deserves some respect."

"I didn't do anything to Ev—"

"Mallory barely knows him," Sunny adds.

Kate looks at Sunny and furrows her brow then slowly turns back to me. "Is that so?"

By the insinuation in her tone, she knows more about my brief history with Evan than I'm ready to discuss. I decide to remain silent because anything I say might be used against me. I'm also embarrassed that this is playing out in front of Sunny since I haven't told her about my tryst with Evan yet. Fortunately, I'm saved by the bell—the food's ready. Sunny leaves to deliver their order.

Both Kate and I watch her stride over to their table, precariously balancing the food on a tray.

Kate crosses her arms over her chest and cocks an eyebrow up at me. "She doesn't know about you and Evan?"

"No, it hasn't come up in conversation. Believe it or not, I don't even think about the time I spent with your brother and I know he doesn't think about me, so it doesn't matter anyway."

She smirks and it's unsettling in its familiarity. "I think you're thinking about him more than you're letting on, new girl."

Anger burns inside as I feel my embarrassment over falling for Evan's smooth lines and hard abs. "No offense, Kate, but your brother is an asshole."

She bursts out laughing. After catching her breath, she says, "Mallory, I think we're gonna be good friends."

"I'm confused. Yesterday, he was renting porn with two

sluts. Today, you, *his sister*, wants to be my friend. Yeah, so a little confusing, don't you think?"

"You're different. I can tell. You've got a brain, first of all," she says with a smile. "You seem cool and if I'm being direct, which I always am, Evan had some nice *and* interesting things to say about you." She stands up and rests her hand on the bar. "When's your next day off?"

I'm too stunned to respond. This is the absolute craziest conversation I've had in a while and naturally it's with another Ashford. I'm so fascinated by her that I reply, "Friday."

"Great." She looks at Sunny, who has returned. "Are you off on Friday, too? Mallory and I are going to get together."

Sunny is puzzled, her expression mimicking exactly how I feel. "I can switch shifts with Johnny. I'm sure he won't mind."

"Perfect! I'll make plans." Kate pulls her phone out and I give her my number.

When she walks back to the table, I see Evan looking at me out of the corner of his eye. Kate sits down, and he immediately leans forward and starts to whisper. He seems angry. Kate laughs and pats him on the shoulder, blowing him off and turning her attention to Murphy.

Evan stands abruptly and stalks straight to me. My breathing stops in stunned anticipation of the inevitable confrontation. Before the movie store run-in, we hadn't spoken since I told him to leave almost two weeks ago. Acid fills my stomach as the hurt and anger come flooding back, and it pisses me off that even with the incident yesterday fresh on my mind, I've actually missed him. His looks didn't change to me. I thought my anger toward him, the hate I was feeling, would make him uglier to me, but it hasn't. He's beautiful, still too beautiful for his own good.

"We need to talk," he says, placing his hands on the edge of the bar as if he needs the support. "When's your break?"

Sunny gives me an *'uh-oh'* look then disappears into the kitchen.

"Evan, you can go—"

"Mallory, are you ready to go?" Noah asks, interrupting. Both Evan and I both turn in his direction, neither of us noticing his arrival.

"Ashford," Noah says with a nod. His voice is laced with detest, but he's still polite enough to acknowledge Evan's presence.

Evan returns an equally distasteful response. "Noah." When he turns back to me, his expression is pained. Without another word, he turns and walks back to his table. After yesterday and now this lame interaction, I don't know how I feel about his mood swings or anything else having to do with him.

Noah says something, but I miss it.

"Um, sorry, what?"

He smiles, and says, "I was just asking if you were ready to go."

I glance over at Evan one last time. Though he's scowling, his eyes seem to plead with mine. Taking a deep breath, I reply, "My shift's over. Sunny, we're gonna cruise now."

She hugs me, and whispers, "Are you sure, Mal? This whole situation is heavy, like you're making a choice right now."

"I'm positive." I can be stubborn and mysterious too. I don't need Evan Ashford, and refuse to give him anymore of myself than he already got.

As I walk out with Noah, I feel a pull at my back. Sneaking one more peek backwards at Evan, I have to stop to catch my breath as my heart races. I quickly remind myself that he just had a threesome yesterday. He's not interested in me. *Get that through your head, Mallory!* With those thoughts swimming in my head, I catch up with Noah.

We drive Sunny's bus to his parents' house where he works on cars out in the back. The weight of Evan hangs over us, but we remain quiet on the subject. As he works on the car, I resume the spot that I've become familiar with over the last two weeks—a tree stump I use as a stool. I'm comfortable here. It's easy with no expectations, just friends.

He scrubs at the rust. "I have a competition out on the south shore in a few weeks. Maybe you can stop by and I don't know ... cheer me on or something."

"Those have big waves this time of year, right?"

"The waves are bigger in the winter. We're hoping for seven feet, but I bet it's only about five at best." He looks up with a wide grin, his dimples deeper than usual, his enthusiasm contagious. "You think you'll come out?"

"Of course. I'd like that." Looking around, I see an old, tropical wreath on the back door of the house. This feminine touch makes me wonder why he never mentions his family. "You never talk about your family."

"Because I'm surrounded by them all the time. It gets really old. It's nice to have the break."

"You live with your cousins, but you work out in this shed?"

"Yeah, my parents set this up for me in high school when I took auto shop. I've customized all of their cars."

"Do you have a large family?"

He laughs hard. "That's an understatement. Sometimes I wonder who I'm not related to in Hawaii." He chuckles again. "It's hard to get away with stuff when everyone knows your family."

"I've wanted to ask you about that—"

"Here it comes, the island gossips have been talking. What'd they say?"

"Confession time. What'd you do to land such a bad boy reputation?"

"Don't believe everything you hear, Mallory."

"I don't. But, usually there's some truth down deep in the gossip."

He tells me about his rebellious years and how he started getting into trouble around thirteen and by fifteen he was hanging out with some kids that were wild like him. They would one up each other until his father caught them trying to steal a car. Noah's jaw tenses as he stares out into the distance.

"What is it?" I ask. "What happened after you were caught?"

"My father said I couldn't hang with 'those troublemakers' anymore. My cousins made up the rest of the gang, and he couldn't forbid me to see them since our family is always together."

"So you weren't allowed to see your friends? What happened to them?"

He stands, pulling me up with him, and states, "I don't want to talk about it anymore."

I notice the immediate change in his demeanor over the topic and decide it's best not to push.

"I think that's the last of the rust. Next time I'll start repainting this beauty. I should get you back. Sunny will be getting off work soon."

He holds the door open for me to climb into the VW. Before he shuts it, he says, "Monday night, remember?"

"Of course, the bonfire Monday night. I didn't forget."

15

MALLORY

Friday is lunch with the girls. Kate, Sunny, and I sit at one of the most stunning hotels I've ever seen. The restaurant on the deck overlooks the turquoise water and the view is incredible.

"I'm glad I came today. Thanks for the invite." I smile at Kate though I can't help the feeling that there's more to this than just a girls' day out.

"No worries," Kate replies, tossing her hair behind her shoulders. She leans forward conspiratorially. "And this is just the first part of our day. We're going to take a surfing lesson later."

"Surfing, I've always wanted to try it, but it looks hard," Sunny says, tapping her fingers anxiously on the table. "Is it safe?"

"Isn't there reef or coral down there that can hurt us if we fall?" I ask.

"Don't fall off and you'll be fine. I'm sure the instructors will be happy to help hold you on the board." Kate is confident in everything she says and does. I like her already.

"*Ladies*, fancy meeting you here." Zach walks up, smiling. Sunny grabs her soda and starts sucking. I put my hand on her forearm to calm her. He kneels down next to her and asks, "How are you today, Sunny?"

She slurps the dregs of the soda. "I'm good." Lowering her voice, she says, "How are you?"

"Actually." He pauses and takes a deep breath. "I was wondering if you'd like to go out on a date ... with me ... some time?"

I feel like I'm eavesdropping, but this is happening at the table. Keeping my attention on the ocean, I try to give them as much privacy as I can while attempting to hide my smile. Kate doesn't bother with a charade and just stares at them.

"Yeah, I'd like that." Sunny blushes and looks down.

"Great! I'll call you and we can set something up."

They are so cute that I can't stop the smile that spreads across my face. Sunny deserves a good guy and one who looks as good as Zach with his chiseled features and abs is just the cherry on top.

Kate taps the table, directly all eyes on her. "Sooo, what exactly went down between you and Evan at the porn shop?"

Shocked at her bold question, I say, "We weren't at a porn shop." My stomach twists at the mention of him, but I don't have anything to be embarrassed about, so I tell her how I ran into Evan and those skanks at the video store. I also add my own editorial analysis for emphasis. "Just like everything else with him, it's only about the mindless sex."

"Listen, Mallory," Kate says, her voice is calm and her expression thoughtful. "I may not know you very well, but I know my brother. He can be difficult and confusing sometimes." She laughs lightly to herself. "But he can also be kind, and loving, and he's really fucking loyal. I don't know what the story is between you two, and I can't say I'm not more than a little curious. But, I need you to know that what you saw the other day, those girls, he didn't do anything with them. He was with me at home."

"I saw him with the videos ... and *those girls*, Kate. He most definitely had plans with them." I grab my stomach at the memory as a pain shoots through my chest.

Kate sits back. "I wasn't there when you saw him, but I was right after and he dropped them off. I'm only telling you this because I know you're not going to believe him. I can already see you shutting him out, but please believe me when I say this, he's a better guy than you're giving him credit for."

"This is exactly what I don't understand. Why am I having this conversation with you and not him? Why won't *he* talk to me? He won't open up and just talk to me. It's all games with him and I don't want to play. I can admit that I was stupid. I did things that I thought I could handle and got burned when I couldn't. I don't blame him for that. But all the hurt, the emotions, those girls. I just can't. I won't put myself through that pain anymore."

"He's been hurt in the past too and he's now hurting over you. I know the past is not your problem, but it haunts him."

"Well this is news to me because I didn't even know he liked me."

"Of course, he likes you."

"You make it sound so obvious and yet Evan seems to have gone out of his way to make sure I didn't like him." I huff, crossing my arms over my chest while staring out into the blue water. It seems everyone else is so willing to talk to me except the one person I wanted. I shake my head irritated even more than I was a few days ago. A few days earlier, I was angry and humiliated, but most of all hurt. I cried myself to sleep the entire past week and I'm tired of crying. "We've all been hurt!" I snap.

The three of them look at me, surprised by my outburst. I close my eyes and try to rid myself of the strong emotions that seem to engulf me when it comes to Evan. When I open my eyes again, Zach is shaking his head at Kate and whispering something about me knowing, but I didn't catch it. She uses her eyes to answer him silently which makes me feel I'm definitely missing out on something.

"Is there something I should know?" I demand.

Zach looks at Kate one last time before turning toward me. "No, we were talking about someone else."

As much as I want to delve into whatever they are secretly discussing, emotionally I've lost the energy, so I let it go.

When we finish our drinks, we follow Kate down to the surf shack located on the beach for our lesson. Zach and Sunny lag behind, chatting to each other and holding hands. It warms my battered little heart to see them together like that.

After catching up with Kate at the shack, I look up from my sandy toes and see Evan's sea-blue eyes gazing right at me. "Mallory."

"What are you doing here?" My tone is too harsh as my heart races because of the confusion of seeing him here.

Kate's phone rings interrupting us. "Hey ... *Oh!* I'm on my way." Frantic, she says, "Mallory, I have to go. My friend ... *cousin* ... I just have to go." She dashes off across the sand to the path.

"The lesson is already paid for," Evan says. "I hope you'll still take it. I'm not allowed to give refunds and I could get in trouble if you deny me. Well, deny the lesson that is." He comes out from behind the counter, stopping in front of me with his hands on his hips ... or should I say, right at the top of the sexy V his muscles form that leads to a dangerous and delightful place. I sigh out loud, missing those hands on me and missing that V.

"She's staying," Sunny says, her voice firm. "Zach said he can show me the basics. Evan, you can give Mallory a private lesson."

Trying to set her on fire with just a look, I give her the evil eye, but she doesn't back down. Zach reappears holding a board and takes Sunny down closer to the water. Looking back to Evan, I bow my head, and concede. "Sure. This should be interesting."

Ten minutes later, I'm in a bulky life jacket, boobs squeezed tightly together—I think he tightened it like that on purpose. "Why am I in this life jacket? Sunny isn't wearing one." He chuckles and looks down. I'm pissed. "I don't need this do I?"

"Technically, no, but I feel better that you're wearing it if that makes a difference."

I unsnap the clasps and pull the jacket off, tossing it into the sand. "It doesn't." Although it kind of does make me feel all better that he seems to care, warm inside too, but he doesn't need to know that. "We should get back to the lesson."

The next thirty minutes pass as I practice pop-ups on a large foam board set on top of the sand. Evan is analyzing my action, I mean my pop-ups, and smiles. "You look good. You ready to get in the water with me?"

Um, no ... I would rather stay here on the beach feeling this awkward for the rest of the day. I just think that, but don't bother saying it. I know Evan will get all analytical on me saying that I'm just defensive. *Damn right, I'm defensive. Why am I having pretend arguments in my head?* I'll tell you why.

Because the pretty boy next to me has my soul and emotions all twisted and I don't like it, not one bit. I roll my eyes, a little because of him and a lot because of me. "Let's do this."

He takes the board and carries it waist deep before setting it on top of the water. I follow, jumping as the waves hit against my chest. "Hop on," he says, smiling. His voice is light and playful and I can tell he's in his element.

I roll onto the board like some fat seal that has flippers instead of arms. "Are you sure you're ready for the task at hand?" I ask, referring to my obviously not ready for surfing skills.

"Getting on is one of the hardest parts. You'll get better at it." He starts swimming next to me and dragging the board with him. He's strong and I watch his muscles working beautifully together across his shoulders and back, but I scold myself for still finding him so damn attractive.

We go out quite a distance from the beach, when he says, "Let's try once from here."

Sunny and Zach have already caught a wave riding tandem. They make it look so easy.

Without warning, Evan says, "I've missed you."

"You have?" I ask, surprised by his revelation.

"I've been thinking about you a lot." I quickly remind myself that he's a paradigm, he's setting the mold. He's not changing for me which helps keep my guard up. "Can we talk about that?" he asks, floating next to me.

"Talk about what? How you acted after our night together, those girls at the store? I don't think we have much to talk about." I look ahead and see Sunny and Zach on the beach waving at us. I sit up on the board to get a better look. "They're waving *'hello'*, right?" I ask concerned, and wave back.

I start paddling and look back at the wave coming up behind us. But Evan's holding me steady in the water.

Then I see Zach grab Sunny's bag off the sand and they walk away. "Are they leaving?" I'm nervous she's gonna leave me with Evan all alone. "Get on. She's my ride."

He slides onto the board, bumping against my back then onto his knees looking over my head. "I think they are leaving."

I lift my legs up onto the board and paddle with my hands even faster. "Harder, faster, Evan!"

He chuckles behind me. He's got such a dirty mind and I like that. It makes me smile.

By the time we reach the shore, they are long gone. "I'm starting to think we've been set up," I say, more to myself than to Evan.

He smirks like he always does and my knees weaken just as they always do when he does that. *Why does my body have to react like this to the bad boy? Why not the good guy, like Noah?* "I can drive you home."

"No. That's fine. I'll call Sunny to pick me up." I look around the shack for my stuff, but it's all gone. "She took it, didn't she? Ugh!"

Evan goes into the shack and tosses me a shirt. "I only have the one shirt, but you're welcome to wear it, but I have to say you're looking really hot in that bikini."

I catch it. "Thanks, I guess." *Don't fall for his charms. Don't fall for him again.*

"Let me change into some dry shorts and I'll take you home."

I don't have much of a choice, so I wait. He starts stripping his swim trunks off and although I should be polite and give him some privacy, it's Evan, and he's hot.

"*Mallory?* Mallory, you've got a little drool right there on the side of your mouth," he says, mocking me. I have no response because I was busted and deserve the sarcasm. "You can change here or up at the hotel, wherever you feel more comfortable." He walks out swinging his arm out to allow me entrance into the shack.

I look around and can tell that no one can see in there, so I walk in and duck down. After untying my bikini top, I set it on the counter and slip on the t-shirt. It's large on me, but does the trick. I've actually seen dresses shorter than this, so I decide to take off my wet bottoms and place them on the counter. But one big gust of wind will defi-nitely expose my hoo-ha to the world, so I tug at the bottom of the shirt to hold it in place, standing there— shoeless, braless, panty-less—with no money, phone, or dignity.

Evan tilts his head, slightly amused by my situation, and makes me an offer I can't refuse. "Would you like to wear my briefs?"

"Very much," I answer without hesitation.

He steps back into the shack, keeping his eyes on mine and takes his shorts off. Everything is in slow motion and I find the sexual tension almost stifling in the small shack. He lets his shorts drop to the ground, still not losing eye contact, and steps out of them. My eyes leave his and roam downward.

His skin is like a satin sheet revealing every perfect muscle underneath. I want to touch him. I really want to lick him and taste the dry, salty ocean water on him. When I look up at his face, I know I'll find his standard smirk firmly in place, but it isn't there. I've just ogled him, he should feel a little violated or proud, but he doesn't. His eyes are too busy appreciating me, but it feels more personal than that, like he appreciates my body because it's me. I open my mouth to help counteract the lack of air while trying to calm my heart that's pounding in my chest.

His voice cuts through my wondrous thoughts. "Why are you fighting this?"

My head bolts up. His eyes are curious, but sad.

I know what he means, but he doesn't deserve any more of me. He's a taker, and I'm not willing to fall for his game again. I look down at his black boxer briefs and point. "Are you going to let me borrow those or not?"

"Of course," he says, sliding them down and exposing himself to me.

It hardens as I watch him strip the underwear completely off. *How do I keep forgetting how perfect his erection is?* "You like what you see, Mallory?" He holds the briefs in the air in front of my face.

I snatch them. "Thanks," I say, grinning then licking my lips for some odd reason.

Turning around, I slip one leg at a time into the briefs. Sliding them up so he gets a glimpse of my ass, an unsubtle reminder of what he's been missing. *Yes, I can tease, too.* As I adjust the waistband, his hands grab my hips, pulling me to him. Pressing his hardened self against my bottom, his warm breath hits my neck, and he whispers against my ear, "I think about you all the time."

Stepping forward, freeing myself, I walk around him. Without looking back, I say, "Except when you're sneaking out in the early morning to avoid the mistake you made the night before, or when you're fucking other girls." I leave him in the shack, alone and naked.

I'm almost to the hotel by the time he catches up with me, swim trunks back on. "I left your required little courtesy note." He takes hold of my arm, and I turn back to face him.

"It's not about etiquette, Evan. After what we did, you

should want to tell me goodbye. When you don't, I not only wake up alone but feel like a whore." I yank my arm from him and turn to walk again, but he blocks my path.

"You're not a whore and I didn't use you, I—"

"Ashford! Over here. Now!" Some guy in a staff shirt yells from the patio of the hotel.

"Shit! I'll meet you at the car. This conversation is *not* over," Evan says before jogging toward the man.

The man seems to be griping at him, but Evan glances at me then stares out at the water with his arms crossed, giving him no respect. *Typical.* I watch him nod and then argue.

The employee parking lot is huge and I don't see his car anywhere. Suddenly, Evan grabs my arm directing me to walk with him. "Let's get out of here. I'm parked over here." As we're walking, he hands me my wet bikini then releases my arm, and says, "You left this." His pace is quick and I can tell he's anxious to leave. At the edge of the parking lot, he stops where the grass ends and the rest is cement. He turns and looks at me. "The pavement is hot. I'll carry you the rest of the way. Hop on."

Being stubborn, I touch my foot to the pavement to test it.

"I'm parked six rows over. You can walk if you want." He shrugs, but looks confident.

He starts walking, but the ground is too hot and I don't want to scorch my feet. I huff, putting my hands on my hips. "Fine. I'll take the ride."

And there is that self-satisfied smile. If I wasn't anxious to get out of here myself, I'd protest just to spite him. But I want to get home, so I swallow my pride.

He comes back and bends over and I hop onto his back wrapping my legs around his body and my arms loosely around his neck. My cold, wet, bathing suit is in my hand, dripping down his bare chest, and I find a tidbit of pleasure in that annoyance. He's getting me back five times over with the friction of his body against my nether region as he moves though. All that separates us is the soft cotton of the briefs I'm wearing.

He makes me want him! It's hard to give up the best sex of your life over stupid stuff like principles and pride.

We reach the car and he grabs me from the side, spinning me to his front and pinning me against the vehicle with his body.

"Whoa! What are you doing?" My feet don't reach the ground and he's holding me by my ass and enjoying himself at that.

"I told you our conversation wasn't over."

"Do we have to finish it with your cock pressed against me while your hands fondle my ass though?" I ask, sneering.

He laughs then leans his head against my forehead. "You're right. We shouldn't be talking." His lips graze mine and my body relaxes under his grip. Sensing the tension dissipating from my body, he kisses me. I hold out for exactly point two seconds before I kiss him back.

The kiss is heated from the moment our lips touch, on fire by the time our tongues meet, and burning when I wrap my arms around his neck giving him everything he wants—everything I want. His bulge presses against my sex and I moan into his mouth. Lifting my legs up higher, I wrap them around him tighter as he adjusts his hold on me, so we both benefit. I can feel how much he wants me and that thought alone brings my buried desires to the surface.

His mouth pulls away and he rests his head on my shoulder. "God, Mallory. How do you do this to me?" He sounds as if he's selling his soul to the devil. "I can't fight you. You're all I fucking want."

I tilt my head back to get a better look at him, understanding exactly what he's experiencing. I'm battling my urges for him too. It's been a struggle and is much easier when I don't see him, when I'm not reminded of our chemistry. I bring my legs down, straightening them down toward the ground. His hands loosen and he lets me slide down his body, but his hands remain on my hips, his grasp tightening. When I look into his eyes, he needs me too much and yet not enough—conflict.

My senses take hold of me. "I think you should drive me home now, Evan."

Just as my feet touch the hot parking lot, he opens the door for me without question or further intention. Sliding into the driver's seat, he lowers his head, running a hand through his hair aggressively as if he's struggling inside. He doesn't speak. He just shifts into reverse, and starts driving.

We need a distraction. *I* need a distraction from the tension filling the car. "It looked like you were arguing with that man back there. Are you in trouble?"

He doesn't look at me. I can tell it's on purpose. "No. He was just mad."

"About me? You know, dressed like this?"

"Not about your clothes." He explains, "He asked me if I had sex with you in the shack. I told him no. Then he asked if I wanted to keep my job."

"Do you?"

"Yes, but I told him to go fuck himself—"

I turn, shocked. "Why would you say that to your boss?"

"They won't fire me." He looks at me, the smug slowly reclaiming his gentler features. "They use me to draw in the clients. I benefit them just as much as the job does me."

"Is that how you met those girls? You gave them a lesson—"

"I know you won't believe me, but I didn't sleep with them, Mallory. I swear."

Belief is a powerful commitment. I want to believe, but everything I saw overrides any trust I consider giving him. "The porn, the girls, it didn't look innocent."

"Have you ever watched porn?"

"Don't turn this around. I've watched those kinds of movies and I'm not judging you for that." I scrunch my nose in disgust, and say, "But you were obviously going to have sex with them."

He pulls to the side of the road, slamming on his brakes, and throwing the car into park. "I was. You're right or I wanted to. *FUCK!* I thought I wanted to. I thought it would help." I can feel his anger through his words. "But I didn't. I didn't sleep with them. I didn't have sex with them. I didn't even kiss them, but honestly, does it matter? Are you going to believe me?" he asks, his voice suddenly softer in the confined space. "I screwed up and I'm sorry. I need you to believe what I'm telling you. I was only going to hook up with them to get *you* off my mind. When you kicked me out that night, it upset—"

"I didn't kick you out *forever*," I say, sitting up while standing my ground. Tears well in my eyes and I say more than I should. "*You hurt me.* How many times am I supposed to let you come into my life and do that? I'm a girl and emotional. I need you to be there when I wake up so I don't feel used." I turn away to look out the window.

I can hear him trying to bring his breathing back under control. Seconds later, his hand runs gently down my arm, and he whispers, "I'm sorry I hurt you, but I don't know how not to."

Absorbing his words, I let them enter my soul. Minutes pass before he starts the car back up again. We remain silent the rest of the trip. When Evan pulls up to the apartment, he cuts the engine. There are two possibilities here: he's going to talk to me or he's going to walk me to the front door and end this once and for all.

He opens his door and comes around to open mine. Guess he's made his decision. He offers a hand and I take it though I know by this stage in our convoluted relationship that I shouldn't. I'm weak to him and touching him removes the last of my will-powered walls every time.

We walk in silence. At the front door, I stop and point at the shirt I'm wearing. "I'll get your clothes back to you soon."

"I was actually hoping to collect them now," he says, adorable with a sweet tilted smile in full effect.

"No, Evan."

"*No?* Just like that?"

"Exactly like that."

"Mallory?"

"Yes."

He licks his lips, and sighs, pausing too long for my comfort level.

"I have to go." My words burst out, ending both of our unease. Pulling the key from under the potted plant, I say, "Goodbye."

I unlock the door with haste and walk in, immediately closing it behind me. Resting my back against the door, I close my eyes trying to block out the feeling of his presence on the other side, his heat easily penetrating the metal and my soul.

"You okay, there?" a male voice asks.

My eyes flash open and my hand covers my heart. "I didn't see you."

Zach smiles, and I can't stop myself from comparing the lightness of it to Evan's troubled one. "I gathered that much."

We both look out the sliding glass door and watch Evan get in his car and leave. "You want to talk about it?" he asks casually.

"No, but thanks. Is Sunny here?"

"She's in the shower."

I walk into the bathroom and shut the door behind me. "I need to talk."

"Mallory," she says, moving the curtain to the side, and poking her head out. "Why are you home already?"

"Yeah, about that. I don't appreciate you and Kate ditching me."

"C'mon, it was for your own good. You've got some sorting out to do. We can all see it and everyone within fifty yards can feel the sexual tension, chemistry, whatever you want to call what you two have. It's there, Mal." She closes the curtain. "Why are you holding out? Are you worried about his rep?"

"It's too late for that," I mumble to myself.

"What was that? I can't hear you because of the water."

"Nothing. So you and Zach, huh?"

She turns off the water, grabs a towel off the rack, and flips open the shower curtain. Stepping out with the towel wrapped around her body, she smiles. "Yeah, I like him a lot." She leans toward me, and whispers, "We've hung out a few times and he's been up at Kehones a lot lately. He's nice, polite and he's sweet to me."

"I'm happy for you."

She lifts my chin up so I face her. "You deserve happiness, too. Now, get the hell out of here and let me get dressed."

I walk back into the living room and see Zach sitting there. "So you heard all that?"

"Yeah." He chuckles.

"Any thoughts?"

He puts his hands up in surrender. "Not getting involved."

"*Ohhh*, now you're not getting involved? Where was Mr. I'm-not-getting-involved earlier when you abandoned me at the beach?" I ask, rolling eyes.

"Abandoned is a strong word and that wasn't really my idea, but I tend to agree with Sunny. You and Evan have some stuff to work out—"

"I don't even know Evan."

"Maybe you should get to know him then. He's a good guy despite the reputation that precedes him, and it's just that, a reputation." He laughs looking down at his feet as he stands. "I mean, some of it's true, but some has definitely been exaggerated."

"Does he sleep with a lot of girls?"

He ponders the question then says, "I think you should ask him."

"I don't trust him or his rehearsed answers."

"Why do you think he would lie to you?" Zach studies my face, trying to read me. He reminds me a little of Evan when he does that.

Remembering Evan's words from the first day I met him, he told me not to rely on him, but to trust him. He was honest with me. I got hurt because I did exactly what he told me not to do. I relied on him even though I didn't trust him.

16

MALLORY

The revelation from the day before shrouds my thoughts like a wet towel—a constant drip, reminding me of Evan. Maybe I played this game all wrong. He told me he's not a relationship guy. It was one of the first things he said to me. His actions with the girl at the airport and after, backed that, but his actions with me, didn't.

I stand there lost in thought and staring at the wooden bar that I'm supposed to be cleaning. How he treated me was nothing less than caring for the most part. Yes, he screwed up and hurt my feelings both mornings after we had sex, but he also seemed to be in a constant state of turmoil when around me too. I think he likes me, but doesn't know how to deal with those feelings. Pretty similar to how I feel about him, which is a bit distressing. I didn't come here to find a boyfriend. I thought it was fun to have sex with someone so beautiful on my summer vacation. There would be no strings, no commitments, no obligations, or responsibility, just a one-time thing that I was never bold enough to do back at school. But I was wrong because the minute I got in that car, I knew there was more. I knew he was different. I just didn't allow myself to recognize the feelings I had for him and he had for me. *Evan Ashford has feelings for me.* I say it just loud enough for only me to hear, letting it permeate the air around me.

"*Maalllllory*, earth to Mallory."

I look up. "Yeah ... Oh, Noah, *hi*. What are you doing here?"

"I was dropping the VW off. You wanna see?"

"Definitely."

I walk around the bar and head outside with him. My hands fly up, covering my mouth as it drops open in amazement. I run my finger down the newly painted, shiny, red Volkswagen Bus. "Oh my god, Noah!" I say, pointing at it. "It's incredible." I turn around and jump on him out of pure excitement.

He catches me as I hug him tightly. "Sunny is going to die when she sees her bus."

Noah laughs then sets me back down on the ground. "I hope so. But, you know, Mallory, I can't accept your money. I know you offered to pay me for the work, but you paid for the paint and I actually enjoyed doing the bodywork."

"This looked like it belonged in a junkyard, but now ... well, look at it. It looks like it was just driven off the showroom floor. I need to pay you for your time."

"No, absolutely not. But, you can promise me that we still get to hang out together sometimes. I'll miss that."

"Deal," I say, sticking my hand out to seal it. "We're friends. Of course, we'll hang out."

We go inside and since it's a slow day, he stays, and we enjoy the time chatting and laughing together. When I get off at six, he says he has a surprise for me at his house. I drive the beautifully restored VW and Noah over to his place, an old house down the street from his parents.

When the garage door opens, I see a white surfboard with *'Wahine Nani'* painted across the length in gold. Silver and purple Hibiscus flowers encircle the edge with the University of Colorado Buffalo mascot anchoring the image fin side.

Nudging me with his elbow, he says, "I thought you'd like your own board since you're here all summer, haole girl. Maybe we can surf together sometime."

"You didn't! This is so bad-ass! Oh my God, Noah, I can't believe you did this." I look at the design, running my finger along the edge. "It's amazing. More than amazing. It's perfect." I point to the words, and ask, "Wahine Nani?"

"Beautiful Girl," he looks down as he says this. "You are. You're very pretty."

My cheeks heat under the compliment. "I don't know what to say other than thank you. So you're going to take me out surfing sometime soon?"

"Next week, I will. I promise, but I have that competition coming up, so it'll have to wait until after that."

"I look forward to it."

He follows me back to the car. I drive the VW, and he drives his Jeep with the long board up on surf racks. Sunny isn't home. I'm suspecting she's with Zach again. Noah drops the board off, but can't stay because he needs to work-out to prep for the competition, so he takes off. I'm not disappointed because I really need some quiet time to myself to think about everything.

I spend my evening practicing the 'pop-ups' that Evan taught me in my lesson and feel confident to try this in the ocean on my new board. I love this board so much that I lie down on it to watch TV and eventually fall asleep. Sometime in the night, I feel weightless and warm. I dream of Evan, but I always dream of Evan in some form lately, so that isn't strange. I shift onto my side burying myself into the couch cushions, but don't wake until morning.

The sun hasn't risen and just like so many other mornings in Hawaii, I decide to go to the beach to watch the sunrise. But today, I have a board and the excitement of owning it gets the better of my patience. I throw my bathing suit on, pull on my cut-offs, and slip on flip-flops. I grab the board which is awkward to hold, but settles nicely into my side as I walk.

At the beach, I drop my board into the sand and strip down to my swimsuit. The waves look gentler this morning which eases my worries. I run Evan's surfing lesson through my mind as I paddle out past the first set of breaking waves. The water is smooth out here and it's easy to navigate without much effort. I look back at the empty beach which is now a fair distance away. All the nerve I had maintained abandons me for a brief second with the rush of danger I feel from suddenly realizing I'm a solitary surfer. I look across the ocean, further down the beach, and see the usual 'real' surfers and find relief that others are at least in the vicinity. Newbies aren't allowed to surf with those guys and especially not a haole girl, so I keep my distance.

Looking over my shoulder, I spot a small set of waves coming toward me. These look good, doable. With all my strength and nerve, I start paddling as a wave approaches. I face forward and when my board rides high onto the waters ledge, I pop up. Life is perfect for that one fleeting second before I lose my balance and wipe out.

My body plunges into the turquoise waters and I'm dragged under and spun around like a ragdoll in a washing machine. I open my eyes for one brief moment, but can't focus to find the top of the water. I'm flung to the surface long enough to take one last breath before I'm forced down again by another crashing wave, spinning wildly under the water. I swim and kick, fighting against death and Mother Nature's attempts to keep me down. Vertigo sets in and I start to lose clarity. That's when I hit my head on something hard, temporarily stunning my thoughts to fight for my life.

Everyone tells you that their life flashes before their eyes when death is near. I expected that. I welcome the happy memories, wanting them to wash over me as I'm relieved from this existence, but that doesn't happen. The whole of my thoughts are of Evan. My short time with him replays rampantly through my mind. The pool, him worshiping my body in his bed, the devious, but sexy glint in his eyes, the sincerity that slips through when he looks deep into my soul, and the energy that binds us together. I'm consumed with thoughts of him touching me as I feel my last breath escape me.

My eyes open in the calm of my surroundings while my body becomes one with the ocean. I see him so clearly above, staring at me, staring *into* me, calling me to him though it sounds distant and detached. He yanks me by the shoulders from the watery confines and air hits my skin as he takes me in his arms one last time. I relinquish myself— body and soul. I give in because until I was dying, I didn't know how much I was in love with him.

My throat burns, and I feel sick and heave, but I want Evan to stay with me. My dream teeters on the edge of disappearing and I want to stay asleep forever. One swift punch to my chest sends me flying, spitting out the salty water that had invaded my lungs. Immediately falling back down, I open my eyes. It's real, the dream or death, but it's real because Evan is with me.

I cough, and the last of the water is expelled although I still feel lifeless. Evan's beauty is all I take in against the blue expanse of the sky above. Confusion takes hold of me when he says, "You're going to be all right, Mallory. Focus on me."

I can't do anything else, but concentrate on him. I cough again as I try to speak, "Am I dead?"

His assaulting smirk appears, and I relax, knowing I'm in heaven.

"I think you almost drowned, but you're not dead." He leans down and kisses me on the forehead. I feel strange and wondrous at the same time.

"You're here—"

"Do you think you're in hell?"

His question is too bewildering right now. I know where I am, so I say it. "Heaven."

"Is that where you think you are, baby? You think you're in heaven?"

I close my eyes, letting his words soak in. When I gulp, my throat hurts, my body hurts, and now my heart hurts. *I'm alive.* The aches I'm feeling tell me so, but now I've exposed my feelings to the one person who can damage them the most. Reality sets in, and I sit up with his assistance.

I grasp hold of my throat, hoping to ease some of the burn. "I know where I am now. Thank you for ... did you save me? Why? How are you here?" I ask, strangely disappointed that I wasn't actually dreaming *or dying.*

"I should ask you why you're here, alone. You should never surf alone. You don't even know how to surf. What were you thinking, Mallory? Where'd you get this board?" His voice gets more upset with each question.

Suddenly, I feel defensive, but not enough to lie to him. "Noah gave me the board."

"He's an idiot. It's like giving a car to a child to drive."

"Shut-up, Evan." That's all I can think to say right now which is very immature, but does the job.

He stands up and with an offered hand, calmly asks, "Do you think you need to go to the hospital?"

"No. I'm fine ... or will be. How did you save me?"

I take his hand and stand up slowly, my eyes meeting his. He supports me by the elbow then grabs me into an embrace. While stroking my hair away from my face, he kisses me on the forehead. "Shhh."

Leaning against his bare chest, I savor the warmth of his skin against my cheek. He pulls back and looks me in the eyes. "What were you thinking going out there like that?" His tone is reprimanding.

I turn away and start walking toward my shorts and shoes, but he grabs my arm. "Don't walk away from me."

"Evan, let go of me!"

"No, I want to know why you pulled that stunt—"

"Why are you so mad?"

"Because you fucking drowned out there. What if I wouldn't have been here ..." His head drops into his hands and he runs them upwards through his hair. "I can't lose you," he whispers.

"What?"

"Nothing." He turns and walks over to the board tossing it into the sand a few feet away.

I storm after him, thinking I actually might have heard what he said, and demand, "No! You tell me what you mean by that."

He picks up one end of the board, reads the words, and studies the personalized design before he lifts his foot and stomps down in the middle of the board breaking it in half. As I scream in protest, he does it again, breaking each half into quarters.

Tears fill my eyes, and I scream. "Are you crazy? Seriously, are you insane? Unbalanced? Why'd you do that?"

"This board is luckier than Noah will be when I find him."

I point right at his face, and threaten, "You won't touch him!"

"Your head is bleeding again—"

"I don't care what you think has happened, but you won't lay a finger on Noah. I swear if you do, I'll never speak to you again—"

He grabs me by the shoulders, and steadies me. "Calm down. Your head is bleeding. You need stitches."

"Huh?" I raise my hand to my head and look at it. My hand is covered and dripping downward. "Oh my god, I'm bleeding!" I sway and instantly fall forward to my knees.

"Mallory, stay with me. Stay with me," he repeats, scooping my failing body into his arms and running to his car. His chant lies just on the surface of my consciousness.

When he sets me down on the passenger seat, I mumble the only coherent words I can form. "The blood, your car ... expensive."

17

MALLORY

I wake up on a tiny, uncomfortable bed. Looking around, I see Evan slumped against the wall looking down.

"Ev," I stop and clear my throat. It's sore.

He dashes to my side and strokes my cheek. "Don't talk, baby." He leans over and pours me a cup of water. After he helps me sit up, I sip from the straw.

My hand races to my head and I gently pat the bandage covering the side of my temple. "My head?"

"You blacked out. Fortunately, you only needed three stitches. You hit the reef when you were under water, so the doc said he wants to see you when you wake up."

I chuckle. "I remember the beach and the blood."

He sits on the edge of the bed still stroking my face. "You were super cute before you passed out if that makes a difference."

"Super cute, huh?" *Why do I like that he thought I was super cute?*

"Yeah, you were worried about getting blood in my car."

"I didn't, did I?" I ask, worrying again that I might have ruined the beautiful leather interior.

He drops his hand to his lap, then stands and backs away, suddenly unsure of himself. "Uh, no, there's no damage to the car. I'll get the nurse."

Evan leaves the room so fast that it makes the pain in my head throb to watch. After a few tests, silly questions about fingers being held up, my birth name, and presidents—I could name all of them in order—the doctor said he was not only impressed, but releasing me.

I walk into the hallway, and Evan stands up from a nearby chair, and says, "I hear you're free to go."

"So they say," I reply, a little snark seeping into my tone.

Thirty minutes later, we drive back to the beach in relative silence. When he parks, I say, "Thank you again for paying my bill. I guess my insurance isn't as good as I thought."

"Its fine, Mallory." His tone has changed, just like the ocean tides in front of us.

We both get out, and I walk over to my shorts and slip them on. I grab my shoes, dusting the sand off of them then put them on. Evan walks to the broken board and carries the pieces to his trunk. He returns to the driver's seat at the same time I get back into the car. "I still don't understand why you broke my surfboard."

"I'll buy you a new board ... when you're ready and you're not ready." He shifts the car in gear and peels out. The short drive back to the apartment feels long and tension filled. He lets me get out without protest.

I lean back in, and say, "Pop the trunk and I'll throw the pieces away."

"No, I'm keeping them for now then I'll dispose of them."

Irritated, I slam the door harder than I should. I'm

pissed that once again I'm being wound up and cut loose. I need a cigarette like nobody's business.

He slides out his open window and sits on his door frame. "C'mon, Mallory, don't leave mad. It's a board, that's all." I have flashbacks of him saying something eerily similar to me that first morning after he dropped me off.

I turn around furious by his lack of respect and out of frustration. "Noah gave me that board. He put a lot of thought into it and spent money that you know as well as I do that he doesn't have a lot of. So, it's more than just a board, it was a gift from a friend that's become close to me."

"He's using you to get to me—" His arrogance is revealed once again.

"No, he's not! He likes me. We've spent time together." I walk back, angry and irritated, and poke him on the chest. "Don't talk to me about him using me. You used me, you asshole." I know I'm also to blame, but he flipped this around on us. We were supposed to be easy, no strings then he said things like 'make love' and a string slowly attached itself to my heart.

I turn around and rush to the door. This conversation is pointless and doesn't matter. *I'm done with Evan Ashford!* I stop to dust my hands together to emphasize my ending with him when I'm brazenly pinned against the door from behind. His breath hits my ear, and he whispers, "Don't be mad, sweetheart. Although, I do think you're sexy as all get-out when you are."

I squirm, aggravated by the shameless entrapment of my body. His hands whisk around to my stomach and then separate—one goes north and the other one heads south. I threaten, "Let me go or you're going to be feeling some major pain in two seconds."

"Your feistiness is such a turn on," he says, pressing his bulge against my ass. Wet kisses follow his remark, landing on my neck, and for some reason, I don't fight him. My body caves, allowing him fuller access for his lips, hands, and cock, which is currently hard.

With my sensibilities still intact, I whisper, "I'm not yours for the taking. I ... I can't play this game with you anymore." This is my only attempt at saving myself, and for some reason, I hope he doesn't believe me.

His body leaves mine cold and alone, and he walks away. He stops and looks back at me. "That's too bad, Mallory, because we are so good together."

I want to stop him. I want to shout that he can take me whenever he wants, but I also know my heart can't handle his hot and cold temperaments anymore.

THE NEXT MORNING, I wake up with a pounding headache. I take ibuprofen and lie back down on the couch. It's early and the bright day hurts my eyes. I roll over covering my head with my blanket and fall back asleep.

"UH!" I hear Sunny gasp above me. "Mallory, what happened?"

My eyes flash open causing me to wince from the light flooding the room. "Sunny," I grumble, "you scared me. What is it?"

She drops to her knees besides the couch and gently rubs over my bandage. "What happened to your head?"

"*Oh*, that." I roll over being careful not to put pressure on it. "I drowned, went to the ER, and got three stitches. It looks worse than it is."

"Holy shit, Mal. Are you all right?" Hearing Sunny curse means she's concerned.

"I'm fine—"

"What do you mean you drowned? You're here."

"Noah gave me a surfboard—"

"Wow! That's nice."

"Yeah, but I took it out surfing and wiped out. I was trapped under water, but Evan saved me—"

"You were with Evan?"

"No, I was surfing alone." She looks confused and I'm starting to feel a little confused myself. He never actually told me how he just happened to be there. "I hit my head on a reef and guess I drowned. He pulled me out and saved me. I started to bleed and he took me to the hospital where I got bandaged up. They told me I was fine, so don't worry."

"Let me get this straight. You and Evan spent time together?"

"Really? That's all you got from my harrowing adventure. I drowned, Sunny!"

A huge grin covers her face, and she says, "But, *Evan saved you*. That's so romantic."

"Can you stop swooning for one minute and stick with me here?"

"Okay, I'm sorry. I'm focused again. You'll be okay, right?"

"Yes, but my head hurts."

"What can I get you?"

I look at the cable box clock and see that I'm due into work in an hour. "Nothing. I just need a shower and to eat something before I go to work."

"You go take your shower and I'll make you a sandwich. Sound good?"

"Sounds better than good. Thanks," I say, getting up and walking to the bathroom.

Later, Sunny drops me off at work and I dive right into the busy afternoon. I prefer busy because it lets me put my attention on work instead of other things or certain other people. I have so many questions for Evan and don't know when I'll get answers since I told him to leave me alone, so it's best to not think of him at all.

By eight, Noah shows up, smiling and handsome, as always. I still wish my heart could love him the way I don't want to admit that I might be in love with Ev ... No, I won't even think about him.

I greet him with a hug.

Worry colors his expression, and he asks, "What happened to your head?"

My hand covers my wound. "Oh, this, yeah, it's nothing."

"It's definitely something, Mallory. Tell me."

I look down knowing my story will hurt his feelings, but he deserves honesty from me. I tell him all the gory details, but leave out the part about Evan breaking the board. He looks troubled and guilty. "I knew I shouldn't have given you the board. I knew better, more than you'll ever understand, but I wanted to be the one to teach you. I wanted us to have that to share so we could spend more time together. I'm sorry. It was a stupid gift."

"Please don't blame yourself. It was a wonderful gift. Really, the best gift I've ever gotten. It was very thoughtful. I'm just sorry it got broken."

"Boards break. They're just fiber-glass. I'm glad you're all right. I might owe Ashford a thank you. That's not going to be easy to do."

"You don't owe him anything. Please don't feel bad, okay?"

Looking at his watch, he says, "You've been off work for a half-hour. You ready to go to the bonfire?"

I'm relieved he's not upset about the board being broken. "Let's go have a good time. I think we both can use one."

When Noah and I approach the bonfire at the beach, he takes my hand and smiles. I can see the innocence in his eyes, so I don't mind the gesture. There's already a large crowd of people, and I don't know any of them. Noah introduces me to a couple of his friends and then I hear Sunny. I turn and see her running toward me. Grabbing me into a hug, she whispers, "This is gonna be a great night." She then hugs Noah, thanking him again for the paint job. Taking my hand, she turns to Noah and laughs. "I'm stealing Mallory for a little while."

As soon as we walk away, she says, "Zach built a bonfire and there's a small group over here."

"You're dragging me from one bonfire to another? Why?" I ask her at the same time I see him—Evan.

Zach greets us with a drink for both of us. I can smell rum and know I'm going to need it.

"Mallory," Evan says, acknowledging me.

"Evan," I say and take a large gulp from the plastic cup.

I maintain a safe distance from him and continue sipping my drink as Sunny chats about work, a new outfit, and the bonfire. She whispers Evan's name several times, but I can't say I'm really listening. I'm too caught up in him. Our eyes are locked, bonding us across the small fire.

That is until a girl bounces over to him, wrapping her arms around him like she owns him. She's tan, pretty, blonde, and desperate for his attention. From what I can gather, his standard brand of girl. I, on the other hand, am not, which is why his interest in me is confounding.

He shifts, looking uncomfortable while keeping her at a distance. He seems surprised by her presence, yet anyone here can plainly see that she's obviously with him. We remain wordless as our gaze remains locked until the blonde kisses him. Turning away, I see Sunny who looks like how I feel—upset. "I'm sorry, Mal."

Turning my back on him, I ask Sunny who the girl is.

"That's what I've been telling you. Didn't you hear anything I've been saying? I'm not sure what's going on with him."

I down my drink and leave the scene with my heart lying wounded in the pit of my stomach.

The wind is blowing and the ocean is loud, but I still hear Evan yell from behind me. "Mallory! Don't leave." His tone is demanding and I stop then continue to Noah's side. A few people are watching us, my back is to Evan, but I know he's coming. Like me, that string that bonds us together is tightening around his heart as much as it is mine. I wonder if I should give in, like he's starting to.

"Hey, stay here and you'll be fine. I can handle him," Noah says.

He doesn't understand. Hell, I don't, but I know I'm going to have to deal with whatever this pull is between us and either end it or embrace it.

Evan calls my name again and I glance back over my shoulder. I hadn't noticed his un-tucked, wrinkled shirt, or his worn jeans. I hadn't noticed that his hair is messier than usual or that his beard has grown since I saw him yesterday. And when we were staring into each other's eyes mere minutes earlier, I hadn't noticed that he'd been drinking, heavily. But as he stumbles towards me, the whole picture is much clearer. He's a mess and drunk. The problem is that I'm not drunk enough to not notice these things about him now.

His chest presses against my side, his whole being intrusive. "Mallory, please. We need to talk," he says, his voice but a whisper.

"I don't think you should talk to him while he's wasted," Noah says. His hand grasps my shoulder and squeezes.

"I don't think you have a say in it, there, Nohea," Evan strikes, his anger apparent in his tone. He takes a step back from me. "Oh, and by the way, interesting choice in gifts. Did Mallory tell you she died yesterday? I should fucking punch you for that."

Reflexively, my hand touches the white bandage on my head. I look down feeling sorry for the guilt I know Noah feels. He's apologized endlessly and he seemed relieved to know the board got destroyed, or so I told him. I just didn't tell him how it got destroyed.

I look to Noah and then back to Evan, caught in the middle, and unsure of my next move. Zach comes up behind Evan, and takes him by the arm. "C'mon, dude. Not here and not now."

Evan shrugs him off. "It's cool. No scene." He looks back at Noah and says, "Just give me a few minutes ... alone."

Noah shakes his head. "Ashford, you're fucking trashed. You should leave."

When Evan's eyes come back to mine, his anger filters into pain as if I've stabbed him in the heart. *Betrayal—that's the look he gives me.* His voice softens, and he asks, "May I speak with you, privately please?"

Stepping forward, without a word, I walk away from Noah, heading for the parking lot and out of everyone's judgmental line of sight. Evan doesn't say a word either, but I know he's following me. When I reach his car which is parked in the shadows of the lot, I turn around. He's still walking, head down, hands in pockets, broken.

As he nears, I gulp. I need to be strong, but around him I feel weak and vulnerable. He comes so close to me that our bodies are almost touching. My breath deepens as he leans forward and I lean back, away from him, my back hitting his car as his arms trap me in place. "Are you trying to scare me?" I sound bolder than I am.

"You know I would never hurt you," he says, his breath hitting my face as he presses his body to mine. He smells of cigarettes, whiskey, and perfume, *her* perfume. My hands fly to his chest and I push him off. His hands grab my wrists, trying to still me.

"Let go of me. Your date is waiting." I struggle to free myself.

"I'm not with her—"

"Well, she's with you—"

"Don't be silly. She's a girl that thinks she's with me. You and I both know better."

"I don't know anything about you, Evan."

"You know I want you—"

"You want to fuck me and eventually throw me away just like every other girl that you come in contact with."

He stares deep into my eyes and I detect a tinge of vulnerability. "If I wanted to do that, I would've, but here I am *again*."

"I don't know why you're here. You never cared about me. It was all a game to you and I was just another fuck."

"You're breaking my heart, sweetheart," he says, his words callous as he buries his real feelings like he's so good at doing. But I can see through the façade.

"We're even then."

"Don't tell me Mallory Wray got her feelings hurt? You've put on this whole tough girl act since you arrived on the island. Yet, to Kalei, you're warm and fucking cozy. Well, you made your choice tonight, didn't you?"

I stop struggling, shocked by how his words wound and yet make me want to defy everything he says. The tears that threatened seconds earlier dissolve as my anger takes over. Looking him dead in the eyes, I say, "I hate you, Evan. I hate you with all my heart." Pure lies I pray I believe one day.

My hands are dropped. He releases them as if they'll burn him if he holds them any longer. He laughs, but there's no joy behind it as I move around him and start walking away. I stop when he says, "Hate, huh? Well, it looks like we're back to square one, baby."

My head hurts and my hand once again goes to the bandage covering my temple. The tears return. "I revealed my true emotions to you yesterday on the beach." I look down at my bare feet, keeping my back to him, and say, "I didn't make a choice because there was never one to make in my opinion. But tonight, it seems you've made it for me. I have had such strong feelings for you and yet ... whatever, Evan, it doesn't matter and ... you've never made me laugh—"

"That's what you want?" He comes stalking toward me. "What the hell! I've been killing myself trying to figure out how to win your heart when all I had to do was tell some lame jokes to amuse you."

Allowing one last indulgence for us both, I rub my nose against his scruffy chin. Steadying myself, I whisper, "You're going to regret having this conversation while you were drunk. You're not going to remember some of the details, so take note, *baby*, because this is the moment I walk out of your life for good."

Caught in a limbo for what feels like minutes, but is probably only seconds, we stare into each other's eyes. He's upset as reality slaps him across the face. "*Please*, don't give up on me."

Knowing I'll give in if I hold his gaze any longer, I turn away. "I already have." Gathering my gumption back together, I leave him there and return to the bonfire.

Noah offers me his drink. I take it and down the alcohol.

"Guess we need another round." Noah signals his friend for two more.

I bum a cigarette from one of Noah's friends and inhale deeply, impatient for the calm I know it will bring.

Luckily, I have another drink in my hand before I have time to regret my words to Evan. I take a few quick gulps then sip the rest.

"You want to talk about it?"

"Is there really anything to talk about?" I ask, unable to look at Noah. He'll see through me and then I'll break down and I just can't have that happen right now, right here. I'll save that for when I'm alone tonight.

"You know I don't care for the guy, but it's pretty obvious you do. As your friend, I'd tell you to stay away from him. He's bad news, Mallory."

I finally look up, and smirk. "What would you tell me if I wasn't your friend?"

"I'd tell you to stay away from him because he's bad news."

I laugh, acknowledging the humor in his advice. "Yes, he is, but I can't resist a wounded soul."

"Some people are beyond repair. You're fighting a losing battle."

"Honestly, Noah, I don't know if I'm fighting him or myself anymore. All I know is that I'm tired of fighting."

I'm thankful Evan doesn't stay at the party, but I'm also disappointed that he's gone and worried since he drove drunk. I turn to look for Sunny, but sway, off-balance. Noah chuckles as he steadies me. "You okay?" he asks.

"I'm being stupid. I'm just drunk. Will you take me home?"

"Yeah, I think you've definitely had enough to drink."

I fall asleep on the way back and am barely awake when Noah scoops me from his Jeep and carries me to the door. "Key?" he whispers.

Digging into my back pocket, I produce the front door key and he unlocks it easily while still holding me. He brings me inside and I direct him to the couch.

"You sleep on the couch?"

"Yep," I answer, keeping my eyes closed.

He lays me down and kisses me on the back of the head as I snuggle into a tight ball burrowing into the cushions.

"Get some rest, and I'll see you in a few days."

Noah leaves and I lie there with my eyes closed drifting into unconsciousness.

The sound of light rain pattering against the glass door wakes me. Making my way to the bathroom, I notice Sunny isn't home. I'm careful as I walk back to the couch hoping I don't run into any furniture in the dark apartment. The time catches my eye—3:49 a.m.

I slide my skirt off and take my bra off, dropping them to the floor, preferring to sleep in just my soft T-shirt. Just as I start to lie back down, I see someone on the patio through the glass. I freeze as my heart races with fear.

My adrenaline spikes and my eyes adjust to the dark. I'm able to make out Evan's profile slumped in the chair. I hesitate, although deep down, I want to see him. I may not like how he affects me, but I'm realizing that it's not changing no matter how much I want it to. Walking over to the sliding glass door, I open it, and he stands slowly—sluggish. He's wet from the rain and tired in appearance.

I reach my hand out to him, and he takes it reluctantly.

"I don't want to hurt you anymore," he says. He's not able to look at me and I can hear the shame in his voice, and see it in his demeanor.

"Then don't," I whisper, pulling him inside.

18

EVAN

"You said you hate me, Mallory." She doesn't throw words around carelessly, so those words were meant when she said them.

"I don't hate you. *I want to hate you*, but I can't," she replies, looking down briefly.

I have to know if it's too late. The knots in my stomach tighten, and I ask, "What about your heart?"

Her head jerks up, and there's a conviction in her eyes. "My heart feels strongly about you, but it's not hate that it feels." She notices my clothes, and offers, "You're dripping on the carpet. You want to take those off? I'll put them in the dryer for you."

I don't have time to answer before she starts unbuttoning my shirt and taking it off. I reach down and pull off my jeans not embarrassed in the least to be standing in front of her in briefs. I've been too comfortable around her since I met her. There's something about her that puts me at ease. She's soothing to me like no one else.

"I have some boxer shorts you can borrow, if you like?"

My eyes never leave hers as I try to joke. "Are you trying to get me naked?"

She laughs which makes me smile. "How about I get those shorts?" She hurries over to a small dresser strangely positioned outside the bathroom and quickly finds the shorts. She tosses them to me maintaining a safe distance between us. I don't like that she feels she needs to do that.

She lowers her gaze as I strip my briefs off and pull the dry boxers on. I chuckle at how she is looking everywhere except at me. "You do remember that you've seen me naked before, right?"

"I remember ... quite vividly." With a new found determination, she looks up and then surprises me by walking across the room, and standing well within my personal space. I have to admit, I like that she surprises me like this. But I can't tell what she's thinking. She's unpredictable and that frustrates me. I think she's going to do one thing and she does exactly the opposite. To prove my point once again, she runs her finger down my chest, and says, "I don't want to fight with you, but I need some answers."

"Okay." I agree because we do need to talk. I was just hoping to be rested before we did it.

"Why were you on the beach yesterday morning?"

I grab her exploring finger just as it reaches my happy trail —a trail that if I let her wander down further will lead us to do things we can't take back. Things like three-word phrases being confessed that would end me if I was rejected. Things like selfishly wanting to own her body and doing things to her that would make my fantasies blush. And things like making her promises too soon that won't do either of us any good. She makes me want a future that's not possible, and one I don't deserve. She makes me believe in the possibility of happiness, which is everything I've convinced myself is unattainable. So I stop her because this is not the time for any of that, much less sex, and she's not going to put up with my bullshit anymore.

"I was going surfing, dawn patrol. The surf report said the waves there were decent. I wasn't stalking you or anything like that." Even though that's what it sounds like. I leave that part off, not wanting to freak her out, so I stick to the facts.

"But you come here sometimes," she says, looking me straight in the eyes, and cocking an eyebrow, waiting for me to answer. Not a direct question, but she needs an answer.

I'm not sure she really wants to know that I cruise by her place like a horny seventeen-year-old, so I resort to my usual tactics. "Do you want the truth or do you want me to tell you what you want to hear?"

"You already know this about me. The first day we met you knew the answer to that."

She's right. I knew she'd only want the truth. I'm going to confess my dirty secret, though I know that she's not going to be happy to hear it.

"I'll admit that I've driven by hoping to see you, but tonight is the only time I came up here. I just needed to see you. I needed to know you were home and safe." I sigh, running my hands in my hair out of frustration. "Wait, I have come to the apartment before without you knowing."

Her eyes widen. But when her lips part, I get momentarily distracted looking at them, the fullness, the deep pink color, the way she licks them. It's all very distracting.

"Evan?"

I look up, my eyes meeting hers again. "Sorry," I say with a light shake of my head. "The other night I couldn't sleep, so I drove over here, too. I just wanted to check on you. In some fucked up way it brings me peace to know you're safe on that couch, but that night you fell asleep on the surfboard—"

I see her mind turning as the dots connect. "You put me on the couch, didn't you?"

The problem with honesty is that it leads to hope that things will work out the way they should. That's bullshit though because it rarely does. "Like I said, I don't usually come up to the apartment, but ... I did when I saw you on the floor. I was hoping you wouldn't remember. I know from personal experience that a surfboard is not a good place to sleep."

"You stalk me?"

Stalk? *Stalking* ... I wouldn't consider what I do stalking. "No, I'm more like a peeping Tom—"

"Peeping Tom is better than saying stalking?"

"Not better, just more accurate," I correct her. "Like I said, it's usually just a drive by. We've all done that shit before." I scrub my face with my hands, knowing how deranged this all sounds when I say it out loud.

She should be just as upset by my admission as I am by my own creepy behavior, but she's not showing any emotion which makes me nervous. Once again, she surprises when she says, "Tell me about the morning I drowned."

I don't over think this or try to cover to make myself sound better. The truth is good. "Right when I pulled into the lot, you were heading out, attempting to surf. A very poor attempt, I might add."

"What can I say?" she says nonchalantly, "I had other things on my mind during my one and only lesson."

She's cracking jokes. Maybe there's room for a little hope after all. But the memory of her wipeout takes precedence in my mind. "I was already in the water before you fell. That's probably why you didn't see me. God, Mallory, if I hadn't been there ..." I look away as memories of her drowning collides with my past, blurring the lines between long brown hair and short black hair. Different people entirely, but so similar I feel my stomach churn. Instinctively, I reach for her hips, my hands gently on her body, tentative, but reassuring to me. "Can I hold you?"

Her concerned eyes look down. She's unsure of how this is going to play out. My fear is that she might not even want it to. Stepping forward, she closes the gap, and I wrap my arms around her. The tension between us is thick and heavy, weighing us down.

"Hold me, Mallory," I whisper so quiet that I'm not sure if she heard. Maybe it's best if she didn't. I don't know anymore. I've lost myself. I'm lost in all that she is and I need more.

She touches my shoulders, both of us knowing this is not how two lovers embrace. It's not even how two friends embrace. This is how two enemies who've decided to call a truce hold each other and it's painfully frustrating.

"Damn it, Evan! Hold me like you did that first night." She probably thinks she shouldn't have said that, but like me, I can tell she's tired of playing this volleying match. Lowering her voice, she says, "You made me feel beautiful and cared for."

Wanting to also feel that same connection, I squeeze my arms around her. "You are beautiful and I do care ... too much." Enveloping her body with mine, I risk it all and lightly place kisses across the top of her head. "I'm sorry for being a coward. I've just never met anyone who means so much and I don't want to hurt you again."

As she rubs her cheek against mine, I regret not shaving. I have a lot of regrets when it comes to her, the least of which is probably not shaving.

"Can I stay?" I ask, hoping she doesn't throw me out just from the suggestion alone. She'd have every right to do so, but I hope she doesn't.

"You can stay," she replies though she doesn't sound convinced she's doing the right thing, but I'm not going to argue. This perfect angel has given me another chance and I won't blow it this time.

"It's late. You want to go to bed? I'll hold you while we sleep. I promise not to do anything else." The alcohol from earlier mixed with the emotions of tonight has worn me down.

She takes me by the hand and leads me to the couch. "I'm sorry we have to sleep on the couch."

Through my exhausted brain, I offer, "We don't have to. We can go to mine."

"I don't know," she says, shaking her head with worry.

"Nothing tonight, but holding and sleeping. Scout's honor." I hold up the Boy Scout's promise sign.

She acquiesces as she leans her cheek against my chest. "Evan?"

I rub her back, giving her any comfort I can because I know I'm damn lucky that she's letting me back in even if it's just for tonight. "Hmm?"

"Promise me tomorrow that you'll be there when I wake up."

My chest aches as her words stab my heart. I can't show my weakness, but I can give her what she wants because it's what I want, too. "I'll be there, I promise."

She releases a sigh then says, "Okay, let me grab a few things and we can go, but first, I really need to know who the girl at the beach was. You said you weren't with her, but it looked—"

"I've been with her before." I feel ashamed of my past, but I won't lie to her. "One time. Over a year ago."

"She kissed you—"

"I didn't kiss her tonight. I didn't bring her to the bonfire or leave with her. She was there and wanted to hook up. I told her I wasn't interested." I look back up because I know this might set us back again. "I think it was obvious to everyone there *who* I'm interested in. You know my history or rumors of my history, Mallory. I can't change it, so please don't hold it against me. It's not who I am anymore."

I turn back around feeling exposed and fucking vulnerable. I don't like this feeling. I don't like that I have to admit my deepest secrets to her, but if it opens the door to her heart even just a little, it's worth it. Staring out the glass door, I watch the rain turn to a light drizzle then stop. Hawaiian showers happen often, but don't last long.

She doesn't say anything as she moves about gathering her stuff for the night. I realize the boxers I'm wearing fit too well, too well to be hers. *She put me in some other guy's underwear.* I'd be bothered if I wasn't impressed by her nerve. When she's ready, I take her hand and we walk to the car. She's different tonight—fragile—more careful. I've done this to her. I've broken her spirit and her trust. Silently, I vow to never hurt this girl again.

"You drove drunk tonight ... a couple of times. You shouldn't do that," she says, not reprimanding, just informing me. "I'll drive." She holds her hand out for the keys.

Placing them in her hand, my fingertips scrape lightly across her palm and our eyes meet. "You're right. I shouldn't have."

She nods and walks to the driver's side of the car.

It's quiet in the car on the drive over, and yet feels

calming under the circumstances. We walk hand in hand down the path, and I open the door allowing her to enter first. She stops, and peeks in, hesitant to enter. I wait a few seconds, and then ask, "Are you all right?"

She walks all the way inside, turns with an unconvincing smile on display, and says, "Fine."

I set her bag down and step into host mode. "I'll grab you some water, unless you'd like something stronger?"

"No, water's good." She takes her bag, and asks, "Do you mind if I get ready in the bathroom."

Although I'm disappointed I won't get to see her naked, I'm eased by the fact that I'll be holding her all night. "Make yourself at home."

I bring the waters to the nightstand and stand there looking down at her boxers on my body. After taking them off, I pull a pair of my own boxer briefs from the dresser and slip them on. I sit on the edge of the bed listening to the various sounds coming from the bathroom: the faucet being turned on and off, the brushing of teeth, and the zipper of her bag. The door opens and she appears like an angel in the doorway with the glow from the bathroom light illuminating her from behind. She's the hottest damn angel I could ever imagine even dreaming of, much less seeing. She's wearing a tight white tank top and a pair of white panties. So simple and yet, she's gorgeous.

Heading straight for me, she sits down on my lap. Her arm wraps around my shoulders, and she smiles at me. "I didn't think I'd ever be back here and now that I am, I'm glad I came."

"Why are you glad? I need to know. I need to hear you tell me."

She crawls on top of the covers then tucks her body underneath. Flopping back onto the pillows, she says,

"Because this is where I slept the best since I've been in Hawaii."

Her playful side makes my heart pound from pure happiness. I lean down and kiss her on the shoulder before getting up to brush my teeth. Not able to contain my own theories on the reason she slept here so well, I say, "You sure it wasn't exhaustion from that night's activities?"

She grabs the pillow next to her and tosses it at me as hard as she can. Scrambling out of the line of fire, I laugh as I run into the bathroom.

When I return, she's curled up on her side, facing my side of the bed. I slide under the covers and brush a section of hair from her forehead. "Hi, beautiful."

"Hi." There is a lightness in her eyes that eases my worries. "You still sleepy?" she asks.

"No, I think I've gotten my second wind."

"I think I did, too," she whispers as her fingertips stroke feather light over my cheek. Her hand comes to rest on my neck. "Can I ask you more questions?"

"Sure, but only if I get to ask some."

"That's fair." She acts as if she doesn't know what she wants to ask me, but I can tell it's a ploy. "Why aren't you in school?"

I glance away, chuckling before I respond because one thing I've learned about Mallory is there is always more going on inside that pretty head of hers than she lets on. "I've gone two years. Technically, I'm a junior."

"Why aren't you in school? I mean, Kate told me you didn't go last year and you're not registered for the fall either. Why?"

I try to formulate the perfect answer. Usually, I try to avoid this line of questioning and yet this is the first thing she wants to know about me. *Figures.* "I got into some trouble. I didn't want my grades to slip and there was no way I could've stayed and not ruin my grade point average."

"That seems contradictory. If you cared that much about your grades then you wouldn't have gotten into trouble in the first place, right?" She raises her eyebrow at me not scolding, but curious, sincerely interested in what I have to say. "What kind of trouble?"

How do I answer this without saying too much? "I got a little out of hand with my professors."

She doesn't say anything, but a fresh smirk on her face signifies she understands completely. I think she has me figured out more than I want to admit.

"I kind of thought I was smarter than them," I add.

She laughs softly, rolling onto her back. "Why does that not surprise me?"

"Geez, I have no idea," I say, letting a little sarcasm slip out.

She rolls back over and rubs my arm. Her gentle touches affect me more than she knows. She is warmth and sunshine and the light to my dark. She makes me want to bare my soul even though I shouldn't.

"Where'd you go to school anyway?"

This always reveals more than I'm comfortable sharing with people. I'm usually embarrassed because they will instantly think I'm an arrogant prick, like I'm bragging. "A school in England for a year and then I transferred to one over in Connecticut."

Her eyes narrow and I can almost see her brain cogs turning. "Where in England?"

I roll over, avoiding eye contact, draping my arm over my eyes, and whisper, "A small town outside of London."

"Oxford?"

Um ... I don't answer.

"And, the school in Connecticut, *Yale?*"

Closing my eyes, I think of my cover. I always have a cover with girls and yet nothing comes to mind to help me out when I need it most.

She shimmies against me, resting her body half on top of mine. I take a deep breath, wanting to grab her and rub against her and kiss her breathless. I desperately want to be inside of her, but after taking another deep breath, I come to my senses. I promised her I wouldn't make a move and need to keep that promise.

"Evan?"

"Yeah?"

"You went to Oxford *and* Yale?"

"Yeah."

I move my arm, bringing her tighter against me so she can't see my face. "Yes, those are the two schools. Have you heard of them?" I ask an octave too high to sound natural and once again sarcastically. I'm kind of hoping this will throw her off the scent. I also know she's smart, so I know this plan won't actually work.

She moves over me, hovering above and looks down into my eyes. Her minty breath is warm and makes me feel dizzy from the close proximity. This is a similar feeling to how I felt the first day I spent with her.

She hits me in the arm. "You're really fucking smart then?"

"Just because you go to those schools doesn—"

"Admit it! You're a smarty pants." She giggles then says, "I already knew it anyway. So you can just admit it now."

She's adorable. "Fine," I say with a smile plastered on my face. "I'm a smarty pants. Happy?"

Lowering all the way down, she rests on my chest. "But not just smart. You're like super intelligent."

It's not a question, so I don't feel the need to say anything more about it. "Can we change the topic? It's my turn anyway. What year are you?"

She pauses as if she's now a little uncomfortable being the center of the conversation. "I'm a senior this fall. You already know where I go to school, don't you?"

"Yes."

"Because you're observant, always paying attention to the details. What gave it away?"

"Beside the University of Colorado t-shirt you slept in the other night, Noah put the mascot on your surfboard."

"Ahhh, yes, that's right. The surfboard."

"I don't want to talk about him or that board. Do you have a boyfriend back home?"

"Oh!" She seems surprised. I hear a hint of irritation as if the topic itself is offensive. "If I had a boyfriend, do you think I would've slept with you?"

"No, but making sure, just in case. I don't want to have to deal with an angry haole. And for the record, we haven't done that much sleeping together." I snicker.

With a loud laugh, she rolls onto her back and rubs her stomach. I place my hand on top of hers and she doesn't move it, which lets me know I haven't overstepped any boundaries.

She surprises me by continuing. "I had a boyfriend last year, but we broke up a few months ago."

"Why'd you break up? Better offer? Did you have a line of guys waiting to take his place?"

An annoyed scoff escapes her and she replies while entwining our fingers. "He broke up with me for another girl. He'd been cheating on me for a while though."

"He's an idiot, baby." I say this with more passion than I probably should, but he is a total asshat for cheating on her.

Looking on the bright side—she's in Hawaii because he was stupid for letting her go. Maybe I should thank him.

Her hand leaves mine, and she brushes my chin with the back of it. "You're sweet."

"I'm super intelligent too, remember?"

"Yes, I remember," she says.

I can't keep my hands off of her any longer. Screw the promise. I roll over maneuvering between her legs while holding her by the hips and kiss her belly button. She smiles down at me, and asks, "How long you were you planning on torturing us?"

"I promised I'd be a good boy." I lean down again and dip my tongue into her belly button and swirl it. "Is this being a good boy?"

Her uninhibited laugh is an angel's voice pulling me from my life's wreckage. "That's being a *very* good boy." Her fingers roam through my hair and lightly tug.

With my fingertips, I push her tank top further up her body to expose her stomach, but keep her breasts hidden from view. I slide my hands up and down her curves several times then rest my cheek on her stomach. I need a moment to collect myself, to gain control over my urges because even if this girl begged me, I wouldn't make love to her. *That might be a lie. Okay, that's totally a lie.* If she was begging me I would take her in an instant, but I shouldn't, not tonight. I close my eyes and wonder at what point in the last few weeks I started caring about anyone other than myself. Sensing my unease, she strokes her fingers through my hair in a comforting manner, gentle. "Hey, what's wrong?" she asks.

I sigh, keeping my eyes closed. "Nothing."

"Come on, Evan. You told me you wouldn't lie to me."

She's got a point and she's not afraid to use it. "I haven't felt like this in a long time." I keep my head lowered, knowing what she's going to ask next, so I save her the trouble. "I like you." Suddenly, I feel like I'm ten years old and telling a girl that I have a crush on her. "I care about you."

"You haven't opened your heart in a long time. I know that was hard for you. Thank you for opening it for me. I care about you, too." Then she adds, "Sometimes I worry that I care too much."

I look at her and our eyes connect. Her sweet soul visibly displayed just for me in the soft moonlight of the room. My lips part and my breathing slows as I analyze my beautiful girl's face. *My girl.* I still need to make her my girl, only mine, and tonight I'll do whatever it takes to make that happen.

19

EVAN

Mallory Wray is stunning, especially when she goes after what she wants.

"I know you said you'd be good, but do you think you might be a little bad for me?" she asks. Her cheeks turn the perfect shade of rose petal pink, embarrassed for being direct.

I could easily give her all she wants right now. I want the same, but she deserves more than a few tried and true smooth moves and a certain perfected smile. I have to use my mind with her which turns me on so fucking much.

Exhaling loudly, I'm frustrated that my conscience has decided to intervene. The words fall from my lips before I have a chance to stop them. "I want to be with you so bad, baby, but I think we should wait." She moves a few inches higher on the bed, purposely positioning the apex of her thighs right above my mouth. "Are you trying to drop a hint here?" I ask.

"Am I being too subtle?" She tilts her pelvis up and taps me on the chin ... twice.

"Subtlety is my specialty."

"Really? I never took you as the subtle type," she says, mocking me.

"Watch out little girl, I can do subtle." I look her in the eyes and take her challenge. Taking her panties in hand, I, oh so slowly, slide them down. I lift up on bended knees and start removing them from her ankles when she playfully kicks them off and they go flying over my head. "That's not so subtle," I tease. "Oh, screw subtlety!" I pin her ankles to the bed beside me and bend forward.

Giddiness overcomes her, but her impatience shines through. She tilts her middle up toward my mouth again.

I don't do this. I don't go down on women. I have done it before, years ago, when I was a horny-assed teenager in high school. But even then I did it only to my girlfriend at the time, never casually and never to a girl I was fucking for the week. It's way too personal for that. But this is different, not cavalier at all. Mallory has awakened something in me that's long been dormant.

Desire bubbles inside of me. I haven't *desired* anyone in years. I've lusted and I've always gotten what I lusted after. But *desire*, desire feels like an old friend that I didn't know I missed until it returned. *I desire this girl.* I need to taste this girl. It's something I mistakenly didn't do the first couple of times we were together. I took her for granted. I won't make that mistake again.

I adjust my scruffy face toward her wet center. The phrase '*be careful what you wish for because you just might get it*' comes to mind. I dip my tongue, worried this might be the end of me in the best of ways. I want her like I've never wanted any woman before in my life. I just don't want to screw this up. I need her to like this, to like me.

The first contact makes my head swim as she wriggles and releases a quiet moan. I take her by the hips, holding her down. I want her to feel how beautifully connected we are. I stiffen my tongue and swirl it quickly where I know she'll react. I start to relax and indulge by bringing my tongue into my mouth and savoring her sweetness. My eyes close at the sensation, and I quickly delve back in wanting to devour her. Her hips move beneath my hands as I lick. In this moment, I can be everything she needs me to be and use my tongue to make love to her.

"Oh God! Yes!" She cries out.

Surprised by such a strong verbal response, I back up and slip two fingers inside. She thrusts with pleasure, grabbing my hair tightly in her hands and squeezes, tugs, pulls, and encourages me. I'm not done with her. I bring my fingers to my mouth and suck.

She's not pleased by the pause in action, and looks up. When she sees what I'm doing, her mouth drops open, and she watches as I push them into her again, methodically, while resting my other hand on her abdomen. I watch as she tosses her head back, panting. I've never felt possessive over a girl, ever, but this girl is different. She challenges me in so many ways and owning her so completely right now makes me feel powerful just from the thought.

"Look at me, Mallory," I demand, but keep my voice low.

Her head shoots up and our eyes meet as I swirl my tongue around her gloriousness. The sounds of her pleasure make my cock throb, so I press it into the mattress seeking some kind of relief. My body seems to have its own agenda and I'm thinking this mattress isn't going to satisfy that need. She drops her head against the pillow maintaining our eye contact. Her eyes look how mine feel, heavy with lust, but a depth of something more hidden behind the beautiful color.

The grip on my locks tightens, but the pain is nothing

compared to the pleasure I'm receiving from this simple act of intimacy. *That's it.* That's why I haven't done this in forever. This is something I can do to her to show my feelings through my body. *This is intimacy.* I think my heart stopped at the exact second I discovered that I'm in love. *I'm in love with Mallory.*

As I continue, she struggles to keep her eyes on me, so I give her a reprieve. "I want you to come for me, baby."

Her head drops back and her body jerks forward, harder against my mouth and she cries out in ecstasy. I enjoy the sight of her so tense and yet euphoric, and it's all because of me. As she settles back down, relaxing onto the bed, I leave a wet trail of kisses on her stomach.

Just as I lower the hem down to cover her midsection, she says, "I want you in me, Evan." Her eyes go wide like the words accidentally slipped out.

Crawling up her body, I press my hardness against her stomach. "I think you can tell how much I want to be inside of you, too, baby, but, not tonight." *I can't believe I just fucking said that.* This is the girl of my dreams. I'm in love with this girl, but that is the exact reason I shouldn't do it. "I don't want to screw this up," I say as her hands rub my back, "so I think this should be all we do tonight."

"But I want to," she says, bringing my cupped face to hers and kissing me, still encouraging me.

I pull back, brow furrowed in confusion, to gaze down at this siren beneath me. She runs her nose along my jaw and ends near my ear. She whispers, "I want you, Evan. I *need* you."

"Fuck, Mallory. What are you doing to me? I don't have the willpower to fight you. We should stop." I sound authoritative and in control, but even I can hear the slight whine in the back of my throat.

She giggles. *So much for control.*

She kisses me again then licks the side of my mouth. Maybe I have died and actually did get into heaven despite my mother damning me to hell. My eyes close at the sensory overload of her plush lips on me.

I jump, pinning her by the wrists to the bed. "No! You must stop." Me and my throbbing erection roll onto my back and I slam my arms down next to me.

Rolling onto her side, she props her head up by her elbow. "Evan Ashford, I think your façade is slipping. I think you like me."

With an epic roll of my eyes, I laugh with mild irritation. Okay, it's actually sexual frustration, but I play it up as I look over at the temptress next to me. She's glowing and beautiful and her expression is proud. "I'm not playing games with you. I can admit defeat."

"So, you're comparing *liking me* to losing?" she asks incredulously.

"That's not what I meant. It … it feels like freedom. Does that make any sense?"

"Because you don't have to put on the charade for me." She leans forward and kisses me on the tip of my nose then retreats to lay flat on her back. "I like you, too by the way. There, we're even. Does that make you feel better?" She asks smugly. "It is freeing, isn't it?"

"Like jumping off a cliff."

"Or falling in love for the first time."

I'm stunned by her ability to say that so easily. She smiles and my heart fucking melts and I think for the first time in my life, I know exactly what she means. I reach over and pull her against my side. After bringing the sheets up to cover our chests, I kiss her on the forehead. "It's exactly like that," I whisper. "Goodnight, baby."

MORNING COMES TOO SOON when I'm holding Mallory in my arms. Morning means daylight, which means getting out of bed, which also means not holding her much longer. I sigh in discontentment at this bothersome predicament.

She shuffles, snuggling closer as her breath warms me with its steady cadence. I tighten my arm around her shoulders and appreciate what I can tell are her last few moments of sleep.

Looking down at her, I allow myself to indulge in her natural beauty and how she fits so perfectly into my side. I can't hide my smile just as her eyes open and she looks up at me. In the cutest groggy voice, she asks, "What are you smiling about, gorgeous?"

Her name for me comes as a surprise. "You think I'm gorgeous?"

She looks down, drawing her hand across my bare chest, and adds, "Who doesn't think you're gorgeous?"

I am well aware of the attention I get from the opposite sex, but none of it ever mattered because it's superficial. It's meaningless, but for some reason I care that Mallory thinks I'm attractive. "I don't care about anyone else, just what you think of me."

Her eyes flicker back to meet mine and with a smile reflected in them, she says, "In that case, I think you're really fantastically gorgeous, Evan."

"Well, I think you're really fantastically gorgeous too, baby." I back my words with a lingering kiss on her forehead.

She giggles, encouraging me to ask, "What has you all happy this morning?"

She sits up and slides her face closer to mine. Her

expression goes from playful to genuine within the flash of a second, before she says, "You're here. You're here with me this morning just like you promised."

I gulp, not wanting to be anywhere else but with her, and I want her to know that. "Mallory," she remains calmly looking at me as I continue, "I should explain about that first morning when you woke up mad."

"I didn't wake up mad. I was hurt when I discovered you left me here alone."

I pull her back down into my arms. "I know you were, but that wasn't my intention. You thought I had just screwed you over, but it wasn't like that for me. It was actually the complete opposite." This is the part that still gets jumbled in my own mind, much less trying to verbalize it to sound like I know what I'm talking about.

My hesitation causes her to look up and rest her chin on my chest, waiting. "Are you okay? We don't have to talk about this right now. I mean, we did just wake up."

"No, I want to say this. You need to know that I wasn't abandoning you. I didn't treat our night lightly. It was so much more to me than that. But, I had to organize my thoughts and get some clarity on the situation, *on us*. I did that by surfing."

I take a deep breath and finish. "Surfing helps me clear my mind of the extraneous stuff that's not important. I can focus on the waves and what I need to, which for me that morning, was you."

"Evan, I should apologize—" She sits up trying to talk, but I quickly cut her off.

"No, don't. You don't have to apologize. I really need to tell you this because it's important and yet I feel like such an asshole for letting this get out of hand." I sit up, touching her arm, wanting to touch more. "I knew you were different.

I knew as soon as you made your smart-ass comments to me at the airport. Then during our conversation at the diner, I realized you were too good for me. You became a challenge. So when we got to my place and kissed, it was surprising. You let me make love to you. I almost couldn't contain myself. I fucking won the lottery that day and I tried to play it off like what we were sharing was just a standard fuck for me. But you sensed how I really felt and you kept going. Why'd you go through with it? That's not you. I knew when I met you that you didn't do that kind of stuff and yet you did with me. Is it because you're on vacation? Wait, I might not want to hear the answer. Do I want to know the answer?"

I wait for her to respond, but I can tell she's processing everything I just laid on her.

"When you say you 'won the lottery' are you referring to me?"

I nod my head, unsure of why she's focusing on that tidbit out all of the other stuff I said.

"Let me get this straight. You went surfing to think about the feelings you had already developed for me starting at the airport and you were shocked that a girl like me would come home and sleep with you? And now, you want to know why I had sex—"

"Yes, that sounds about right, but I prefer the term make love."

"Okay, you want to know why I let you *'make love'* to me that day?"

"Yes."

She narrows her eyes in analysis of me and starts to say something, but then stops. Her mouth opens in confusion, but nothing comes out again. Finally, she scratches her head, leaving her hand to lightly rub against the bandage across her temple, and says, "Thank you. Thank you, Evan." She throws her arms around my neck and using me as resistance, she pulls herself onto my lap.

I try to captivate her mind and soul, embracing her fully. "Why are you thanking me, baby?" I whisper into her ear while inhaling her in. She's flowers and beach, sunlight, and beauty combined.

When she looks down, her dark lashes lie in beautiful contrast against her pink blushing cheeks. Slowly, she lifts them up and looks me in the eyes. "No one has ever treated me like that before. You look at me like I'm special."

I don't comprehend her words because I can't understand their meaning in the context. What does she mean by that? "Special? You're everything," I say, running my hand softly across her cheek and bringing her in for a kiss. Our tongues meet eagerly and as I'm absorbing every taste and sound that she makes, I pull back and look at her. "Mallory, you're beautiful and smart. You are special. Promise me you won't ever settle for being treated less than that, even if it's by me. Because if I ever forget even for a second how wonderful you are, you should leave me. I'm not perfect as you already know. I didn't feel worthy that first night and I still don't, but I'm going to try to be the man you deserve. I want this to work out—"

"I'm here for the summer, but I only have just a little over a month left." Her tone is solemn, and the reality that she's going to leave me squeezes my heart.

"We'll just make the most of our time left together—"

"But you sounded like you meant more than just a month." She phrases this more like a question and it makes me feel that maybe she's not into me as much as I'm into her. Maybe I just misread everything that's happening between us.

"I was just, you know, rambling. I know you only have a month. There's no pressure from me," I say, silently berating myself for opening up to her too soon.

She's still looking at me, waiting for me to say something else, but I don't know how to back track and I don't want to lie, so I change the topic. "Should we get some breakfast?"

20

MALLORY

"I have to be at work in a little while. I don't usually sleep this late." I wanted him by my side when I woke up and he is, but he's probably wondering now what?

"So breakfast?" He asks.

"Coffee?"

"Don't tell me you don't eat breakfast, Mallory. It's the most important meal of the day," He leans over and kisses me on the forehead. Taking my hand, he smiles as he looks into my eyes, searching them. "I need to know we're good. We told each other stuff that we shouldn't have confessed this soon into a relationship, but I think I'm good with that. I like this, that we're this comfortable."

I gulp, realizing he used the word *'relationship'* while referring to us. My insides warm at the thought there might be an actual 'us.' I swallow the building tension and sit up. "You're right, Evan, and I like our honesty, too."

Swinging my legs off the side of the bed, a light touch on my shoulder stops me. "Mallory." He looks me straight in the eyes. "I don't want you to date anyone else, and I won't date anyone else either."

I'm speechless by his declaration. His eyes beg me to say something, to let him know that I'm not rejecting him, making me wonder if he's ever been rejected before. I also wonder if he's even been exclusive with a girl before.

"Evan," I say, getting as close as I can to him and brushing my lips against his.

His hands go to my waist and hold me as his eyelids drop close. I inhale the moment, savoring every second. With our eyes closed, I whisper, "I only want to be with you."

I've been holding back on my true feelings for too long. Giving in, body and soul, I become one with him. It's no longer Mallory and Evan. It's us as one now and I kiss him.

He gently uses his weight to push me back onto the bed. His chest presses into mine as we deepen the kiss, his hand finding their rightful place on my chest, right over my heart. His lips work their way down my neck to linger between my breasts then he sighs in satisfaction. I slowly drag my hands up his back and hold him to me. He asks, "When do you have to be at work?"

"Eleven."

"It's ten. You get ready, and I'll make you coffee. Then, I'll drive you to work."

"That's an offer I can't refuse. Do you work today?"

"Yeah, but not until noon."

Fifteen minutes later, I step out of the shower and wrap a towel around me. Standing in front of the mirror, I see beautiful Mallory again. I laugh that a boy affects my self-esteem like this, but there are definitely worse things he could be affecting, that's for sure.

I'd taken the bandage off before my shower and lean toward the mirror to get a better look at the stitches. It's starting to heal and doesn't look that bad.

There's a soft knock at the door.

"You can come in, Evan," I say, rolling my eyes. "We've slept together, so I think we're past knocking at this point."

The door opens and he leans against the frame holding a tall travel mug out to me. "You look beautiful," he says, admiring me. I feel a little embarrassed under his adoring eyes, and blush, feeling the heat reach my cheeks. "Especially when you blush ... you have ten minutes until we need to leave. If you keep that up, you're going to be calling in because I'm not gonna let you walk out that door."

My cheeks flame at his heated insinuation, knowing that's *exactly* what I want to do with my day—not walk out that door. Memories of our time having sex flood my mind and I unknowingly smile. "Seriously, Mallory, you've been warned. One more adorable gesture like that and I'm calling Alana myself to tell her you're not coming in." He comes over and wraps his arms around me. He whispers, "I'm here for you. I'm not going anywhere. We're together now."

My heart melts at the sweetness of this man.

He kisses me on the cheek at the same time I feel his hand slide under my towel and rub my ass. I smirk, and he smacks it. "Your head looks good," he says, referring to my stitches. "Get ready, good looking, you've only got five minutes now."

I burst out laughing when I notice how the sting on my butt cheek is delightfully tingling. Evan Ashford is going to be the death of me—one way or the other—and yet I'll happily walk hand in hand towards that death with him. I don't have time to dwell on the joy I feel, the happiest I've been in ages. I've had boyfriends in high school and a couple in college, but I've never felt for them what I feel for Evan.

After throwing some clothes on with light makeup—lip

gloss and mascara, we hurry out the door. He holds my hand while he drives me to work. Racing around to my side of the car, he opens the door when we arrive. When I stand up, he pulls me against him, and says, "Can I pick you up after work?"

Sunny parks next to us and gets out with a devious look on her face. "Good morning, Mallory. *Evan*."

Evan releases me and returns the greeting. "Good morning, Sunny. If it's all right with you, I'm going to be spending an inordinate amount of time with your best friend for the remainder of the summer." He leans towards her, lowers his voice, and adds, "I'm kind of smitten with her."

They share an elbow nudge then laugh. "Well, I guess that's all right by me," she says sassily. "I'll see you inside, Mal."

I grab two handfuls of his T-shirt and pull him closer. "I'll see you later then."

"I'll be here."

"*Goodbye.*"

"Goodbye, baby."

We say this, but remain standing there still staring at each other. The fire building in his eyes reflects the same in mine.

"So, I guess I should go in now. I think I'm officially late."

"Uh-huh, late, definitely late."

I can't resist him any longer. I lift up on my toes and kiss him hard. He returns the favor.

"We should probably open up for the lunch crowd. Don't ya think, Mallory?"

We jump apart as if we were just busted by our parents. Alana is standing between us and the entrance to Big Kehones with her arms crossed.

"Hi, Alana," Evan says, nodding at her, smirking, and adjusting his pants.

"Aloha, Evan. If you're not here for lunch, I suggest you remove your hands from my employee so she can get to work."

His hands immediately drop to his sides, and he chuckles. "Yes, Ma'am. Sorry, I was just dropping Mallory off."

"Okay then. She's here, so you have a good day. Mallory?" Alana looks at me, waiting. She's teasing, trying to refrain from smiling.

I rush past him, smacking him on the ass, and whisper, "See you later, sexy." With a smirk and a little extra wiggle to my hips, I walk inside with Alana.

Sunny is at the bar. She's busy filling ketchup containers when Alana and I come inside. Alana looks at me, all knowing, and says, "You and Evan Ashford are dating." It's not a question, but she seems to ponder it.

Discussing who I'm dating is an embarrassing conversation to have with my boss, but the relationship is so new it's weird to talk about it with anyone. I'd hate to jinx it. I start filling a napkin dispenser, keeping my eyes on the task at hand. "Yes, we are." I sound too giddy to appear casual.

Sunny giggles then interrupts, "They're cute, aren't they?"

"Cute, just like you and Zach," Alana says, enjoying what is obviously going to be the topic of discussion today.

She points her finger, swinging it between me and Sunny and adds, "Don't fall in love too fast, girls. You're strong, independent women. Don't ever feel like you have to rely on a man. You're educated and smart. Let life take you where you're supposed to be. Never hold back."

Letting her words sink in, it makes me wonder. "Even in love?" I ask.

"Especially in love. But true love allows you to be who you're meant to be. It doesn't dictate your potential."

"Work hard, play harder?" Sunny asks, looking at Alana for advice.

"Live life with passion and have fun, but do it for you." She waves us off as she turns around, and starts walking toward the back office. "Enough of the lecture. Are we ready for the lunch rush?"

NOAH COMES in for a late lunch with his friends. He sits at the bar as the others grab a table.

"Hey, you took the bandage off. How are you feeling today?" he asks.

My hand reflexively goes to my wound. "Yeah, I had it on long enough. It's healing and I'm fine."

"Good to hear because you had a lot to drink—"

"I slept it off."

"So, I was thinking we could hang out sometime this week. What's your schedule look like?"

"Oh, um ..." I feel weird saying this, but I respect Evan enough to know it's the right thing to do. "Listen, this may sound crazy, especially after last night, but I think you should know ..." He readjusts on his barstool, giving me his complete, undivided attention. "I've started seeing Evan."

"Seeing?"

I make myself clearer. "Dating."

"I left your place less than twelve hours ago. After the bonfire, how'd you ..." Everything seems to dawn on him as he searches my eyes for answers. *"Oh."* He closes his eyes as if he's coming to grips with this new revelation. He slowly shakes his head then looks at me again. "You know I don't like the guy, but I can see you do." He analyzes my face. "You just need to get him out of your system. I get it—"

"No, it's not like that, Noah. It's like he's a part of my system. I like him ... *a lot*."

"Mallory," he says, his tone almost condescending, "you're not the first girl to fall for Ashford and you won't be the last. Hell, you're only here until the beginning of August. How serious can it really be?"

I lean forward, putting my hands flat on the counter in front of me. "It's pretty damn serious."

His hands go up, and a small, arrogant smile crosses his usually charming face. "Okay, okay. I get it. I just want you to know when you need a friend, I'll be here for you."

"That sounds like you mean when he dumps me you'll be here for me?"

"That's exactly what I mean."

The air stills around us as I come to terms with the harshness of his words, the real possibility in his warning.

"I need you to respect my decision here, Noah."

He sighs in obvious disappointment. "I'm just surprised you'd fall for his ... never mind. Does this mean we can't hang out anymore because he's so damn jealous?"

Taking Alana's words to heart, I say, "We can still hang out. Now, can I get you something to eat?"

I WALK out of the restaurant and find Evan leaning against his car holding a large flowering plant. My knees weaken as he smiles at me.

"Hi, beautiful. I brought you flowers." He holds the potted plant out to me.

"You brought me more than flowers, Evan. This is a bush."

"I wanted you to always have flowers blooming around you."

I take the hibiscus bush and hug my arms around it and remember how my ex-boyfriend only gave me flowers twice. Once when he was trying to woo me into having sex with him—sadly, it worked. The other time was when he cheated on me and that felt more like he was really trying to say, *'Sorry I cheated on you and I like having sex with other women better than with you, but I still want the option of having sex with you when I can't find it anywhere else.'* So, needless to say, receiving flowers just because someone cares about you is a foreign concept to me. "I love it. Thank you."

His hands work their way through the bush, pushing the branches aside until he sees me. He leans through the parted plant, cups my face, and kisses me. "I missed you," he whispers against my lips, "but," he releases the branches which smack back together in front of my face, "we need to go. I've got plans for you, sexy girl."

He opens the car door allowing me and my plant to slide down into the seat and then takes the pot. After wedging it in the back, we drive out of the parking lot, but before leaving the lot, he asks, "What are you smiling about?"

"You ... this." I stumble through my words because I feel so good. "I'm just really happy right now."

He rests his hand on my bare knee and gives it a little squeeze. "So am I." I can see the sincerity in his eyes and know he means what he says.

"So, are you going to fill me in on these big plans of yours?"

"No."

"I had a feeling you might say that."

"Do I need anything for these so called plans?"

"Definitely no."

"That's intriguing." I sit back and enjoy the rest of the ride to his place. We have the windows cracked open and the music becomes background to the sounds of the ocean.

As we park and then walk the side path to his house, he carries my plant for me and holds my hand. Once inside, I flop onto the couch and he retreats to the bathroom for a minute. Upon his return, he says, "Follow me."

We walk out the door to a set of flagstone steps that lead down to the back of the property, a strip of beach. With the setting sun as a backdrop, I see a large blanket spread out on top of the sand, a picnic basket, and champagne. My eyes go from the set-up to the smiling man before me as I realize the efforts he went to make this romantic and memorable. "You did all this?"

He's beaming. "Ms. Chart put the basket together and I set it all up. It's all for you, Mallory. Do you like it?"

"I love it."

"Good," he says, taking me by the hand and over to the blanket.

We sit down, and I flip off the sneakers I wore for work and lay back on the soft blanket and staring up at the sky, never feeling more content. "This is paradise."

I sit back up and he hands me a glass of champagne, and says, "In celebration of us."

We toast and sip, and then I ask, "Who is Ms. Chart?"

"She's our house manager."

"What's a house manager?"

He laughs to himself, but not in a mocking way. "She runs the property and oversees the other employees to keep things running smoothly."

"Since your parents are away?"

"She works here year round, but occasionally flies to New York to help out there. My parents spend about two months out of the year here. A month in winter and a month during the summer. They're flying in later this week."

"Will I meet them?" I watch as he looks out into the ocean as if searching for an answer out there.

When he looks back at me, the happy I saw a second earlier has disappeared. "If you like, you can."

His hesitancy makes me nervous.

"Do you want me to?" I ask the question although I fear his answer.

"I want to introduce you to everyone special in life, like Ms. Chart, but my parents and I aren't that close these days." He lies down on the blanket, and sighs. "I don't like talking about my family situation that much, but I know you need answers. I know you need them for us to work out. I'm not trying to hide anything from you. I'm just not used to talking about this stuff and usually try to avoid it."

I lay back down, placing my head on his shoulder. "Tell me when you're ready."

"I want to tell you. I, uh, I just ... I'm a disappointment to them. I don't want you disappointed in me, too."

I slide my fingers down the palm of his hand and inter-twine them with his. "I won't be. Remember, it's you and me now."

He chuckles lightly, watching as the sun sets into the ocean. Then he surprises me by opening up. "Something happened right before I went to England and it messed with my head. I had trouble concentrating and I developed an attitude. I guess I probably already had the attitude, so it just got worse. I was about to get booted from university, so my adviser called my parents. He was a good guy and only did it out of concern, but a decision was made and that's how I ended up at Yale."

"What happened before school?"

He rolls towards me and strokes my hair. "I don't want to talk about that. I'm sorry. I will, but not yet, not tonight."

I whisper my reassurance that it's fine, and he continues, "Yale was a disaster from the start. Some of the big guys on campus didn't appreciate me swooping in on their territory. They were legacy, but really, I think it's that they didn't appreciate their girlfriends liking me." He laughs at the memory. "Maybe they didn't like me screwing their girl-friends. That's probably more accurate."

I roll my eyes, but I'm not surprised by his statement.

Lying on his back, his hands drop to his sides, and I already miss his touch. He says, "I lost interest in school and just wanted a break, so I dropped out and went home. It only took a month before I was on my parent's last nerve and they were on mine. I packed a suitcase and came out here. That was the biggest crime in their eyes. They had already plotted my whole life out in New York. I was set up with a job, an apartment, even a girlfriend if I wanted, but it was just one big fucking social climbing game there. I didn't want anything to do with it." He squeezes his eyes like he's wishing the memories away.

His eyes flash open and he looks at me. "I'm sorry. Tonight wasn't supposed to be about this crap—"

"No, don't apologize. I like when you share with me. I want to know all about you. I know you in a very intimate way, but I really don't know who you are as a person."

"I want to know all about you, too."

I sit up and finish my champagne. He's there, ready to top it off as I soon as I swallow.

"I'd rather kiss you," he says.

He leans over and kisses me, making me want more of this man than I should. He brings out a slutty side of me and I'm really starting to like the benefits of that side. The slut is powerful and confident. She knows what she likes and isn't afraid to ask, or wiggle into position to give a strong hint, for what she wants. *I'm Evan Ashford's slut!*

I kiss him with the pent up need of, well, of a girl from Colorado who discovered her very own personal life-size Hawaiian sex god. I jump on top of him and kiss him feverishly, pinning him down and continue on my kissing tirade of his body until my stomach growls. It growls so loud that we both—lips still attached—open our eyes and look at each other. I slowly lift up as he props up on his elbows. "I want you, Mallory, but we should eat."

"If we must," I say, disappointed.

After settling down onto the blanket next to him again, he pulls a container of cut-up pineapple out of the basket. "Don't worry, we have all night and I'll make the wait worth your while. Can I feed you?" he asks, eyebrow raised in anticipation.

I've always wondered what the big deal about feeding someone else was all about, so I reply, "Sure."

I take another gulp of my champagne and look at him, unsure of what I'm supposed to be doing other than waiting for food to enter my mouth. He moves closer, confident, as he picks up the first piece of fruit and brings it to my mouth. With a smile, he says, "Open wide, beautiful."

While waiting for the fruit, I'm convinced my mouth hanging open is completely unsexy and I start to feel awkward. His eyes and expression turn lusty and he pauses as he stares at my open, waiting mouth. With a lift of my eyebrows, I encourage him forward. He sets the pineapple lightly on my tongue and I close my mouth around the fruit and his fingers. His fingers linger and then he slowly pulls them out and sucks them into his own mouth seductively one finger at a time.

Watching him stirs my most inner desires. Letting my own desires take over, I say, "I want you!" Without a second thought of someone seeing us here, I jump on top of him, knocking the bowl of pineapple over. He flips me down on to my back and straddles me while attacking my mouth with wet kisses.

We grab at each other's clothes, pulling and tugging, until our shirts are off. Never looking down, his hands unbutton my shorts as he roughly pulls at them with one hand. I lift up and using both his hands, he takes the sides of my shorts and underwear and yanks them off. He removes his swim trunks and tosses them carelessly away from us. When he drops down on top of me, my legs instantly spread wider. I gasp at the sensation as he rubs his length firmly against me, hitting the perfect spot. "Baby ..." His voice trails off as he sucks down on one of my breasts.

Suddenly, he looks up and his smile is mischievous. "Mallory, I'm hungry." His words sound more like a moan than a request.

I lift up and look at him, confused. *"What?"*

"I'm hungry," he says as a piece of pineapple appears in front of my face. He holds his hand steady as my eyes flicker between him and the pineapple. *Seriously, he wants to eat right now? I want to feel him inside of me and he just wants to eat?*

"I thought we had decided to wait on the food?" I signal to our naked bodies.

He cocks his head to the side, and says, "I'm going to eat ... you, baby."

"Oh!" I drop back down onto the blanket. I wave him

onward. "I'd like that, too. Yes, you should eat." I put my forearm over my eyes embarrassed that I've become so sexually open with him. At the same time, I like who I am with him more and more. He makes me feel beautiful and brave, confident in myself.

His body moves down mine and I jerk when I feel something cold against my most personal place. Bolting upright, I see and feel him rubbing a piece of pineapple on my aroused sex. "Um … Evan … *Oh dear lord*." That's all I manage to say before falling back and enjoying his tongue maneuvering on me down there. I look over to my side and see his hand groping at the blanket searching for more of the Hawaiian fruit, but with no luck. I grab the bowl and put it in his reach because this feels fan-fucking-tastic and I absolutely want to encourage him to eat more— since he's so hungry and all.

He chuckles against my wet insides, resulting in even more pleasure. My hands go to his head, gently holding his face to me, and all I can say is, "Oh my God! Yes, Evan, eat."

I close my eyes and get lost in the sensation. His tongue and fingers work me over in opposite motions, making my eyes roll back into my head. The ocean, the breeze, the pineapple, Evan, it's all too much. His fingers enter as his teeth graze across my sensitivity, and I lose it. With a gasp and the calling of his name, I hold his head tightly to me as his tongue does one final lap around my holy land before I relax into the blanket a complete mushy mess.

Looking up, he rests his chin on my pelvis and smiles at me. His eyes are glistening with happiness, his more arrogant side tingeing his irises with pride. He's gorgeous.

"Promise me you'll do that again. That was in-cred-ible," I say, enunciating every syllable for extra emphasis.

"Honeydew melons are in season," he says, and we both burst into laughter.

He climbs up my body, hovering over me, and kisses me. It's tender and lovely, much like the feeling blooming inside.

The sun has disappeared into the horizon and when I turn back, Evan kisses me again. The taste of pineapple, him, and me commingling in his mouth inspires a moan from me. He sits up, his face suddenly pained. "I can't be with you until I know you want it, want all of me. I need you to know that you're more to me than just this, than just sex."

"I don't doubt your intentions," I whisper, running my nails lightly down his back. "I want to be with you, Evan. But … I think I should rinse off first." I can feel the stickiness and though it was quite the turn-on at the time, I worry that it might become an issue later.

He pops up then takes me by the hand, helping me to my feet.

Now I feel self-conscious. "Can anyone see us down here?" I ask, standing there naked on the beach.

"There's a public path further down the beach, but no one really knows about it, so don't worry," he says, reassuring me as he leads me into the water until we're waist deep.

His hands hold me and we come together and kiss. This time we're much slower and tender. I let my hands explore, skimming over every taut muscle and defined feature of his strong back. His hands start their own exploration and grace down my sides to cup my ass. He pulls me up, holding my body tightly to his. His erection is solid and ready, making me moan into his mouth again. The first course was nice, but I'm ready for the main course now. He picks me up and I wrap my legs quickly around him. Trudging through the water with my body fully attached to him, he grunts into my mouth as a wave hits the back of his legs. Wobbling slightly, he tries to hold on as the next wave crashes against him and he stumbles forward. We fall down, but he catches me by breaking our fall with his hands.

He looks up and the playfulness of the moment is gone, a dark desire replacing the light in his eyes. I scurry out from under him, going for the blanket, but he grabs my ankles and drags me back down under him. "Where do you think you're going?"

The depth of his voice is mesmerizing. It's like in those old black and white movies where Dracula approaches the distressed damsel and then suddenly she decides, hey, he's hot. I'll let him end my life. Yeah, it's a lot like that right now. "Don't move," he says, jumping up and running to the blanket.

I don't move an inch when the water surrounds my body as the tide comes in softly then glides back out. I don't even think I blink in the time he's gone. He resumes his position over me and then licks the water droplets on my stomach. The tip of his nose dips into my sex and he lingers there, inhaling me. His hot breath makes me squirm, causing his eyes to flicker up to meet mine. He crawls up my body, owning every inch of me, as I lay there helplessly under his spell, paralyzed by the sexual heat of the moment. Sitting up, he takes the condom between his teeth while telling me very pointedly with his eyes what he's about to do to me. My breathing deepens as he adjusts back down and covers me, skin against bare skin, on the sand, in the water, in paradise.

I can tell he's waiting for me to give him the go ahead. He already told me I hold the power, so I end the misery for both of us by stroking through his sideburns and over his ears into his hair. "Evan, I want to be with you. Please."

He exhales in relief, running his hands from my elbows

towards my wrists and dragging them above my head, pressing them into the sand as he enters me. I gasp at the fullness, which reminds me of everything I've been missing for weeks. He fills me completely as he pushes himself as deep as he can go. "I've missed you," he says, verbalizing my sentiments.

Our fingers intertwine and he uses the leverage to move quickly in and out. The frenzy deep inside begins to twist and build. I squeeze him with my legs, sand grating between us, and move against him, needing more of everything. My mind blurs, but keeps that tightening feeling in focus.

His lips brush against mine as he stakes his claim, not knowing he already owns me. "You're mine, baby. *Only. Mine.*"

I nod, confirming his declaration.

Our bodies move erratically as he drops his head against my forehead. He releases me and pounds his hand solidly into the sand, leaving it there for balance. His other hand goes to my cheek. Although I feel sand rubbing against me, his touch is tender and sweet.

With jagged breaths, we look into each other's eyes as I hold him to me with my legs. Leaving my cheek, he lowers his hand to my flaming center. Awakening my whole body, little earthquakes erupt from deep inside. "Oh, Evan, yours, only yours, *always*," rushes from my mouth without thought, but knowing it's the truth revealed.

"Oh, fuck, Mallory." He leans down to attack my mouth with his tongue. "*Always. Mine.*" His orgasm hits any unshattered nerve that remained in my body and makes me twitch with pleasure.

We collapse, laying there in the sand with no will to move. I turn to look at him, but he has his eyes closed, exhausted from the activity. The water surrounds my body one last time before I sit up. He does the same though no words are spoken. The lust in his eyes has been replaced with love, and I move closer to him, curling into his side and letting him envelop me with that love. I kiss his chest and then look out in awe of how amazing life can be when you're happy and in love.

21

MALLORY

After a night of sexual escapades, we lay in the dark of the early morning hours, the curtains drawn open and the moonlight hitting the edge of the room. It's just bright enough to see his features. Evan has a handsome profile, and I take the time to really look at him, to memorize for later when we're apart. My heart clenches at the thought, but I wish it away, so I can enjoy the time I do have with him.

I lie on my side, letting my gaze trace from his forehead, over his nose, making the transition over peaks and dips of his kissable lips and detour down to his chin.

He's different to me now, different from the night at the bonfire where he was all arrogance, and pride, pained and vulnerable, wrapped up in the whirlwind tornado of his emotions. He's also different from the first day I met him at the airport. Evan was just cocky looking for a lay then. He didn't know about me and didn't care to. It makes me wonder when it all changed for him.

"Did I not do my job properly?" he asks, his eyes remain closed as the corners of his mouth lift up in a smile.

"What job is that?" I ask, restraining my own smile.

Evan rolls onto his side, his eyes opening. He looks tired and utterly breathtaking, but I don't say that. That would give him the upper hand in the moment and I'm liking the little control I do have.

"I was hoping to wear you out earlier."

With a light laugh, I say, "I got a second wind."

He leans over and kisses the tip of my nose. It's a sweet gesture, almost playful coming from a man who has trouble showing his true feelings.

There's an opening with this kiss and I decide to broach the subject I've been most hesitant to bring up. I'm curious and it's beginning to get the better of me. "I heard you and Noah used to be friends, close friends. What happened?"

He appears thoughtful as he looks down, his hand slipping under the covers and finding mine. He drags it up and uses his fingertip to draw on my palm. "Yeah, we were. It's stupid kid stuff. We got into some trouble and his dad wouldn't let him hang out with me anymore."

"You two tried to steal a car, right?" I put the two stories together.

When he looks up, I can tell he's not happy that I know about the car situation. "Is that what Kalei told you?"

I nod and look away from this narrowed gaze.

"That's kind of bullshit coming from him," he says, keeping his voice low in respect to the time of day. "The car was my dad's. He wouldn't have pressed charges on us. I even had the key, so it's not like we were 'breaking in' technically. His dad is just old-fashioned Hawaiian. He wants his kids to hang out with descendents of the great Hawaiian Royals, not haoles. It's pretty ridiculous if you ask me. I mean look at Noah." My eyes flicker up to meet his as his tone changes to angry. "He's part of this tight local culture and preaches about it, but hits on you. I mean, I understand why he's hitting on you, but it kind of goes against all his beliefs."

I don't say anything because I don't know what to say, first off. Secondly, I don't know what to believe either.

"I don't want to talk about Noah," he says, putting his arm behind his head and lying back on his pillow.

I don't want to push even though I feel like we have so much more to talk about and discover about each other, but for the first time, it also feels like we have enough time ahead of us to do all that.

I wake up in the morning to the sound of the shower. When I look at where Evan should be, I find a note instead. Taking it in hand, I smile. It reads:

To My Beautiful Girlfriend,

   I went for a swim. I'm hopping in the shower now and then I'm going to take you to breakfast. I'm in the mood for pineapple. Go figure. I also want to take you somewhere special today. Dress to go swimming.

   Love,

   Your Boyfriend – God, I like saying that!

I flop back down onto the bed, holding the note to my heart and smiling with an uncontrolled reverence for the man who left it for me. The water shuts off and a minute later, Evan appears, wet with a towel wrapped around him. His voice is soft, testing. "Are you awake, baby?"

"Yes, come over here," I say more seductively than I intended. I guess he brings it out in me.

He saunters over, dropping his towel, and climbs back

under the covers. Leaning over, he kisses me, leaving me breathless.

"You summoned?" he asks, his tone and expression matching in their slyness.

I hold the paper in front of him. "You left me a note?"

"I'm a little slow on how this whole relationship thing works, but I've learned my lesson with the note."

"You know, you don't have to leave me a note whenever you're not in bed. It's just ... it's just that first morning I woke up and waited for a long time. It made me feel that night meant nothing more than just another," I lower my eyes, and say it, "another fuck, just a one night stand."

"Look at me, baby." His finger lifts my chin until my eyes meet his again. "You were never just a fuck. At the airport, I was attracted to you and thought you looked like a good time, but when you told me my bullshit wasn't going to work, I knew you were different. Yes, beautiful in such a fucking sexy way, but you challenged my mind, too." He places his fingertips on my forehead and slowly drags them over my nose, continuing down my neck and stopping between my breasts. "You're the whole package, Mallory. I've never met anyone like you before." He leans in and kisses me by pressing his soft lips against mine, barely moving, but with more unsaid emotions than we've kissed with before.

His hand flattens on my chest, and he admits, "I'm afraid I'm going to screw this up."

"I'm no expert here, but as long as we talk we'll have a lot better chance at this."

His wet hair drips on my face and he swipes away the drop. "Mallory, I know you only have a month left, but I ..." He turns away from me, and sits up hunching his shoulders with his head downwards.

"What?" I ask. My heart races with hope, but knows his next words could be just as devastating.

His voice is just a whisper. "I really like you. I like to think that we're more than just a month's worth of fun." He gulps loudly, emphasizing his nervousness.

Resting my head on his back and wrapping my arms around his waist, I kiss him lightly on his shoulder. "We are and I like you, too." It's my turn to open up to him like he has to me. "I want more with you, but is it silly of us to think this can go beyond this island?"

He turns, pulling me onto his lap to hold me. "I guess we shouldn't worry about that, but I'm scared for this to change."

"It will change, but that doesn't mean it will change for the worse." I climb off of him and stand, looking back. "Come on, let's not waste time. Give me ten minutes and I'll be ready."

He lies back on the bed and watches me wiggle my ass for him as I go into the bathroom. I hear a loud catcall before I shut the door and laugh as I lean against it in complete bliss. I'm in way deeper than I ever thought possible, but he is too. That thought carries me forward to see beautiful Mallory staring back at me in the mirror. Evan not only makes me feel this way, but also loved, and in my heart, I know he's right. We've wasted too much time. One month will never be enough.

22

MALLORY

It does not escape me that the boats are growing progressively larger the further Evan and I walk down the dock at the marina. My curiosity finally gets the best of me. "Are you going to tell me what we're doing today?"

"Nope," he says then laughs, enjoying his surprise a little too much.

I huff in annoyance. Not real annoyance, but I play it up and mope, hoping he gives in and spills the secret.

As we approach one of largest boats in the harbor, I stop. "Did you rent this for us?"

"No."

I put my hands on my hips and look at him skeptically. "Please tell me your family doesn't own this boat."

"Okay. No, they don't own this boat, but they do own this yacht," he laughs again, referencing the same boat. "Mallory, it's too big to be called a boat."

I hit him on the arm. "So were going on this *yacht* today?"

"No. We're going on this." He points to a small boat that

has two planks for seats, a cooler and beach towels inside with an engine hanging off the back.

"A fishing boat?"

"A dinghy to be exact."

"Why are we taking this when we can be taking the Ashford yacht? Where are we going anyway?" I can't help my disappointment as I eye the little boat.

"All of your questions will be answered in due time, my dear. Remember, patience is a virtue," he jokingly scolds. "Now, c'mon, let's get going."

He helps me down into the rocking little boat and starts the motor. As we putter away from the marina, I look back at the yacht once more. Evan's money and access to money gives me another clue to the man he is and how he was raised. Even though I don't get to go on it today, I can't help but be impressed by that boat ... *I mean yacht.*

I settle into the dinghy and kick my feet up on the side, letting the wind whip through my hair. It's a glorious day and not just because the weather is perfect. Looking back at Evan, I start to wonder if I'll ever get used to his handsome face. A more perfect man couldn't have been created if I'd made a wish list. I eventually turn my whole body around, wanting to watch him as Master and Commander of this small water craft. He has such a presence that everyone in his orbit notices him. He lifts his right eyebrow up knowingly at me before moving his attention back to the bright Hawaiian horizon.

Twenty minutes later, I see a small land mass with people, wave-runner's, and boats all around. As we get closer, he slows the motor, and announces, "This is the sandbar. It will get busier as the day goes on."

"What does everyone do out here?"

"Swim, drink, cook-out, build a bonfire, play music, and

just be. It's very laid back and locals come out here to hang out and get away from all the tourists. It's made of sand, so we only have about five hours before the tide comes in and it's all underwater again."

He stops the engine and jumps into the water which is hip deep. After tossing a small anchor overboard, he looks at me. "Let's go, I want to introduce you to some of my brah's."

I kick my shoes off and get a piggy back ride to shore. He sets me down on the sand and walks back out to the cooler to grab two beers. Popping one can open, he hands it to me, and takes my free hand in his. Everyone I meet is friendly and seems to love Evan in a small town hero kind of way. That's exactly the opposite impression I was given by Noah, which doesn't really surprise me since they're enemies. I just wish I knew how they went from good friends to arch-rivals.

Evan holds my hand, or is wrapped around me from behind, or has his arm draped over my shoulder the entire time. He's got a possessive side that I find extremely sexy. No one has ever been possessive over me before.

An hour later, Sunny, Zach, Kate, and Murphy arrive in a ski boat. Murphy stands at the front of the boat with his arms wide open and makes a loud booming announcement, "The party has arrived!"

Gotta love that guy.

Sunny makes a beeline for me, and Evan releases my hand so I can greet her. When we hug, she whispers, "Look at us, both in love and with best friends, no less."

We see Kate walking over and eye each other, the plan silently formed and agreed upon. As soon as she gets close we both grab her. She's so surprised that she stumbles forward and it's all legs, screams, and long hair flying to the ground with us landing in a heap in the sand.

"Shit! I hate getting dirty," she whines as she tries to hide the smile that's creeping up the side of her cheeks. "Thanks!" She bursts out laughing.

We fall back and lay there as the boys 'take a meeting' in the water. "Are they pissing?" Sunny asks, disgust seeping into her tone.

"I think they're comparing their manhood," I say.

"Zach will win that contest hands down and down and down ... oh, and wide and wide ..." Sunny moves her hands down and then out to emphasize his size.

"*Ewwww!* That's gross, Sunny," Kate says, gagging as we all sit up to watch the guys. "Anyway, it's no contest. Look at Murphy—his hands, feet, huge build—need I say more?"

"You sure are quiet there, Mal," Sunny says, pushing me with her hand.

I smile to myself thinking about Evan and all he's blessed with.

Kate stands up using me for support then playfully pushes me back down into the sand, saying, "Look at her face, Sunny! And that's the ultimate ew. That's my baby brother you're having naughty thoughts about."

I blush, and say, "There's definitely nothing baby about—"

"Who's not a baby?" Murphy asks, walking up and grabbing Kate from behind.

Sunny stands up, and stating matter-of-fact, says, "Mallory was just telling us what a large cock Evan has."

All three of the guys' eyebrows shoot upwards in shock.

"Is that why you're blushing?" Evan says, offering me a hand up. "Don't worry, beautiful, these guys know they pale in comparison. It's a fact."

"Fuck you," Murphy says, punching him lightly in the gut and running off laughing. Evan takes off after him. Zach puts his arms in the air like he's exasperated, but starts laughing as he gives into the antics and runs after them.

We grab another beer from the cooler before stripping off our shirts and shorts. The three of us crawl onto a large floating raft and lay, soaking up the sun in our bikinis.

Kate asks, "You're coming to the 4th of July party, right?"

Sunny quickly replies, "Yep, I've already been thinking about a shopping excursion. You two up for that?"

Lying in the middle of them, I feel the lift in the raft as they turn their heads toward me, so I feel the need to answer. "Evan mentioned the party, but we haven't really talked about it."

Kate tosses her empty beer can into the boat nearby, grabs my hand and gently squeezes. "You're coming. It's our family's biggest event here on the island. Everyone comes to this party. So consider yourself formally invited."

She sits up, and adds, "Anyway, the food is amazing and it's open bar. We can get ready together at my house beforehand."

Shielding her eyes, she asks, "Want to go shopping after work tomorrow?"

"I'm in," I reply, hoping Evan wants to go to the party. He may not since his parents will be there and they seem to be a big source of contention with him.

The boys drag themselves through the water looking worse for wear after wrestling on the beach.

"Fore!" Evan lands next to me and that sends Kate and Sunny off the sides into the water.

They scream and curse as their guys laugh their asses off at their soaked sweeties. Evan rolls on top of me and kisses me gently on the lips. He whispers, "I've missed you."

I'm about to tell him how much I missed him when Kate and Sunny get their revenge by flipping the raft over, which sends us toppling into the water. When we stand, I expect laughter, but Evan weaves his hands into my wet hair and brings me into a searing kiss that takes my full attention.

His lips move against mine, and he says, "I want to be inside of you. I need to make love to you, baby. Can we leave?" My knees weaken and his embrace tightens. "I'll take that as a yes."

We give quick goodbyes and launch our small dinghy back into deeper water to start the motor. We're about half way back to the marina when he catches me staring at him again.

Evan tilts his head, making eye contact with me. His tone is soft, concerned, and caring when he asks, "Are you happy?"

"Very much," I reply without hesitation.

"I'm glad."

"Are you happy?"

He runs a hand through his hair and briefly looks past me as he continues navigating the boat. His eyes flick back to mine, and he says, "Today was a great day. I haven't felt this happy in a long time. It's good. Life is good."

I smile, feeling the good vibrations growing stronger, and in this very moment, I've never been more happy.

23

MALLORY

"I'll give you a two count head start and then I'm coming after you." His warning is not playful or teasing and is a direct threat to my girly bits. Suddenly, he slaps my ass and says, "Go."

It doesn't matter that I'm tired from a day at the sandbar with the gang. My adrenaline kicks in, and I take off running without looking back. Giddy mixed with a little fear sends me straight into the pool. He jumps in over my head. With anxious anticipation, I wait for him to surface as I hold tight to the edge. He stays under longer than I expect, but then I finally see his darkened figure swimming under water towards me. My swaying legs cross underneath the water in sex protection mode. He grabs my hips, pulls me under, and kisses me. I relax after taking hold of his shoulders, and we break the waters' surface together. Our tongues mingle as I wrap my arms around his neck and he presses me against the side of the pool.

Breathing much heavier and with a much huskier tone, he says, "You have entirely too many clothes on."

He pulls my shirt off and gets my shorts undone with

precision and speed. Tossing them both onto the nearby grass, he turns back and tugs each string of my bikini one by one until it's untied, letting it fall to the ground. He leans forward to kiss me, hard with determination and passion. His roaming hands glide over my naked body until he finds my hand and takes it, pressing my palm against his cock that is clearly ready to bust out of his shorts.

Together our hands rub him, and I groan in desire, not able to stop myself. I start pulling at the drawstring to rid his body of this barrier. Just as his breaths turn to pants he stills my hand. He leans into my neck, nipping his way up to my ear, and says, "I'll be right back. I need to get a condom and towels."

He swiftly lifts up on the side of the pool, and I ogle the muscles in his arms as he does. He dashes away, but stops and looks back. "Don't start without me, baby."

"You better hurry up then," I say as seductively as I can muster and add a moan for good measure. With my back to him, I hear him running and the opening of his door.

Just as I giggle, the shaking of ice against the sides of a glass grabs my attention. I turn in the direction of the sound and when I find it, I also hear a female voice. "I'm glad to hear my son is smart enough to wear a condom."

My heart and breathing stop in unison as I watch a very petite, slender golden blonde-haired woman stand from one of the chaise loungers facing the ocean. She finishes what appears to be the last of her drink and stares at me in the pool. I drop one of my arms over my chest which I know is visible through the water and with the other arm I hold the cement edge to keep me afloat.

She puts a hand on her hip. "I'm Mrs. Ashford and this is my pool that you're skinny dipping in." She walks around the far side of the pool as I remain in place—speechless and mortified. Stopping opposite of me, she stares down as if a thought has occurred, but doesn't voice it.

Delving down deep, I find the one tiny nerve I have left and start to say, "I'm—"

"Shhhh!" she says, holding her hand up towards me to shush me. "I don't need your name, your life story, or why you felt the need to contaminate my pool by having sexual intercourse with my son in it. I just want you gone."

I'm embarrassed, but turn when I hear Evan. "Mother?" She turns toward him and watches as he stands above me. "When did you get in?"

"Evan." Her tone is as chilly as the ice that tings against her fancy glass. "I landed a few hours ago. I'm tired and I'm going to bed. We'll discuss *things* in the morning."

"All right." His reply has no emotion attached.

She grabs the handle of the back door, and says, "And, Evan?"

"Yes?"

"Make sure your *friend* doesn't stay the night and please don't make me have to drain the pool."

"Mallory is staying the night." But his words fall on deaf ears as the door slams closed behind her. "Hey," he says, squatting down next to me.

Lowering a little further into the water, I can't muster any gumption as shame fills me. "Can I have a towel please?"

"Sure."

I use the steps in the corner, wrapping the towel around my body as I emerge from the pool. Walking towards the guesthouse, he takes me by the arm to stop me. "Hey, it's okay. You don't have to leave."

"Evan, you heard her. She doesn't want me here—"

"But, I do."

I finally have the courage to look up to meet his eyes although tears fill mine. "She thinks I'm one of your skanks. You haven't told her about me and—"

"Have you told your parents about me?" He searches my eyes for the answer he already possesses. "No? Why haven't you told them about me?"

"It's different because you won't be meeting them. I'm leaving in a month, so I didn't think it mattered. But you knew I'd be—"

He releases me, and stalks towards the beach.

Shit! Realizing how that sounded, I feel horrible. "Evan! Wait!" I jog after him, holding the towel tightly around me. "Stop! Please. I'm sorry. I didn't mean it like that."

He does stop, but an instant later I kind of wished he hadn't. He turns and looks at me, hurt written all over his face. "It doesn't matter because I'm just the here and now, right? I'm just a summer fling to you and a dirty secret to your friends and family. What the fuck, Mallory? I thought ... this whole past week ..." He runs both his hands through his hair and then knots his fingers at the crown of his head and turns to face the ocean. "I thought this meant something more to you too." He sits down on the sand and pulls his knees toward his chest then drops his head.

I sigh in frustration. I'm frustrated with myself, and I'm a lot frustrated with what just happened with his mother. Sitting down next to him, I whisper, "You mean more to me than that. I'm sorry. I didn't mean for it to sound like—"

"You said exactly what you were thinking and I got burned by one of the qualities I admire in you the most— your honesty." He finally looks over at me, and says, "I think over the course of this past week, deep down, I'd hoped that maybe I would mean enough to you to stay beyond the summer, but I can tell that's not where you're head is at right now. I understand that your school, your friends, your family, all that's back in Colorado waiting for your return." His voice is steady and cold. I can almost see his walls go up as his eyes focus into the distance. "I get it. Your life is there and mine is here. I was just being stupid. That's all."

I touch his arm, but he flinches, clearly not wanting to be touched by me. "Evan, you aren't being stupid, but you're right, my life is there and I can't change that now." The distance between Hawaii and Colorado is too far for my liking, causing the distance between us emotionally to grow. My heart hurts over the thought of leaving him. I've grown too attached to him.

"Fuck, let's not do this." He stands abruptly and looks down at me. "I told you I get it, all right." He takes a step back, away from me. "I think I should take you to Sunny's tonight."

"Why?" I demand, jumping to my feet.

He searches my eyes once again then turns to walk away from me. "Grab your stuff and I'll drive you back."

"No! You're not pulling this bullshit with me. Stop walking away, Evan!" I run up behind him and grab his arm to stop him, needing him to face me. "Look at me, damn it!"

His head tilts to the side and out of the corner of his eyes, he looks at me. But I can see this conversation is pointless. He's already withdrawn from me, and it's probably best if I just give him time. But this hurts and I care too much for him. I want to fight for him. My selfish side just wants him to hold me again and make *me* feel better.

As I follow him inside, I stop and drop the towel. I'm shameless. "I'm not fucking leaving, so you can just get that right out of your mind."

I watch as he walks in silence to his dresser and pulls boxers from it. He tosses me the same pair that I had given him to wear a week ago. He strips his wet shorts off and slips on another pair. Without warning, he demands, "Why the fuck do you have some other guy's boxers?" He walks back to the second drawer and pulls out two t-shirts and once again, tosses me one and then pulls one over his head.

I remain there dumbfounded by his lack of attention to my nakedness and by his line of questioning.

"Those shorts are mine. They aren't some guy's. I like to sleep in boxers at home—"

"By home, you mean Colorado, not Sunny's?"

It's clear what he's getting at. "You knew I was leaving. I'm a senior. I would lose credits if I transferred now."

He yanks his cargo shorts up and walks over to the door after putting on his flip-flops. He doesn't look at me, but says, "I'll wait for you in the car."

"Fuck you, Evan!" I yell.

He pauses, but then walks away.

I'm so pissed that I throw the t-shirt on haphazardly and storm across the lawn to grab my wet clothes and bathing suit. I stomp my way to the car with my mind reeling in anger. The door is already propped open and he's sitting in his seat with the car running. Tossing my soaked clothes onto his carpeted floorboard, I make a production of getting in then slamming the door shut. He glares at the clothes that we both know are drenching his carpet and backs out leaving tread marks at the end of his driveway.

I try to calm my pounding heart. I don't want to fight with him, and garnering some logic, I decide to try a different approach. "Evan?"

Nothing.

"We need to talk about what's going on here," I say, trying to stay calm.

"I think we've said enough already."

"Well, I don't—"

"Well, I don't want to fucking hear it. How about that?"

I flinch when he yells, the car feeling way too small to contain this important of a conversation. Turning toward the window, the beauty of the crashing waves mimic the way his words hurt my heart. Silence is the best tactic, and I remain that way the rest of the ride.

He slams on the brakes, coming to an abrupt halt when he pulls into the parking space near the apartment.

After taking a slow deep breath, I try again, attempting to keep my voice from shaking. "Your mother started this. You realize that she ruined tonight, don't you?" He shakes his head before resting it against the window. "You were happy. We were happy. Evan, we were about to have sex until—"

Sitting straight up, he slams his fists onto his steering wheel, and yells, "Fuck, Mallory! I told you not to do this. But you have to push, always with the fucking pushing. My mother didn't ruin this! You did!"

"I didn't say she ruined 'this'," I correct him, swaying my hand between us while a sinking feeling sets in. Barely above a whisper, I say, "I said she ruined tonight, *not us.*" I sit there staring at him, waiting for a response, but his emotions are void of true feelings. My voice is trembling as I let the words fall from my mouth. "Are we over?"

He doesn't look at me, but it's more that he *won't* look at me. I watch him and my breathing catches as everything begins to move in slow motion. He rubs his eyes with the heel of his palms and turns away from me, hiding his face.

I'm confused by how this day took such a drastic and harsh turn. Opening my door, I get out before he has a chance to stop me, needing a cigarette like yesterday. He jumps out and runs after me, grabbing me by the arms. "We're not over—"

"Then why does it feel like we are?" I lost hope in us, and the stress of my life falling apart makes me crave a nicotine relaxer.

Sounding just as hopeless as I feel, he asks, "Why are we so bad at this?"

This might be a rhetorical question, but I feel the need to respond anyway. "I don't know, but it doesn't seem like it should be this hard." I start walking for the door again. As I near, I can see Sunny and Zach sitting on the couch talking, laughing, and basically making it look so fucking easy.

"Mallory, I only wanted us to talk tomorrow. I don't want us to be over, but what you said … or slipped up and said, it's how you feel and it might not be good for me to think that this can be more than it is."

This is one of those times I wish I hadn't wanted to talk it out. *Why couldn't I have left it until tomorrow?* We wasted so much time not communicating before and now I try and it backfires. Fuck, I hope I have a cigarette inside.

He lifts my chin up. "Get some rest. It's been a long day. We can talk again tomorrow."

I feel like I'm going to throw up. He leans toward me with his lips lingering against my temple before he finally pulls back. *This is it, I can feel it.*

"Goodbye, Mallory."

I watch, unable to move, as he shoves his hands in his pockets and walks back to his car.

As he gets in, I rush around the corner and lean against the front door, praying he can't see me. I slide down the door in agony as my heart is ripped from my chest by the string that had bound us together just an hour earlier. The imagery of it dragging behind him makes my chest ache all the more. I drop my head between my knees and cry.

I cry because of this fucked up situation. I cry because of his mother. I cry because I don't have a cigarette. But mostly, I cry because the only man I've ever truly been in love with just left me.

24

MALLORY

I give myself all of three minutes before I stand up, dust the dirt off of my ass, and enter the apartment. Zach and Sunny both look up from the couch, surprised to see me.

"Hey there," Zach says, smiling like his usual happy self.

Sunny takes a second to analyze me before she asks, "Have you been crying?" She stands up and rushes over to me.

I nod, embarrassed to be breaking down in front of Zach.

"What happened?" she asks.

"I don't ..." I stop to choke down a sob not seeming to be able to get out what I want to say. "I can't talk about it."

She strokes my hair back off my forehead, and says, "Is it Evan? Did he hurt you?"

I stare at her not sure if she means physically or emotionally. She's seen the emotional damage from him already, but she should know he would never physically hurt me. Hell, he's Zach's best friend, of course, he wouldn't.

"We broke up."

"What?" Zach stands up and exclaims. "That makes no sense."

"Well," I start, but my voice wavers. "I'm not sure, but I think we did. It's all just so messed up. We're messed up." I throw my hands into the air, exasperated.

Walking back to my bag, I squat down and dig through it, but am still not able to find a cigarette. I go into the kitchen and dig one out of the emergency pack hidden in a coffee mug in the cabinet and grab the lighter from the TV stand.

I head to the sliding glass door and let myself out. After settling into one of the plastic chairs, I light up and inhale the nicotine. Right now, this might actually be better than an orgasm.

Sunny and Zach are mumbling to each other inside, probably debating who's going to come out and have to talk to me. "Save yourselves the trouble. I don't want to talk anyway," I shout to make it easier on them.

Silence fills the air then Zach appears in the doorway. *Guess he lost.*

"Mallory, I've been meaning to catch up with you lately." He tries for casual, but his body is stiff, uncomfortable as he makes his way out the door. "You know, me and Evan actually have a pretty cool bond for guys. We have similar backgrounds and—"

"So I should warn Sunny to stay away from you before you two end up a complete mess like me and Evan?"

"I'll let that slide because you and Evan are a lot alike." He takes a deep breath and noisily exhales before starting again. "Listen, I want to say something wise and helpful here, but I don't know what to say other than you have turned Evan's world upside down." I sit up, wanting to hear more as the rain picks up to a steady mist. "He's different with you ... since you've been here. He's better somehow and I thought he was pretty fucking cool before. People say some bad stuff about him, but it's not who he is on the inside."

"Who is he then, Zach?" I stand up and walk closer, standing under the awning for shelter. Lowering my voice, I plead, "Please tell me who he is because I thought we were good and then I said something stupid. The walls went up and he shut me out." I feel bad all over again and try to explain. "I apologized, but he wasn't hearing it."

"He's stubborn, but he heard you. Sometimes he just needs time to process stuff."

"I met his mother."

He looks at me with a raised eyebrow. "Oh! How'd that go?"

"Not good. I want to blame her, but really, we should have been more open with our expectations." I smile to myself. "He can be very distracting."

"Too much information," he says and then chuckles.

After an exasperated sigh, I say, "All I want is back in, and I don't know how to do it. I don't understand how to be in his world and not hurt him."

Sunny steps outside and leans on Zach's shoulder as they take in everything I'm saying. I feel good sharing this with people who care about both of us, who'll listen. "I can't help that I leave in a month," I say. "This summer was supposed to be carefree and now I want to be with him and it hurts to think that I have to leave him, but it hurts even more that he's upset about me leaving. It was supposed to be a one night thing, you know." My hand covers my mouth to stop myself from revealing anything more, but I can see they heard every word and my slip-up.

Zach whispers even though I don't know why since we

can both hear him. "We all know you two were together the first night—"

"I can't believe he told you—"

"No, no, no," Sunny says. "It's not like that. It's just through comparing notes that we all figured it out." She laughs. "Honestly, it wasn't that difficult. But ..." She steps forward and touches my arm. "Maybe it's time to finally admit that you two are more than just a one night stand. You're not in this alone. Evan feels the same about you as you do him."

Zach wraps his arm around Sunny's waist, and says, "Don't waste your time on petty bullshit. You should be together whether it lasts a month or a lifetime. You need to give it your best shot before it's too late."

"That's easy for you to say," I say confused and open to suggestions. "You have each other and go to school together. Evan and I don't have anything past August."

"You need to talk to him," Zach says. "I know talking is the last thing you two are any good at, but you're going to have to share your real feelings." He steps inside the apartment and pulls Sunny behind him. "Now, I'm going to take Sunny to my house and make love to my woman all night long."

I roll my eyes, no smile, but with annoyance clearly attached to my face. "Yeah, rub it in, why don't you?"

Ten minutes later, I'm alone on my couch, *bed*, whatever this little torture device is and thinking hard.

After the long day at the sandbar and then being in the pool, I need a shower. I drench my face under the warm water wishing this crappy feeling away, but to no avail.

I hit the shower lever down, turning it off, and jerk the curtain open. I'm pissed! He's breaking up with me. He broke up with me. We're. Broken. Up. That was a final goodbye if I've ever heard one and I've heard a few. I wrap the towel around my body and stomp into the living room digging my panties out of the top drawer. I grab a white tank top and slide it over my head before heading to my bed. I lay there fuming for five minutes before I bolt upright. "No! No fucking way!" We're not ending like this!

Zach is right. This is petty bullshit and he's been stalking me or peeping Evan-ing me, and making me fall for him. He doesn't mean we're over. He wouldn't have gone to all the trouble if he didn't love me. He loves me. Evan is in love with me. I gasp. *Evan. Is. In. Love. With. Me.*

I toss the blanket aside and grab the nearest clothes—a black cotton mini skirt and slip it on. I run to the door putting my flip flops on and grab Sunny's car keys off the hook.

Before I have a chance to gather my thoughts and change my mind, I'm pulling into his driveway and parking. I sit there numb to what I'm really doing here and what I'm going to say to him. The rain picks up and to me that's a sign that it's now or never. I'm going to follow my heart and screw all reasoning that contradicts this romantic notion.

I get out of the car, duck my head from the heavy drops, and run. Half way down the path, I run straight into Evan's chest. Looking up into his eyes, I stand there pressed against him, unsure what to do. The rain gets heavier, soaking us completely. My hair glues itself to my face and his usually messy hair presses down against his forehead, but he still looks amazing.

I'm nervous and scared, hesitant and anxious. "Evan?"

In one swift movement, he takes my face in his hands and our lips are together. The passion that initially brought us together ignites between us again. Even though the cool rain pours down on us, the heat between us prevents us from acknowledging its existence.

He pulls back and looks at me through dark eyelashes covered in droplets. "I can't be away from you. I need you, Mallory."

I finally drop my guard and let my pride slide away as my tears mix with the rain, covering my face. When I look down, he quickly tilts my chin back up. Through gentle sobs, I confess, "I love you, Evan. I shouldn't, but I do. I didn't want to burden you with—"

His body meets mine in a flurry of hands, lips, and legs coming together. His tongue enters my mouth without warning, weakening my body into his.

Mingled with gasping breaths, he moans into my mouth, *"Mallory."* Our lips never part, and we don't need words to express how we feel. This is natural for us. Our bodies have always said what we can't seem to.

He moves me backward against the side of the house and under the small protective eave of the roof. My hands find purchase against his muscular abs and pull his shirt up enough to reveal his stomach. I need him and he needs me. This is how we find our way back to each other. I know this physical connection will strengthen our emotional one. His hands skim and then stop on my breasts as he attacks my neck with hot, open-mouthed kisses that could melt an iceberg. My hips squirm against him needing more, needing all of him. When his hands slide down my body to the hem of my skirt, they slip underneath. I throw my head back, hitting the hard structure that my body is firmly pressed against. I pull his shorts open in one swift and easy move, and he moans against my neck. "Why does it feel like we haven't been together in ages?"

I feel the same. *Desperation maybe?* There is a neediness we have for each other and it's insatiable.

Lithe fingers slide into my panties and into my own personal downpour, causing me to gasp aloud. He starts kissing me as the sensation deep inside starts to tighten and twist. His fingers slide out and he leans back to look at me. His expression has changed, and the hunger in his eyes ever present as he removes his shorts and rips open the little foil packet.

We come together as the rain continues to pour. Our world engulfed by sighs and moans, frenzied bodies slick and steady, finding a rhythm all our own.

"Mallory, you feel so good, baby. This is ... we are ... perfect."

I wrap my arms around his neck and his lips caress mine. My mind starts going fuzzy and I'm lost in the sensations of him.

I kiss from his ear down across his jaw. Not being able to resist anymore, I lick his stubbly jaw and under his chin, lightly nibbling before moving to that smooth spot behind his ear. His head tilts to the side allowing me access as he softly chuckles, enjoying the attention. During the most intimate of acts, I discover the sweetness that my surfer boy is ticklish.

When he turns and takes my mouth with his, his tongue swirls with mine, making me forget all about giggles and nips. "Ahh," *stubble*, "Ung," *fullness*, "Oooh," *rain*, "Oh, Evan." I come apart on top of him, squeezing my eyes shut and get lost in all that is us.

He buries his head into the crook of my neck and groans through his personal bliss.

We stay still, our bodies interlocked and surrounded by heavy breathing. The rain starts to lighten and then stops.

Evan shivers then slowly lowers me, asking, "Can you stand?"

I can't verbalize a response yet, but I know my legs are too shaky from being held against the house. He lifts me up with trembling arms and cradles me against his chest. Turning, he walks down the path, kissing the top of my very wet head, and carries me over the threshold into his place. On a mission, he brings me into the bathroom and sets me on the edge of the large jetted tub. As the bathtub fills, he continues his kisses, pecking them across my cheek and up my temple. His breath is warm and the contact caring, satisfying the desperation I felt minutes earlier.

"You should take off your clothes. The water will warm you up." The words seem contradictory to the sentiment, but I know what he means.

"I'm warm on the inside," I say, with a soft laugh following.

He laughs gently as he stands to take his own shirt off. It's stuck to him since it's soaked and he has to peel it off over his head to remove it. The sight of his hard body and concern for me makes me feel loved and makes my tummy flutter. "Get in the tub, baby, so you can get warm on the outside."

He steps in and holds a hand out to me. I pull the soaked, see-through tank over my head, and strip off my black skirt. I take his hand and step in. We don't talk as he settles into the water and I work my way down onto his lap, resting my back against his chest. My head drops back against his shoulder and I sigh, content as he wraps his arms around my waist under the water. He kisses my head then says, "I'm glad you came back."

"So am I," I say, not able to hide my smile. "Evan?"

"Yeah?"

"I'm sorry ... for earlier tonight. I'm sorry for letting a summer deadline dictate our future." I slide my cheek against his comforting chest and look up at him. "If you'll still have me, I'm here, completely this time."

He laughs aloud and the sound is music to my ears. I love hearing him happy. "*If* I'll have you? I can't *not* be with you, Mallory. That's what I've been trying to tell you. I don't have a choice in the matter." He rubs his nose against mine and kisses me sweetly on the lips.

"I meant what I said outside." Three words that came from the heart, shared in a moment of passion and closeness I've never shared with anyone before.

"I know you do and I do, too," he says, and I catch that he isn't saying the words I want him to, but his feelings are the same. I try to let that comfort me, but in an emotional girly moment, I really wanted to hear him say those three little words that mean so much.

I gulp down the unimportance of my silly need and bring myself back to the current romantic position I've found myself in. He takes the bar of soap and dips it beneath the water running it across my stomach and under my breasts. Sliding back down my stomach, his hand dips between my legs. A sharp intake of air traps itself and I hold my breath.

"Breathe, baby, breathe," he whispers, tonguing the shell of my ear.

I try to comply, but only short, ragged breaths escape.

"Am I making you nervous?"

"No," I lie.

"Liar."

I relax at his playful banter. He knows me well enough to know I was lying.

"You're right, I am a little nervous, but I don't know why. Maybe nervous isn't the right word."

"I think it's because we had our first fight as a couple. It's new for both of us and we're trying to figure out how to get over it and come together and be stronger because of it."

It's times like these that he blows my mind. He's insightful and brilliant and has so much to offer the world, but chooses to keep his true feelings bottled up inside.

"How do you do that?" I ask, hoping he understands my vague question.

His head tilts back to rest on the ledge. "Hmmm." He hums as I wait for him to share more. "You mean the stuff about coming together?"

"Yes."

"Although I haven't been in many relationships, I want this with you, because of you. I don't want to lose you over petty bullshit."

I laugh when I hear him say that. "*Petty Bullshit*. Did Zach talk to you?"

"Yeah, I got the 'Petty Bullshit Lecture' texting edition."

"How'd that go?"

"Something like, '*Don't let the petty bullshit fuck things up*'."

"I got a similar speech."

"So, what do you think?"

I spin my body around in the water so that I'm straddling him. I kiss him, fondling his lower lip with my tongue and then enter his mouth. It's wet, soft, welcoming, and I can taste a hint of liquor and cigarettes. I moan, craving him again already. That bad boy of mine is such a turn-on. I adjust myself, placing his firming cock right against my most needy spot and then reluctantly pull back to answer his question between heated pants. "I think we should forget the petty bullshit and really give this a go. What about you?"

His dreamy eyes focus on mine, and he says, "If you mean *us* when you say *'this'* than I agree wholeheartedly." His hands pull my head to his and we kiss, not frenzied or crazy, just sweet, sincere, and meaningful.

My body goes on auto pilot and I rub against him searching for that radiance that only Evan can give.

"No one has ever turned me on as much as you do, Mallory," he says, his lips against mine.

Picking up the pace of my grind, I mumble, "Yes, turned on," grind, "like you, Evan."

He snickers then weaves his hands into my tangled hair, still wet from the rain. He holds us together until in unison, we part needing oxygen. I stare down at him, heated and lusty, as he says, "I ..." He closes his mouth and then opens it to start again. My heart bubbles over knowing what he's about to say. "I ...," he clears his throat, *"Mallory ..."*

25

MALLORY

"I ... let's move to the bed," Evan says, his words staggering out, but the *I love you* I know he feels remains elusive.

To say I'm disappointed would be an understatement. My love for him is felt down to my bones, so it was easy to say, but it makes me wonder why he can't just say it. I really hope I don't start obsessing over this. "Bed?" I ask, confirming what he said.

"That will be more comfortable." I step out of the tub and grab a towel, tossing him another. We dry off in companionable silence both knowing that the 'I Love You' elephant is now in the room making its presence known.

"I'll meet you in there," I say, walking out of the bathroom and straight towards the bed. I drop my towel and slide in under the sheets that feel like a cool heaven. Evan walks in looking relaxed and sleepy.

He spreads his arm out and I snuggle into his side, and ask, "You want to talk and then go to sleep?" From this vantage point, I see a bottle of whiskey, a shot glass, and a pack of cigarettes on the kitchen counter which explains a lot about how his night went while we were apart.

"You want to ..." He lets the questions trail off.

"I'm always up for it, but we can just lay here, if you'd rather. I'm just happy to be here."

"I'm happy you're here too, baby," he says, kissing my forehead. Questions fill my mind as I look up at him, studying his face. "Oh no, here we go again. Ask whatever it is you want to ask. I know you want to, so go ahead."

Not hesitating, I go for it. "Why were you drinking tonight?"

"I drink almost every night."

"You drink hard liquor every night?"

"No," he says, sighing loudly. "I'd just had a fight with you. Did you think it didn't affect me?"

"I guess I wasn't thinking about how it affected you. I was kind of caught up in my own pain at the time."

I sit up in bed with the sheet covering me. Evan puts his arms behind his head and angles himself in my direction. "Listen, Mallory, I don't like feeling bad. I've spent years feeling like shit and you made me excited again, happy. So your words earlier cut deep. I'm not trying to drag this up again, but I'm thinking long term here and you're thinking the present. I understand why you feel that way. I'm just saying it hurt to know that you were closed off to the idea of a future together."

I scoot down and roll onto my side facing him, eye level. "I'm not now. It may have taken me awhile to realize it, but I do now. Isn't that what matters?"

He rolls over and rubs his thumb along my cheekbone and smiles. "It's all that matters, but I also have a better understanding of why you were thinking the way you were." He looks down and says, "I just can't help myself when it comes to you."

He looks back up, needing me to reassure him, so I do. I

want to anyway. "I want to be with you, Evan. Sometimes my heart races and I feel like I've never wanted anything more. My feelings scare me as much as they excite me, but August looms over my head, smothering me, *smothering us* and all we're meant to be." Tears fill my eyes as I verbalize my fears.

One falls down my face as he moves closer and kisses my cheek, capturing the tear with his lips. I grab onto his shoulders and get as close as I can. His right hand slides down my arm, working itself under the sheet to graze lightly across my skin. We look at each other and I see that look again, him adoring me, appreciating me with his eyes. I lean forward to give him a gentle kiss, but he pulls back. His voice is thick and husky as he speaks. "I want to make you feel good, baby."

I gulp, already feeling the moisture between my legs from his declaration. His hand presses against my side, so I roll onto my back. He positions himself, his large erection trapped between us. I gasp from the contact as he leans up to my ear, rubbing himself against me, and says, "I'm going to make love to you, but I'm going to watch you come first." His hand slides between my thighs and sparks fly, setting the wick on my coiled dynamite on fire.

I can't stop from wriggling in pleasure as he starts working me over more purposefully. My eyes begin to close, but he demands, "I want you to watch me do this to you. I want you to remember this when we're not together." Two fingers—turning, spinning, exploring me. I want to close my eyes and savor the feeling, but he's right. I don't want to take my eyes off of him either.

He lifts his body off of me and repositions himself lower down. His eyes don't leave mine and his fingers never lose contact. He touches me in a way that makes me jerk involuntarily and push down harder against his hand. A mischievous smile covers his face then he sticks his tongue out, flicking it against my needy sweet spot. I bite my lip to keep it from hanging open. My heart is pounding and my body squirms from the erotic sight in front of me.

My hands need to touch him, but I can only reach his hair, which is not such a tragedy. I move it around unable to put effort into it while he's looking up at me from between my legs. He twists his fingers, knowing exactly what he's doing, my inner dynamite getting close to exploding. My eyelids drop closed despite my best efforts and then nothing. My eyes pop open to find Evan lowering a condom down his length. "Sorry, baby, I need to be inside of you right now."

"No sorries. I want you."

He's at my entrance as he steadies himself on top of me. "Mallory, I uh ..." He slowly closes his eyes and kisses me as he enters me with care. "You always feel so ama ... ungh, amazing," he mutters and then says, "it's never been like this. I've never felt like this."

His body moves on top of me and I can't resist joining him, the intensity of our connection heightens.

"Evan, Evan, make me yours, babe," I say, knowing that I'm needy for him to give me my release. Only he can do this for me, no one else ever has.

I watch as his eyes twinkle, and he smirks. "*Oh baby*, you're in trouble now. Roll over."

"What?" I ask, snapping out of my semi-delusional state.

His tone is firm and demanding, no sign of playful Evan left. "You heard me, Mallory. Turn onto your stomach and don't lose contact. Now move."

Holy Shit, he's sexy when he takes charge! I pull my leg up and twist my body. I can feel him withdrawing as I continue to roll over.

"Mallory! Don't. Lose. Contact."

I stop moving. "I—"

"You can do it. I want you to do this. Go slow, baby."

He sits back and I complete the maneuver, which has my back to him. My lips part, my lungs needing the air while still enjoying the fullness that is a part of me. I happily sigh and inwardly congratulate myself.

"Stay up on your hands and knees. I'm liking this view." He resumes a slow push into my soaked center while gripping my hips tighter. "I'm going deeper," he warns, pausing momentarily. "Hold on."

I nod to let him know I'm ready and arch my shoulders upwards, lower my back, and angle my hips up to meet his every thrust. Each plunge is rapid and with grand intention, and yet I can still tell how much care he's putting into his every movement. He leans his chest down against my back and snakes a hand around to my stomach. His fingers lower, grazing across me down there and I explode, clenching around him and feeling like I might black out from rapture. Holding me firmly against his pelvis, he furthers the depth and then orgasms while sputtering profanities. I drop to my elbows, forcing the back of my body up as I come back to the reality of us still linked together.

As soon as he lets go of me, I drop to the bed not realizing until that moment that he'd been holding me up. He falls next to me and settles by pulling my back against his chest. He wraps around me while protectively holding me inside our little pleasure bubble.

I can't hold my eyes open any longer. The last thing I see is the illuminated clock across the room— 3:19 in the morning. The last thing I hear is *'I ... you'* and I fall asleep.

Mallory gasps, and it startles me. I bolt upright and find her holding the sheet tight across her chest and staring straight ahead wide-eyed.

"Aren't we bright-eyed and bushy-tailed this morning?" Sunny chirps too cheery for this early in the morning. My eyes flash across the room and I see Zach and Sunny sitting on my couch facing us.

Mallory relaxes and flops back down onto the mattress.

Leaning over, I kiss her on the forehead. Her eyelids are heavy and she huffs in frustration. She looks right at me and whispers, "It was fun while it lasted."

I know what she means. After that horrid fight and my mother's surprise appearance, last night was good—really good—great even, and now our bubble has been invaded.

It pisses me off. I wanted a leisurely morning waking up with my girl, maybe make love to her ... definitely make love to her, but that opportunity has passed. Irritated, I ask, "What the fuck are you doing in here?" Sitting back up, I glare at the two people who interrupted what I know would've been fantastic morning sex.

Zach, still looking way too comfortable considering my tone, says, "Calm down. The girls made plans for today and Sunny just wants to sort out the details. What are you doing sleeping in anyway, ya fucking lazy bastard? We're missing some sweet waves today."

My girl looks way too cute this morning tucked into my bed, and I can't resist the soft smile that I know she has just for me. I fall back and cover us both up with the comforter, cocooning us away from the rest of the world. "Go away!" I shout, hoping the intruders get the message.

Mallory comes closer and kisses me on the lips. She whispers, "I guess I should get up and get to work. I also promised Sunny and your sister that I'd go shopping with them this afternoon." She smiles. "When will I see you?"

"I've got a better plan. How about we just stay in bed all day?"

"That would be heavenly, but I've gotta earn some spending money, honey."

Now I'm frustrated. After an overly dramatic sigh, I say, "I'll see you tonight then." I slide out of bed, stretching and not caring that I'm naked with morning wood in front of Sunny and Zach.

Sunny audibly gasps as Zach claps his hand over her eyes, and warns me. "A little respect, dude."

"You worried your girlfriend will finally discover what she's missing?" I laugh at my own joke.

"Brah, that's just all kinds of wrong," he snaps back.

"C'mon, Sunny, we'll wait outside." Zach drags her by the hand out the door.

I turn around and crawl across the covers and lay on top of Mallory, trapping her beneath me. "We might have enough time," I say, wiggling my eyebrows, "to start the day off right."

Before she has a chance to respond, I kiss her. I kiss her how she deserves to be kissed—with all I've got.

My hips start moving, pressing against her, the blanket keeping our heated centers apart. Her hands wind into my hair, urging me on, so I grind harder knowing that just humping could so easily get me across the finish line.

She mumbles into my mouth, *"Evvvvaan."* She pulls back to get my attention. "I need to go. I'm sorry. I really want to stay, but I can't."

I brush her hair away from her face and smile. I want to tell her how I'm feeling. I want her to know how she affects me, but I only manage to say, "You're so beautiful."

A hint of blush colors her cheeks and she takes a deep breath seeming to calm herself. I can tell she knows I chickened out from what I should be telling her, but her hand still strokes across my cheek as she runs her thumb along my bottom lip. "I think you're beautiful, too." And, like me, I know she means more than what she said as well.

She crawls out from under me and makes her way into the bathroom. I throw on some shorts and a t-shirt and join Sunny and Zach by the pool. Stretching out on a lounger next them, I say, "Thank you for the, well, you know, stuff you said yesterday." Zach helped both Mallory and me realize we were wasting precious time last night. The petty bullshit advice allowed us to see the bigger picture. My bigger picture is Mallory, all Mallory.

Zach glances at me. "You're welcome. Now can we get on with our summer?"

I snicker. "Yeah, let's do that. You wanna hit the water?"

"Totally," Zach says, kissing Sunny on the cheek.

I'm jealous because they make it look so fucking easy. *I want easy for a change.*

Mallory walks out and stands on the path, signaling us

to come over. We all get up and make our way, walking together.

"You aren't trying to hide over here, are you?" I ask, cocking my eyebrow at her.

She shrugs, obviously uncomfortable. "No," she replies, keeping her eyes straight ahead. *She's lying.*

"You're a guest of mine. You are welcome here anytime you want, so don't feel like you have to sneak around. I don't want you worrying either. I'll talk to my mother."

She places her hands on my chest and looks up at me. "I don't want to cause any trouble. I especially don't want you to fight with your parents over me." She holds my hand, pulling me over to Sunny's car. "Sunny is at Zach's every night now. She said I can sleep in her bed. We can just stay over there more—"

"We'll stay over there because we want to, not because we have to. I'm not ashamed of you and I'm not going to hide you or kowtow to their every fucking gripe and whim."

She pecks me on the lips, and asks, "I'll see you tonight?"

"Yeah," I whisper with an added nod.

Zach and I watch as the girls drive off and then we make our way back down the path and into the main house.

"I need to take care of some stuff. It shouldn't be long. Help yourself to coffee and breakfast."

"Cool," he replies, following me inside.

When I open the door into the kitchen area, my mother is standing, staring out the window, and drinking her coffee. I can tell by the lack of acknowledgment that she saw Mallory. I gulp and then address her, the proper way—the way she likes. "Good morning, Mother."

"Good morning, Zach," she says, not looking at me. That can't be good.

"Good morning, Mrs. Ashford," he replies, surprised.

She turns toward me, smiling, and says, "Evan, I'd like to speak with you for a few moments if you can spare the time. I know you must have a busy schedule between surfing, partying, and screwing classless girls, but do you think you might be able to squeeze a chat in?"

I'd say I'm shocked or outraged but this is her standard M.O. so I'm used to her passive aggressive bullshit. "I have time now."

I follow her into the library and shut the doors behind me.

"Sit," she says, pointing at a wingback chair stationed in front of the desk. She sits in the chair behind the desk and teepees her hands, resting her forehead against her fingers while closing her eyes, apparently, searching for the words to come to her. I've seen these dramatics before, but usually when we're in New York when she has the grey clouds to back her mood. It all seems silly with the sunshine, blue sky, and palm trees outside the large picture window. She lifts her head suddenly, and smiles. "How are you, Evan?"

"Ummm ... I'm fine." I readjust in my seat. I'm weary of this new approach.

"I've missed you. You should come home for a visit."

"I didn't know I was welcome."

"You're always welcome. It's your home, too." After an awkward pause, she says, "You've changed in the last seven months. You're very handsome and look a lot like your father when I met him." She smiles with pride as she searches my features as if to find contrast. "Your face structure is clearly his, but your eyes match mine." An expression I haven't seen in a long time, a soft smile, appears. "Kate seems to be the opposite. She looks like me, but has your fathers coloring."

"She's a beautiful girl—"

"Let's hope she has the sense to use that to her advantage." She shuffles some papers in front of her as if she's back to the task at hand. "What have you been doing with your time out here?"

"I think you know for the most part. I've been working. It's not full time, but it's steady."

"Your father tells me you decided to take more time off from school. Why is that?"

"I don't feel ready for the commitment school takes. When I return, and I will return one day, I want to be focused—"

"It must be nice to flounder on your parents' dime—"

"Like you did?"

Her eyes lock on mine, her pupils narrowing. "I didn't flounder, Evan. I have a degree from Barnard College. Because I chose to stay home and raise a family doesn't mean I don't deserve respect."

My blood boils as she looks at me spewing these words as if they're true. "You didn't choose to raise us. Nannies raised us. You were too busy getting drunk with the ladies of society to give a shit about me and Kate!"

She quickly rises to her feet, slamming her hands down on the wood desk top. "I will tell you this only once, Evan. You do not swear at me and you will show me respect!"

"Respect is earned. Isn't that why you always told me you didn't respect me, Mother?"

"I don't respect you because you let a small incident throw all my ... *your dreams* away. You let one small bump in the road ruin your potential." I jump to my feet, walking towards the door as she continues shouting. "You will not leave until I dismiss you."

"I'm not your servant!" I yell, not missing her slip up about my fulfilling my parents' dreams. Stopping at the door, I turn around waiting for her retort, the excuse that will allow me to justify once again that we have no real relationship.

"That's obvious because you've never listened to anything I've said." She sits down as if she's calmed down. She straightens her blouse and gently smooths a few loose strands of hair back into her updo. "I don't want to fight with you. I'm actually hoping for us to resolve this mess and move forward. Will you please sit down and talk to me?"

I want to stomp my foot like a petulant child, but I reserve my emotions, knowing I'll take them out on some waves later. I take my seat again and lean down, dragging my hand through my hair twice before fully calming down.

"Let's talk business," she starts, "your father won't be on the island long enough to go into any real details, but you and Kate are expected back for the annual company summer party. There's no arguing this. You were noticeably absent from the holiday party and we missed you at home. I want you to be there for this event. I want my family back together. Can you do that? Will you come home for me?"

I can see the sincerity in her eyes and agree to her wishes by nodding, not able to give her more than that.

"Good. Thank you. In other business, a board meeting is scheduled for that week and since you're still considered an active member you're expected to attend. We've had a lot of changes that I'm sure you are unaware of so please study the details before you fly out. Your father's company is resting in the hands of you and your sister and I expect you to protect what is rightfully the Ashford's."

"Okay."

"Your father and I are still hoping you'll follow in his shoes one day. I don't think you're a lost cause despite how you perceive my opinions. With power comes commitment, and we expect a certain level of respect from you. Your name is being sullied with rumors on a daily basis. You must show everyone that you mean business and you deserve their respect. That won't come about with your flitting about being useless. It's not been easy to squash the rumors thus far and will be even harder if you continue on your current path. So Dad and I need you to make some decisions and since school is off the table for the fall semester, you need to make better choices in your personal life."

Oh, here it is. Here's what she's been trying to get at the whole time—*Mallory*. "Are we talking about my dating life?"

"We're talking about your reputation, your image, and your future. There are plenty of," she laughs with a casual gesture of her arm, "willing young ladies in New York. They're beautiful, smart, and connected. They are the whole package. Surely, you can attend a few events during your visit."

"Those debutantes are shallow and only care about fashion and gossip. I'm arm candy, a prize for them to display and use to make others envious. It's pathetic. Anyway, I'm dating someone, someone that you treated like trash last night—"

She scoffs. "Evan, that girl, she's a passing fancy. Honestly, I didn't see anything special—"

"Don't! Don't talk about Mallory like that. She hasn't done anything to deserve your judgment. She's good. Her heart is good. She's smart and can hold a conversation which is more than most of those twits back home can do."

She waves her hand in front of her like she swatting away a gnat and then stands abruptly, holding in the raging emotions playing out behind the blue of her eyes. "I need to leave. I have a charity luncheon to attend." Walking to the door without looking back, she says, "Thank you for chatting with me." She exits the room leaving the door ajar.

I begrudgingly get up and leave the room too. I can hear Zach laughing with Ms. Chart before I see him. I hit him on the shoulder as I come around the corner. "Let's cruise, dude."

"Good morning, Evan. Nice talk with your mother?" Ms. Chart actually sounds hopeful.

I stop to give her the respect that she has earned from me. "The usual. They want me back in New York, you know, *living the high life*," I say sarcastically.

"Hmmm. I see. Well, what do you want?"

This is why I wish this woman was my mother. I smile, leaning against the marble counter, and say, "Would you be disappointed in me if I said I'm in a quarter life crisis and I've lost my way?"

She nods in understanding then asks, "Maybe this new love can help you find your way home. I don't know her and I know it's been just a short time that you have, but I see a spark in your eyes that you haven't had in a long time. You're happy which is a great start to finding your life's path."

The sentiment is sweet because she actually makes a future with Mallory sound possible. *Is it?*

She walks around and hugs me. I hug her back, leaning down against her shoulder as she whispers, "Bring your Mallory by. I want to meet this special girl."

My eyes are watering, which is really fucking embarrassing in front of Zach, so I will the tears back inside and straighten to my full height. "I will."

Zach nudges my ribs. "C'mon, you know how I get all sappy and shit." He laughs, but I actually do know that he's a sensitive guy.

On the drive to the beach, Zach says, "You've got a lot to think about."

"Why does it already feel like I have to choose sides?" I remain staring out my window at the ocean beyond the break where the waves roll in.

"You don't. You've already decided," he says as he parks the car. "C'mon, we wasted enough time this morning. I need to get my surf on." We do our knuckle, fist, thumb rub handshake and spend the next three hours feeling at peace as we become one with the ocean.

27

EVAN

Time moves so slow when you're anxious. Lying on my bed, I can feel myself getting more agitated with each slowly ticking minute. This is not just about want. It's about need, as selfish as it may sound. Not only do I want to see Mallory, but I *need* to see her.

Moving to the couch for a change of scenery is a momentary distraction, even if it is just fifteen feet from the bed. Propping my feet up on the arm, I toss a tennis ball into the air, wasting another hour before I decide I can't wait any longer. I call Murphy and Zach to come get me and we head over to Big Kehones.

Zach parks and we hop out. I rush ahead too excited for my own good, only to stop in my tracks in the doorway. Noah is sitting at the bar and laughing with Mallory. My heart clenches and anger takes over. I'm about to physically launch myself across the room when I see him lean forward and whisper something to her, but Murphy stops me. The commotion causes them to look over.

As Mallory's eyes meet mine, she tilts her head, silently questioning my expression of rage. I watch the corners of her mouth slide upwards into a reassuring smile and feel the tension starting to leave my adrenaline pumped muscles.

Noah watches as she comes around the bar and greets me. "Hi, babe. It's good to see you," she says, wrapping her arms around me and bringing her lips to mine. We kiss and I know I shouldn't, but I can't help but deepen it since Noah is watching.

She stops, her lips almost against mine. "Stop. Don't do that."

I'm so busted, but feign innocence anyway. "Do what?"

"You know what you just did. Don't use me like that, Evan." Her arms are still around me, but I see the hurt in her eyes.

I lean my forehead against hers. "I'm sorry. I just got jealous seeing him acting too friendly."

She calls over her shoulder, "Sunny, I'm taking five." She pulls me out the back door and onto the beach. Once we're a fair distance from anyone else, she says, "I've told you how I feel about you and more importantly, I feel like I've shown you what you mean to me. You have no reason to be jealous, especially not of Noah, so please don't worry." She holds both my hands between us, rubbing her thumbs over the prominent veins on top of them. "You have really great hands, strong hands."

I laugh, and the small tension that had built falls away. "Thanks."

Staring right into my eyes, she says, "I told Noah I would hang out with him in the next week or so. I'm not asking you, Evan. I'm not threatening you either—"

My mind is already searching for an explanation of why she needs to see him at all, but it's coming up empty for any reasonable excuse.

"... I enjoy his company as a friend and I don't think I should be caught in the middle of some ridiculous war you've got going with each other—"

"Ridiculous? Is that what he told you?" I take my hands from hers and rake them through my hair before bringing one down to my side, clenched. I turn to face the ocean. "You know I trust you. It's—"

"I know, I know. It's him you don't trust."

"Exactly."

"Well, that's not a good enough reason for me not to trust him or to hang out with him. So, unless you're willing to talk to me about what really happened between you two, I'm going to continue spending time with him."

I'm in utter disbelief, and suddenly my mind flashes forward. This is how Mallory is. This is how she will always be. She's stubborn and frustrating and although it's infuriating, I have to let her be who she is. I look at her defensive little body, arms crossed, fingers tapping, hips angled out. She's perfect.

"Did you hear me, Evan? I'm hanging out with him unless—"

"Okay," I whisper, taking hold of her wrists and carefully uncrossing her arms. I'm not ready to share the darkest part of my life, so I have to let her do this.

"What?"

"Okay, you can hang out with him. Obviously you're allowed to be friends with whomever you choose. So if you want to waste your time with him then that's your decision."

I wrap her arms around my waist and wrap mine around hers, bringing her closer.

After kissing her on the forehead, I say, "Some things you've got to learn on your own."

She leans back and makes a funny face at me. Then she smiles, and says, "Thank you, baby."

"For what?"

"For trusting me to make my own choices."

"And to live with the consequences?"

"Blah, blah, blah ... no consequences. You just remember that I lov—" She pauses though we both know what she was going to say. I wish she would again because I'm too scared to do it all on my own. "Well, you know who I'm coming home to." I still freaking love that she calls me home.

I kiss her on the tip of her nose. "Yeah, you just remember that when he's flirting with you."

She rolls her eyes. "I have to get back. Are you staying to eat?"

"If the guys are."

She turns to walk inside and I smack her jeans clad ass —*hard*. She yelps from surprise and maybe a little pain, but I've noticed she kind of digs it when I do that too.

"Revenge is sweet, Evan."

"Bring it on, baby."

"Hmmph!" She struts off, tossing her hair over her shoulder and trying to act like she's mad. She isn't, I can tell beneath the fake pout.

I sit down with the guys and Kate joins us.

"What's the drama today, lil bro?" she asks, not holding back. She's never afraid to hold back when it comes to me.

I feel defensive, but try to keep that emotion in check when I speak. "Mallory's going to hang out with Noah."

All three of them look at me in disbelief, probably because I'm not freaking out.

"*Ummm*, and you're okay with that?" Murphy asks, his mouth resuming the hanging open position.

"Nope, but she's going to have to learn the hard way."

"And what hard way would that be? When he has his *hard* member pressed against her? Is that the lesson you want her to learn?" Kate asks, looking between Murphy and me.

I roll my eyes. "She'll find out soon enough that he wants more than just friendship with her."

"Oh," everyone says in unison. We all turn to look at the current topics of discussion at the bar.

I slap my hands together, which startles them. "So, we eating or what?"

Noah leaves while we're chowing down on burgers and I can't say I'm sad to see him go. He didn't acknowledge my presence after the kiss I forced him to witness and ignored the group when Mallory returned from outside with me. I think he was more bothered than he let on, but that's just my opinion and one I'll try to keep to myself. Before we leave, I kiss her, not for show this time, but because I want to.

Kate is staying behind with the girls for their shopping excursion to Honolulu, but walks Murphy to the car. After their sexual display of pure horniness, I ask, "Hey sis, can I talk to you before you take off?"

She pulls herself away from Murphy like they're chained together, each step a struggle for her. We take a small walk around to the side of the restaurant to talk in private. I shove my hands in my pockets nervous I might upset her, so I tread carefully. "So, um, I talked with mom this morning."

"How'd that go?" She asks, obviously surprised by the news.

"Not as well as I would have hoped, but I'm not going to let them control me. I have a lot to think about concerning the future and I'm willing to do that now."

"That's sounds good. What about New York?"

"You knew?"

"Dad told me before I flew out here that they would appreciate us being there, representing a solid family front for the company ... and for them."

"I told her I'd be there for the board meeting and the party." I look over my shoulder to make sure no one is eavesdropping. I lower my voice just in case. "Does Mom know about Murphy?"

Kate's eyes scan behind me. "She's aware of him, but not to the extent of how I feel."

"How do you feel?"

"I like him ... a lot." She lowers her eyes and a small smile appears as her cheeks pink. The act itself is new for my sister. That's how I know she means what she says next. "I might be falling in love with him."

This new side of my sister makes me smile, but we only have a few minutes, so I continue with our conversation. "How did mom react to your relationship?"

"She thinks it's just a summer thing."

"That's more credit than she gave Mallory."

"She needs to get to know her first and then she'll see how great Mallory is."

When she looks at me, I say, "She's not willing to accept Mallory as part of my life, Kate. She told me on my last visit that she wants me to stay in New York to date girls there. She made that more than clear again today."

I gulp to fill the silence that exists between us. We're both well aware of what's expected for us to fulfill our legacy. Murphy and Mallory aren't considered proper marriage material for either of us, which in turn means they won't accept us even dating them in the long term.

Kate's face contorts from contemplation into sadness.

She whispers, "Our family needs us, Evan. We're the next generation, *the only* next generation. We don't have cousins or anyone else. If we don't run the business, it's like we're selling our legacy to the highest bidder."

"So you're willing to give Murphy up to please our mother?"

She exhales loudly through her nose which is very un-Kate like, and confesses, "I lied. There's no might about it. I do love him. I've already fallen for him. I know I shouldn't. He's the opposite of everything I thought I ever wanted, but since we hooked up last spring break, I haven't been able to get him off my mind—"

"Wait," I interrupt, narrowing my eyes at her, "back up. What do you mean you hooked up over spring break?"

"Oh, don't go all brotherly on me." She raises her hands in the air and says, "I've slept with guys. I know that ruins the virginal image you had of me, but it's kind of ridiculous that we can't be friends and talk about this stuff."

"This is a conversation that I'd hoped I would never have, but since we're here and having it, I'm just shocked that he didn't spill. The boy can't keep a secret to save his life."

"First off, ewwww on the sharing! Thank God, he didn't spill. Secondly, apparently he can keep a secret, so that's moot at this point. And thirdly, let's get back on topic. Back in New York I was dating and all the guys were being compared to Murphy. Listen, I know sometimes he's goofy, but he's funny, and sweet, a romantic at heart, and he can hold his own in a game of Trivial Pursuit. But, most of all, he's sincere."

I reach over and pull her into a hug. It's always kind of felt like *us* against *them*. Things haven't changed. "He's a good guy. That's why he's one of my best friends."

She hugs me, and whispers, "I don't want to lose him and I don't think I can give him up."

My heart breaks for her knowing she's in the same situation, fighting the same battle I am. "It's going to work out, sis. I promise."

We walk around the corner to join the others, but I have a million thoughts clouding my vision. I struggle with believing my own words of reassurance to Kate just a moment earlier. But when I think of Mallory, my heart knows it's a battle I must wage. If this was a month ago and Zach was in this situation, I'd laugh at him. But a lot can change in a month and has. I never saw her coming, underestimated her and then got in over my head, all the while loving every minute I'm lucky enough to spend with her.

I see Kate wipe her eyes, pretending that our talk didn't affect her the way it did, but I feel the same and it's hard to hide a true emotion.

Smiling, Kate shoves me hard, and says, "Go! Have a fun boys' night. I've got a date with your girlfriend." I know she's just embarrassed that she was caught getting sentimental.

"Yeah, yeah, yeah, okay." I walk back towards the guys, but stop, turn around, and say, "Love you, big sis."

She nods and smiles. "Love you back, little brother."

"Can you two stop with the mushy crap for the day? My heart fucking hurts over this angsty shit!" Zach shouts as I climb into the back seat.

"No more today, I promise."

"Good. Let's go get fucked up now," Murphy shouts loud enough for the entire restaurant to hear.

Zach and I both roll our eyes, and I laugh thinking that one day this punk just might be my brother-in-law. Once again, proving how much can change in such a short period of time.

THREE HOURS LATER, we're lounging at Zach and Murphy's house playing quarters and eating pizza. Mallory called me two hours ago to tell us the girls were off work and heading into Honolulu. Then Sunny called Zach an hour ago and told him not to expect them until later tonight. The thought of Mallory being away that long bothered my insides. I already missed her and it was messing with my quarter bouncing skills which really sucked because I was down fifty bucks.

But when Kate called Murphy thirty minutes ago to tell him they were done shopping and now drinking their way through the bars, I was downright frustrated. I just want to spend all my free time with her and the image of my girl drinking with other guys vying for her attention sent me into a pissed off, jealous mind-fuck.

The guys were now sensing a major distraction was needed and fast. So they concocted a plan that was stupid, irresponsible, and completely perfect. As Zach unloaded the BB guns from the shed, Murphy lined up the empty beer cans at the far end of the yard. I poured the whiskey shots.

Not ten minutes later, we are cocking our guns and trying, to the best of our drunken abilities, to aim at our tiny targets. After ten rounds, we had yet to hit one. Yes, we got the tree near the house several times, the metal trash can against the fence three times, but the shed and fence took the brunt of our misses.

When we ran out of BB's we dragged ourselves into the house and plopped down in front of the couch. It was probably best for the neighbors that we were too wasted to continue our outside fun. Inside, I think ESPN was on, but I passed out, so I'm not positive.

"Baby, wake up. Wake up, sexy." I hear a sweet angel calling me, a siren willing me to her. My gaze fixates on the light as my body is weighed down.

I draw my eyes open one at a time and see *my* sweet angel sitting on my lap.

"Hi." Her voice is but a whisper on my skin. Her lips brush across my cheek and then she says, "I want you, baby. Do you want me?"

My body responds to her presence, leaving my foggy brain to catch up.

"I always want you. I think you know that," I whisper in return. My eyes grow heavy again as she nips around my ear. But the discomfort of the room spinning does nothing to help me focus or to be able to satisfy my girlfriend.

My hands grip her hips, stopping her. "Baby, wait."

"Are you drunk?"

I look into her eyes which are looking pretty drunk themselves, and chuckle. "Yeah, a little."

"A little?" she asks incredulously. She takes a deep breath and then sighs in disappointment.

I can't take her sadness. "Where is everyone?"

"They already went to bed."

"Good."

"Good?" She perks up.

"Very good." I may be tired, but never too tired to please my girl. "Come here," I say pulling her down next to me on the reclined chair. I run my hand up and down her smooth thigh, inching under her short skirt. "I like this outfit." I nuzzle her neck and kiss her, dragging my tongue up and behind her ear as my hand reaches her panties. When I move them aside, I hear a faint moan and she wiggles in anticipation.

"I love when you touch me."

I press my lips against her ear, enjoying the feel of my girl getting hot and bothered. "I love touching you, baby."

Her body moves, seeking what she needs and when she finds it, she drops her head back, eyes closed, and mouth hanging open. This girl is going to do me in with that look alone. Her mind and body are already focused, so I need to give her what she craves. She feels fucking magnificent and I'm not even being touched. I move against her, putting more pressure and touching her heat until she lets herself go.

I'm lost in the sound she creates and the feel of her pleasure as her ecstasy engulfs me whole, my body reacting and finding my own release. I grind into her hard as I force everything I've got out, finding relief.

Minutes later, I hold her close. We're panting and tired, satisfied and sleepy. Then reality sets into my slightly dazed and alcohol-filled brain. "Holy shit! I just came in my pants. I've never come in my pants before. Fuck, I've never come without someone else or at the very least me touching my dick." I feel embarrassment take over, covering my cheeks.

She cups my face, and says, "It's because your mind was turned on."

I look down at my pants, which are sporting a wet spot that's beginning to seep through the fabric. "I'm pretty sure more than my mind was turned on." This girl, *my girl*, made me come like a thirteen year old seeing his first pair of tits. *I'm in so fucking deep.*

28

MALLORY

My head hurts.

My body hurts.

What the fuck is stabbing me in the ribs?

Although my head feels like it weighs a ton, I lift up and find the source of the stabbing pain—Evan's elbow. I shift in the recliner, trying not to disturb him, but I do by accident. His eyes open, but they're only slits as he squints to take in the scene.

"Did we sleep like this?" His voice is low, groggy with sleep.

Slowly sitting up, I look around as my eyes adjust to the bright sunlight shining in through the exposed large window.

He pulls me back down on him, and says, "Let's not get up yet."

I cuddle with him, but complain because I feel like crap. "I don't want to get up, but we probably should." Noticing the time on the clock that's hanging on the wall, I attempt to get up again. "It's almost eight. I need to go home and get showered before work. Do you work today?"

"Yeah, at ten."

I kiss his scruffy cheek and sit up, again. He kicks the bottom part of the recliner down, tucking it securely back into place. I stand up and stretch, hurting all over from lying on a cramped recliner all night. "Why do I feel like today is gonna suck?"

"Eh, you're just tired, baby." Evan gets up and walks to the window, suddenly energized. "Look outside, it's beautiful out there." He takes my hand and pulls me toward him. I groan, though secretly I love these kinds of moments with him—the quiet ones when he snuggles against me, embracing me from behind. "C'mon on, sleepy, paradise awaits."

I turn in his arms, wrapping mine around his neck, and say, "I found paradise when I found you."

"I thank the Hawaiian Gods every day for letting me be the first one to hit on you at the airport. Imagine if some other chump had gotten to you first?" He sighs, closing his eyes. When he reopens them they sparkle with an ocean-blue brilliance. "My cocky nature got me you."

"Your cocky nature didn't get me, but your cocky little guy did," I say, rubbing against his erection.

"*Ooohh*, don't hurt his feelings. *Little?* That's kind of selling him ... short, don't ya think?"

"You're right, bad choice of words because there's nothing *little or short* about you, hot stuff."

He leans down and kisses me three times in quick succession. "Let's get out of here."

We walk down the porch and then stop when we see the parked cars. "Shit! I forgot I didn't drive yesterday."

"Neither did Sunny. Kate drove us," I say.

"Fuck, we'll have to take Kate's car." He moans as he turns around and trudges back inside. I follow him in, but he stops at the entrance to the short hallway. "I swear on my Maserati, if Murphy's on top of her, I'll hurt him."

"They make a cute couple, but yeah, it's still your sister. Do you want me to knock and get her keys instead?"

"I don't hear anything. Maybe they're still sleeping. I don't want to wake them. I'll just sneak in and get them."

We tiptoe down the hall and press our ears against the door. Feeling confident that neither of us heard anything coming from inside the bedroom, I whisper, "I think they're asleep."

He carefully turns the doorknob, takes a deep breath then whispers, "I'm going in."

"Be swift like a ninja and good luck." I joke because of all the dramatics.

The door opens without any creaking and Evan starts tiptoeing into the room. I watch him through the cracked opening from the hallway. He sneaks over to Kate's purse that's on the floor and bends down. Suddenly, I hear a moan. It wasn't Evan and it definitely wasn't me. He squats down quickly, glancing over his shoulder at the couple in bed. My heart races as my eyes dart between him and the bed, hoping he doesn't get caught because that would just be all kinds of awkward.

Right when I think it's safe for him again, I see Kate and Murphy move around on top of the mattress. Waving my hands frantically, I try to signal for Evan to stay down exactly at the same time we hear Kate say, "I love your ass."

"Is that all you love, pretty?" Murphy asks.

I'm frozen in place as I lock eyes with Evan who looks like he's about to vomit. He continues to dig around her purse, the stress of the situation making him clumsy.

I cover my mouth to keep from giggling when Murphy

uses a baby voice, and says, "I love when you play with my hair."

"Who knew ass hair could be such a turn on. I think you should let the hair on your back grow out again. I'm getting horny just thinking about it."

"What the fuck kind of kinky shit are you two into? Scratch that, I don't want to know the answer to that." Evan stands straight up, completely disgusted.

I clasp my hand over my mouth in shock and keep watching, unable to look away.

Murphy tosses the covers off his head and throws a pillow as hard as he can, hitting Evan in the face. "Get the fuck out. Ashford!"

"Get the fuck off my sister!"

"Evan! I'm a grown-ass woman. I'm horny for my boyfriend, so get out!"

Evan laughs, staring down at them. "Yeah, I've been meaning to talk to you about your growing ass—"

"Don't make me bring up Sir Mix-Ford." Kate's laugh is more of a cackle than an innocent joke.

With a threatening finger pointed at his sister, Evan says, "You better shut your mouth, Katherine!"

"What are you doing in here anyway, you pervert?" Murphy yells.

"Looking for Kate's keys. I need a car," Evan replies as if his presence should be obvious. "You two have some nerve calling me the perv when," he makes a hairball-stuck-in-the-throat gagging sound then says, "you're getting off on *ass hair*!"

"The keys are in the kitchen on the bar. Now get out before I come over there and kick your ass out of here," Kate shouts. Her expression is serious. She means business.

Evan rolls his eyes, stomping out of the room, and

mumbling. "Figures, the keys aren't even in here. Wonder if Zach has any bleach for my brain after this sick conversation."

"Yeah, save some bleach for us after having to see that dried come spot on your pants. Oh, and, Mallory, don't think I don't hear you giggling out in the hall," Kate says, walking across the room in a tank top and underwear.

I'd be a fool not to take the perfection of the situation and twist it around. "I can't help that I giggle when I get into *hairy* situations."

"Ha! Ha!" She slams the door closed, and I hurry after Evan who is already in the kitchen jangling the keys in his hand.

"I could've lived my whole life not knowing about my sister's sick turn-ons." Evan looks down at his crotch and groans in frustration. Turning quickly, he takes my hand in his and rushes us out the door.

I feel like I'm running to keep from lagging behind him. "Where's the fire?"

He looks over at me, his smirk firmly in place. "I want to get you all sexed up and showered before work." I stop, forcing him to halt, and look at him in shock. My mouth drops open as he asks, "What?"

"I, uh ... Evan!" I'm stunned by his brusqueness.

"What, you have a problem with showers?"

I roll my eyes, and burst out laughing. "No problem with showers."

He leans down and kisses me. Then he whispers, "Well, I'm hoping it's not the sexing part—"

"Abso-fucking-lutely not! No problem with that part at all."

He straightens back to his proud 6'1" height. "Good, let's go and make that happen."

He drives like a crazy person hell-bent on a mission. The tires squeal to a stop in the parking lot and he races around to my side of the car. I delay my exit to let him 'beat' me to opening the door. I know he's a gentleman like that and likes to open it for me. For such a bad boy, he has a romantic side that makes me swoon.

As soon as we get inside the apartment, Evan rushes to the bathroom and starts the shower. When he walks back out, he's naked and my heart races at the beauty of his physique. He's tall with broad, muscular shoulders, lean, sculpted stomach, and strong legs—he's perfect. He waves at me, causing me to look at his hands. My fist goes to my mouth as I watch his long fingers moving in the air.

"Up here ... my eyes are up here, baby," he says, but it doesn't register with my brain.

I bite down on my knuckles and feel my body readying itself for him. *Holy hands, those fingers.* "Unf!"

"Mallory? *Oh, Mallory?*" he calls.

My eyes flash to his at the sound of my name. "Huh?" I do a lame attempt of trying to think.

He leans against the doorframe amused. "Go ahead, baby, ogle away. I'm all yours anyway." His member grows before my eyes, revealing his own naughty thoughts.

I gulp before trying to speak, but only disjointed, gargled sounds come out. I clear my throat, and he chuckles.

"*The shower?*" I finally get something comprehensible out.

He nods and waggles his eyebrows. "Yeah, the shower."

I've already soaked my undies just looking at him, but now I move toward him in a lust filled haze of want and desire, needing him ... *in the shower.* I brush against him as I strip my clothes off, tossing them behind me on my way to the water.

When I bend over, I shake my ass for effect, and test the water. The effect is felt because I instantly feel him pressed to my back side before I even stand back up. His strength and hardness leaves me breathless. I move to the side, slipping out of his grasp, and step into the tub. Under the warm water, I close my eyes, and push my hair back, soaking it. When I open them, Evan is watching me, his lips parted, eyes darkened, and his hand stroking himself.

"How bad do you want me, baby?" I ask, teasing, tempting his carnal desires to the surface.

He licks his lips and takes two steps closer, joining me, making me back up under the water so the spray can cover him. His hands go flat against the wall, trapping me between them and leans in so close I think he's going to kiss me, but he doesn't. With his lips barely touching mine, he says, "More than I've ever wanted anything in my life."

I might have melted a little. Okay, my knees weakened and I can't breathe. His words, his breath on me, his body's proximity, it's all too much. I blink, but it feels like the slowest blink in history. Too much is never enough when it comes to him, so I encourage him further. "Take me then."

A faint gasp slips out as he kisses across my collarbone and nibbles up my neck, pressing his chest against mine. His weight feels raw and needy as if he has no choice, but to be there. Dropping his head onto my shoulder, he says, "We can't do this. It's torture to leave and you have to go to work soon."

"We'll be fast," I say, sounding like I'm begging, which I kind of am.

He looks into my eyes, and says, "I don't want to be fast with you."

Hot steam billows around us, and I agree. "I don't either.

I want so much more." I may be referencing our future as much as the sex.

Thirty minutes later, he's dropping me off at Big Kehones. After opening the door, I get out of the car and lift up on my toes to kiss him. My emotions are heavy today and I feel so much for him that I want to remember the feel of his lips on mine for the rest of the day. I also have a jealous side that wants him to remember mine as well. I'm worried he's going to meet someone better at his work.

He is, after all, headed to work to socialize with pretty girls in teeny bikinis. "I love you, Evan."

He already knows me too well though. "You don't have to worry about us. It's only you, always, okay, baby?" Sliding his hands into my hair, he kisses me with reverence. Our lips part and he whispers into my ear, "Although I love hearing those words from you, I'd rather you say them because you want to instead of feeling like you have to."

I tilt my head against his mouth, his lips to my forehead, keeping my eyes closed. "I love you, Evan." A small smile crosses my face and I savor his full embrace.

He holds me so tight that I feel his crushing love. I've still not heard him say those three magical words, but I definitely feel his love and that's the most important thing to me anyway. After a sweet kiss on the top of my head, he says, "I'll pick you up at six. You want to order a pizza and watch a movie at my place tonight?"

"Yes, I'd like that."

"Good. I'll see you tonight."

I start walking backwards toward the restaurant and blow him a kiss, which he catches with his hand in the air and presses against his heart.

29

MALLORY

Noah doesn't visit me at work today, although I half expected him to. Our friendship has an ease about it, and I look forward to catching up during these times. We don't talk about Evan, for good reason, though he is fully aware that we are a couple. He has the surfing competition soon, and I realize he's probably out preparing.

Johnny comes in at two. He's always good company, and I can see why Sunny likes him so much. We have down time to talk while the place is empty.

"I've been hearing how crazy your life has become. I think Mallory Wray has thrown this sleepy island a curve ball." He stops wiping down a table and looks at me as I restock the beer cans. "What are you going to do come August?"

"I'm not sure. Well, that's not completely true. I'm going back to Colorado. I have to. I can't afford to transfer and I have scholarships there."

"I understand. Your life is there, but how's Evan doing with that?"

"We've struggled with it. He thinks he's alone in wanting

to be together long term. He's not. I've been considering all the options, but there aren't any for me. Change would have to be on his part and I don't ever want to guilt someone into changing their whole life for me."

"What if he wants to?" Johnny asks, sitting on the barstool in front of me. "Have you thought that maybe he might want to go? He only has that part time job and doesn't seem to have any other obligations."

"He has his friends—"

"You're his girlfriend now."

"He has free rent at his family's house—"

"He can shack up with you."

"I don't think so," I say, nodding. "We are definitely not ready for that."

"Take the plunge, Mallory. What do have to lose? If he wants to pack up and follow you to school, let him."

"You sure are full of advice for everyone else. What about you? What's going on in your love life these days?" I ask, wanting to change the subject and simply because I'm curious about the secrecy regarding his love life.

He stands up and acts busy all of the sudden, so I walk around the bar and help him adjust chairs that don't need adjusting. When we're done, I put my hands on my hips. "What gives, Secret Secreton?"

"Nothing, Nosey Noserton."

"*Mmmhmmmm*, sure, nothing at all," I say, taunting him. I hop on top of the table he's currently rearranging. "C'mon, spill it. I won't tell anyone."

He shakes the table and I take the hint and hop off. Sitting on a chair instead, I place my elbows on the table and rest my chin in the palm of my hand, feeling impatient waiting for him to confide in me.

"You promise not to tell anyone?"

"Promise. My lips are sealed," I say, turning an imaginary key to my lips and tossing it over my shoulder.

"Especially, not Sunny. Promise me you won't tell Sunny."

"I won't tell Sunny. Will you get it out all right already? I think I've aged a year just sitting here waiting for you to tell me."

"Fine," Johnny says, grabbing a chair and turning it backwards. He sits down leaning his arms on the top of the chair. His expression goes from light to sad. "I'm in love with," he says with a sigh, "*Sunny.*"

Sitting straight up at his confession, my mouth drops open from shock.

Words fly from his mouth to justify what he just said. "I know I shouldn't, but I do. We just grew so close over the last couple of months. I knew she liked Zach, but it seemed likely it was one sided. Now, all of the sudden, they're inseparable and it seems I've lost my chance."

I rub his forearm gently. My voice is calm, but sad for him. "Oh, Johnny, I'm sorry. You're really in love with Sunny?"

"Yeah, but I don't want to be. How do I stop?"

I smile at his hopeful thinking. "I don't think our hearts work like that."

Resting his chin on his hand, he looks down. "Do you think I should wait for her?"

When I look into his eyes, the words quickly follow. "No, I don't. She's in love and Zach is madly in love with her. I may be a poor judge of what works in my own relationships, but anyone can see that *they* work. I'm sorry. I know that must hurt, but you shouldn't waste any more time pining over something that will never be. I know she cares about you as one of her closest friends and if you want to maintain that, then you need to let her be with Zach." He sits up, pondering my words as I keep talking. "This island has a lot of beautiful women. Any of them would be lucky to have you in their life."

He stands up, and I do too. I sit on a barstool, letting him man the bar instead. I can tell he needs the distraction. Johnny leans across the counter, and says, "You should go home. It's dead here today."

A twinge of excitement shoots through my body at the prospect of seeing more of Evan. Then I remember he's working today. Maybe I should stop by. *Would he like that or hate that?* I decide I'm doing it. He stops into my work all the time. I know he'll be happy to see me. "Are you sure you don't want me to stay?"

"It's cool. Go enjoy your day."

"Thanks. You're going to meet the girl you're supposed to be with," I say, hoping he can find comfort in my words.

"I like your faith."

I wish I could help, but we both know he's going to have to work through this on his own. He also knows what he's up against now if he decides to pursue her. "I'm going to text Sunny and see if she can pick me up." My eyes flash to his when I mention Sunny. I hope she's not a sore subject for him. He sends me a reassuring smile, so I text her then ask, "Hey, are you sure you're okay?"

"Yeah, I'll be fine. It feels good to finally get it out. Maybe I can start to move on."

I walk around the bar and hug him. "If you ever need to talk, I'm here for you."

"I know and thanks. I appreciate that."

When I break the embrace, he stops me and he says, "Hey, Mallory, I'm really happy things are working out for you. I think I misjudged Ashford because of all the bad stuff

I'd heard, but he seems to be a decent guy. I'm glad you're happy."

"I misjudged him too. He is a good guy and thank you."

Ten minutes later, Sunny pulls her VW into the parking lot and Zach drives in right after. She tosses me the keys as she runs over to Zach's car and gets in. "Hey, take care of the bus and we'll see you later at Evan's for the barbeque."

I catch the keys then freeze. "Wait! What? What barbeque at Evan's?"

But they're already gone. I get into bus and start the engine, but feel numb to the thought that dinner might include his mother. I speed all the way to the hotel where Evan works, choosing to park in the distant employee lot, so I don't get him in trouble. I jog down to the beach area, stopping about thirty yards away when I see him with a client near the surf shack. It's a woman—a very shapely, beautiful woman. Beautiful enough for me to be able to tell she's attractive even from this distance. I walk to a nearby bench and sit down. All of the previous excitement to surprise him at work has been sucked out of me as I watch him 'working.'

The woman is flirting. I can see it in her body language —the way she leans toward him when talking, the way she rests her hand on his shoulder to laugh at a shared joke, and the way she lays down on the surfboard attempting to do a pop-up which looks more like a sexual come on.

My stomach turns. This is what he gets everyday at his work, *heck*, this is what he gets everyday of his life. He wears charisma and charm as a second skin. They both come naturally to him and he wins everyone over when he meets them, including me. Who am I kidding? *Especially me.*

The woman's hand slides from his shoulder up his neck and into the back of his hair. I stand up ready to march over there and smack her overly affectionate hands from my man, but I see him duck out from under her blatant pass. He takes two steps away from her with his hands in front of him like he's telling her to back off. His body is firm, tense, leaving no room for misunderstanding. Sitting back down and feeling totally ooey-gooey over his respect for me, I smile.

He loves me. Not knowing I'm here, his actions clearly stated that he's in love and he's in love with me. *My sweet surfer boy, oh how I love you, too.*

The woman seems mad as she grabs her bag from the sand. Evan tries to talk with her, but she's not hearing it. *Rejected! Yeah, that's right lady, you were rejected! So move along now.* I inwardly cackle.

Evan watches her walk away. He looks frustrated until he spies me, squinting then smiling. I start walking towards him, but he hurries over.

"Hey there," he says, pulling me in for a kiss.

"Hey there, yourself. A little girl trouble?"

He looks over my shoulder at the hotel, and says, "You could say that. So, what brings you to this part of the island? Aren't you supposed to be working?"

"It was dead, so I got sent home. I wanted to surprise you, but I got a little surprise myself."

His smile turns into a smirk. I don't have to lecture him or say hooking up with her would have been bad. He knows all that and proved where he stands emotionally, and that's right by my side.

Taking my hand, he asks, "C'mon, she was my last client. You want to hang out while I close up?"

"Sure, I can help."

"Nah, it'll only take five minutes. I just want the company."

"In that case, can I tell you I love you or is that too distracting?"

He stops and turns back to me with a board tucked under his arm. "You can tell me anytime you want, baby."

I rest my hands on his chest; his skin is hot from the sun. "I love you, Evan." I'm not saying it because I need him to say it back. I'm saying it because I feel it deep inside and I'm content with that.

He props the board against the shack and pulls me against his sweaty, fan-fucking-tastic smelling chest and kisses me on the top of my head. In his arms, I feel his love and this feels good, satisfying. His body tells me everything I ever need to hear, everything he can't say ... or isn't ready to say.

Backing up, he smiles and wags his finger at me. "You are a distraction. Let me get this stuff packed up and we can go. I'll let you distract me in private when we leave."

I lean against the counter and watch as he moves in and out of the shack with gear and surfboards. He's strong and his muscles defined, making the task look easy. A few minutes later, he takes my hand and we walk to the parking lot. We talk about our day as he walks me to the VW first, unlocking the door, and starting the engine for me. When he hops out, I see him gnawing on his bottom lip. I've never seen him look so worried before.

Ahhh, the barbeque ...

"What's wrong?" I ask, knowing what's coming.

He takes my hands in his and looks down, focusing all his attention on my fingers. Waiting an uncomfortable amount of time, he's starting to worry me, but then he says, "My mom invited you over for dinner tonight."

"Just me?" I gulp, hoping he doesn't hear it.

"No, Kate and Murphy, and Zach and Sunny. All of us."

I absorb his cryptic non-detailed answer. "She invited me specifically or she told you to invite your friends?"

He looks up at a cloud that suddenly hangs high above our heads contrasting against the blue of the sky.

"Friends."

"So she doesn't know you're inviting me? And, she doesn't know that we are dating? And, let me guess, she isn't expecting me tonight?"

"You're looking at it all negative. She asked me and Kate to invite our friends over. I want you to meet her tonight. I want to introduce—"

"Meet your mom officially? Because, technically, I've met your mom and she told me to leave."

"I want her to meet my girlfriend, not for her benefit, but for us. I'm not hiding you. She needs to know you and to know what you mean to me. I've told her about you," he says, brushing a few flyaways from my face.

I drop his hands and rub my eyes, searching for clarity behind my closed lids. "Fine." I look back at him, and say, "Fine, I'll go for you."

Hugging me, he says, "Thank you, Mallory. And don't worry about a thing. I'm there for you, just you."

30

MALLORY

I push my skirt down in a sad attempt to straighten the wrinkles for the third time since I've exited the car. *Why did I agree to this again?* I try to think back to when I stopped listening to my intuition. *Oh, that's right—the moment I met Evan.* I giggle, but then my stomach flips again. "I feel sick." Grabbing a hold of Evan's arm, I stop him.

He turns back to me, and says, "Baby, if you don't feel comfortable, we'll leave. It's that simple. We're a team, remember? You and me." He leans over and kisses me on the neck, which weakens my knees. His sweet, innocent kiss turns wet with more suction as he attempts to distract both of us from what has to be an awaiting disaster.

I push him off of me. "Do not give me a hickey right now," I whisper in a stern tone. His mother would really love if I showed up with a fresh hickey courtesy of her horny son.

He chuckles and takes my hand, not bothering to comment. I think he's learned when it's best to acquiesce. And on that note, we continue down the path, passing the wall that now holds one of the best memories of my life. The thought lightens my mood in time for us to round the corner and see the gang already gathered. My eyes scan the area and I exhale a breath of relief when I don't see his mom outside. I relax and we continue over to the other side of the pool where a large wooden table has Kate, Murphy, Zach, and Sunny sitting, enjoying cocktails.

"Hey there, guys," Kate greets us, getting up to hug me. "Mallory, how are you doing?" Her tone is concerned while she searches my eyes for some hidden truth.

"I'm good ... kind of. Okay, I feel like I might puke."

Evan squeezes my hand as Kate wraps her arms around me, bringing me into her again. She whispers, "We're here for you. She's decent once you get to know her."

"Ahh, it's getting to that point that worries me," I reply, reaching for Sunny's drink.

Sunny slaps my hand. "Go get your own, Mal. They're right inside on the bar."

"I'll get you a drink," Evan offers.

My nerves kick in again at the thought of encountering his mother on my own, but feel I should probably be brave and try to do this to show Evan I'm making an effort. I also want to make an effort for my own sake. Trying not to think about the first time I met his mom, I answer, "Thanks, but I need to use the restroom anyway. I'll get the drinks."

When I start walking, the party suddenly goes silent. I look back over my shoulder and five pairs of eyes watch me head for the door. "The show is over people. Carry on talking amongst yourselves." I roll my eyes right before I enter the kitchen.

"Hi, you must be Mallory," A welcoming woman says, making her way around the marble counter to shake my hand.

"Yes," I nod, not knowing who this is.

"I'm Gail—"

"Ms. Chart, I'd like you to keep the formalities of the house with our guests, whether they're welcome or not," Evan's mother says, curt in her tone. She walks toward me from a large sitting room that is impeccable and too formal in décor, considering we're in Hawaii.

My stomach flips inside out and I'm rendered speechless. She walks straight up to me, and says, "You're Evan's friend from the other night?"

I nod, completely incapable of using my voice. From out of nowhere, Kate is behind me, placing a comforting hand on my shoulder. "Mother, this is Evan's *girl*friend, Mallory."

"Oh," she responds, placing her hand on her chest as if in shock.

Finally, remembering how to speak, I say, "I'm Mallory." *Gulp.* "Wray. It's very nice to meet you, Mrs. Ashford."

She tilts her head as if critiquing my every move. I watch her, waiting for her to say something else, anything else. I'm on guard, but know I need her approval and don't want to be disrespectful.

Kate walks around me, filling the awkward silence. "Would you like a Mai Tai, Mallory? Evan wants a beer. I'll get the drinks and you can use the bathroom."

"Uh, yeah, that sounds good. Thank you." She'll never know how much I appreciate the chance to escape this uncomfortable situation.

"Ms. Chart will show you the way. Kate, may I speak with you for a moment," Mrs. Ashford calmly directs.

Ms. Chart waves me over to follow. "Right this way, Mallory." As soon as we turn the corner and enter a long corridor, she says, "It's the third door down on the right."

I look at her a second, taking in her rounded features and kindness, and I smile. "Thank you."

Her smile is filled with warmth and makes me feel like we're already family.

When I finish in the restroom, I walk back down the corridor and notice the last door on the left is open.

"Mallory, do you have a minute?" Ms. Chart is sitting on a bed welcoming me inside. I nod and walk in, sitting down next to her. Her words are soft, comforting as she speaks. "I just want you to know that I'm really glad to finally meet you. Evan has told me so many wonderful things about you."

"He's talked about you also, but I had no idea he told anyone about me."

"You're very special. Not only because he talks about you and he never talks about girls, but because, if I may be so blunt," she lowers her voice, "you've brought my Evan back. The Evan he used to be. I hope you don't mind me sharing this with you. I already feel close to you, like I know you. Evan would call me a sentimental fool."

"Well, there is nothing wrong with that and I feel the same about you." I feel at ease considering I just met her. Even her calling Evan 'My Evan' doesn't bother me because I know exactly what she means. "I like that you're honest. I'll be honest, too. It's not been easy and meeting his family, well, other than Kate, is quite nerve-wracking." I look down at my hands. "To say the least."

"I'm not Mrs. Ashford. She has this idea of who Evan's supposed to be and it's suffocating him. Please don't let her scare you away though. She can be very kind and generous once you get to know her." Ms. Chart places her hand lovingly on my forearm while airing a more serious tone. "It might not be easy. I won't lie to you, but he needs you and I can tell he cares for you very much." She leans over and hugs me. Her embrace is sincere and caring. "Thank you, Mallory."

"Don't thank me. It's all him. He's special."

She smiles warmly, and in that smile I see why Evan seems to bond with her in such a familial way.

Standing up, I thank her before walking back through the kitchen. I hear my friends laughing outside as I head for the door.

"He's not as good as you think he is. He has problems he hasn't worked through yet."

I look over my shoulder and see Evan's mother sitting in a pale yellow club chair in the breakfast room. Taking the doorknob in hand, I turn around. I want to ignore her poisonous words, but I also can't hide my thoughts on the matter. "He's also not as bad as you think he is." Opening the door, I exit the house and join my friends.

Evan is all smiles, and my heart soars just looking at him. *This is right. We are right.* I won't let his mother ruin us.

After taking a seat next to Evan, I look around and watch as everyone starts to couple off, getting lost in their own worlds. Murphy is tending the barbeque pit while Kate leans against his back supervising, as if she needs to. It's obvious she just wants to be touching him.

Sunny sits on Zach's lap, whispering to him, making him giggle like they're fifteen-year-olds. He rubs her arm, enchanted by her, which makes me smile.

"Hey there," my surfer whispers in my ear, his voice laced with possibility. "Are you hungry? I noticed a *delicious* looking fruit salad on the buffet."

I giggle at the insinuation, remembering how naughty he was with fruit on the beach just days earlier.

Looking at him, at my Evan—maybe it's the star-filled

night or all that we've been through, maybe it's that I feel in control after giving his mom a small piece of my mind, but I'm not hungry. I'm happy and satisfied and full of love for him. Leaning my body against his, I rest my head on his chest, right over his heart and wrap my arms around him. "I'm wonderful."

His arms gently work their way around me, and I snuggle even closer. "You sure? I'll give you anything you want," he says, both of us knowing he's not talking about food. I nod not wanting to leave the warmth of his body. "Do you want to stay or would you rather leave? We can go to my place or for a walk on the beach?"

"Let's go for a walk."

We stroll a short distance in silence before he takes me in his arms again and kisses me—deep and meaningful, full of hope and a future.

When I pull back from the only place I really want to be, I confide, "Evan, I don't want to leave you. I don't want to lose you either." My voice is a whisper in the wind, but loud enough for him to hear my plea.

He runs his hands on either side of my face then pushes the blowing strands behind my ears. As he holds me, his eyes search mine. With a most confident grin, he says, "Just because you have to go back to school doesn't mean you'll lose me. I'm yours. You marked my heart as yours the day I met you. So relax in the knowledge that I'll be here, soulless, heartless, less of a man altogether until I see you again." He pulls me against him, burying me in his possessive embrace and kisses my head. "I'll visit you as much as you'll let me."

"How can I relax knowing you're living life halfhearted-ly?" I laugh softly. "And I feel the same about you."

"Does that mean if you have my heart and soul and I have your heart and soul then we are whole?"

"Yes, I feel complete knowing I'll have a part of you with me."

He lightly chuckles. "You'll have the only parts that matter."

With closed eyes, I press my ear against him and listen to the rhythm of *my heart* beating in his chest.

Taking his hand in mine, I guide him back down the beach to the stone steps that lead up to the house. I stop on the first step so that I'm eye level with him and wrap my arms around his neck, kissing the smooth skin behind his earlobe that always elicits a smile and laugh from my ticklish man. I whisper, "I love you. You don't have to say it back. You've shown me time and time again how much you love me."

Cupping my face in his large hands, he presses his forehead against mine. I hear him gulp as he closes his eyes, the words stuck in an undercurrent of emotion.

I close my eyes, shivering from the breeze that surrounds us and listening to the waves crashing nearby. "I meant what I said, Evan. This is enough."

"Mallory," he says, and I look up into his dark, deep blues. "I ... one day, I'll be what you deserve. I'll be everything you ever wanted."

"You're everything I never knew I needed."

Our lips meet, and under a full Hawaiian moon, that kiss tells me we were always meant to be more than a fling in paradise.

That summer, we became forever.

PREVIEW

To be continued in book 2 of the Playboy in Paradise Series,
Redeeming the Playboy.
For a preview, keep reading.

REDEEMING THE PLAYBOY

Noah cups my face, forcing me to look at him. His words are urgent as he stares straight into my eyes. "I will never treat you like that. You mean more to me than that, Mallory." He pulls me by the arm and as if I don't have a say in the matter, I go stumbling behind him.

"Mallory!" Evan calls, and though I know better, my heart aches for him.

Looking over my shoulder, Murphy and Zach have him restrained. My eyes catch movement nearby, and I see his mom and Kelly smiling in their victory. I move forward, needing to be free from the hate of their contemptuous eyes, needing a minute away from everything to do with a future snuffed out. They planted the seed and let us destroy each other. A conversation that should have happened during more sober times, forced itself into our lives ... and now we'll pay the price for this devastation. Both of us walk away wounded in a battle over egos and lies, a battle that should have never been waged.

Just as I round the corner, a strangled cry halts my escape and every breath in my body.

"Don't leave me, Baby! I love you!"

Redeeming the Playboy is now available.

ALSO BY S.L. SCOTT

To keep up to date with her writing and more, visit her website: www.slscottauthor.com

To receive the Scott Scoop about all of her publishing adventures, free books, giveaways, steals and more, sign up here: http://bit.ly/2TheScoop

Join S.L.'s Facebook group here: S.L. Scott Books

Audiobooks on Audible - CLICK HERE

Playboy in Paradise Series

Falling for the Playboy

Redeeming the Playboy

Loving the Playboy

Playboy in Paradise Box Set

The Crow Brothers (Stand-Alones)

Spark

Tulsa

Rivers

Ridge

The Crow Brothers Box Set

Hard to Resist Series (Stand-Alones)

The Resistance

The Reckoning

The Redemption

The Revolution

The Rebellion

The Revelation

The Everest Brothers (Stand-Alones)

Everest - Ethan Everest

Bad Reputation - Hutton Everest

Force of Nature - Bennett Everest

The Everest Brothers Box Set

The Kingwood Series

SAVAGE

SAVIOR

SACRED

SOLACE - Stand-Alone

The Kingwood Series Box Set

Talk to Me Duet (Stand-Alones)

Sweet Talk

Dirty Talk

From the Inside Out Series

Scorned

Jealousy

Dylan

Austin

From the Inside Out Compilation

Stand-Alone Books

ABOUT THE AUTHOR

To keep up to date with her writing and more, her website is www.slscottauthor.com to receive her newsletter with all of her publishing adventures and giveaways, sign up for her newsletter: http://bit.ly/2TheScoop

Instagram: S.L.Scott

To receive a free book now, TEXT "slscott" to 77948

For more information, please visit
www.slscottauthor.com